Perfect Intentions

Leona Turner

PERFECT INTENTIONS
copyright 2014 by Leona Turner

www.leonaturnerauthor.com

**Cover Art Copyright 2014
Stephen Bryant**

www.SRBPRODUCTIONS.net

FIRST EDITION

Prologue

He blinks, snorting up the combination of blood and mucus running from his nose he; attempts to cry out, no noise. He tries to inhale again, but it becomes apparent the gesture is a futile one. He starts to retrieve his feelings, pain courses through his body as his befuddled mind struggles to grasp the reality of his situation. Remaining calm, he tries once more to inhale; he can smell something, something underneath the smell of blood and his own fear, something vaguely familiar. Once again he tries again to inhale, the gag still foiling any other attempts to breathe. He can the feel panic rising in his chest, so he decides to try a different tack. Using all his remaining breath, he blows out, and a stab of pain shoots through his face and up into the back of his eyes. Now finally free to breathe, he tries to sit, no luck. His arms and legs are bound. He knows this by the dull aching cramps emanating from them he struggles into a kneeling position. Then a wave of nausea hits him as he pinpoints the smell—petrol. He blinks rapidly, trying to bring his surroundings into focus. A dark open space occupies the area around him.

I must be in some sort of warehouse

Far in the distance, a small flickering light emerges, and he strains his eyes trying to use the tiny pinprick of light as a base.

Christ, I'm not alone, there's a shadow…

Or my imagination

As the light draws closer, he realises his first guess was accurate. The shape starts to move closer, then suddenly a flash of bright light. Momentarily he's stunned, as the sudden brightness assaults his retinas. He closes his eyes to give them time to adjust; he opens them once again as the heat starts to bear down on him. Looking around, he contemplates his changing situation.

I'm trapped.

Inside a ring of fire, bound and terrified, he can swear he sees a malicious face just through the flames; it seems to be laughing. From behind the mask a voice spoke.

"Next to you is a knife and a box of explosives with a timer, the timer is set to go off in three minutes, if you make it to the door on your right you live, if not..."

The sentence hadn't needed completion. Moving quickly, eyes trained on the timer, he scrambles for the knife. Struggling to control the violent shaking of his hands, holding the knife between his two thumb joints, he focuses all his attention on working the serrated blade up and down against the tight rope. Sweat builds on his forehead and rolls down into his eyes, blurring his vision as he screws up his eyes in consternation. This temporary blip in concentration combined with his profusely sweating hands causes him to lose grip, and he drops the blade. The sound ripples through his awareness over the sound of the flames and his eyes flicker uncontrollably over to the timer.

Two minutes ten seconds.

Grabbing unceremoniously once more for the blade, he resumes his work. The first few threads of the rope start to shred, and spurred on by small victory he quickens his pace, sawing faster and faster. He is rewarded to see a few more of the rope threads shred; he glances once again at the timer.

One minute thirty seconds.

Faster and faster sawing, sweat stinging his eyes and hindering his progress, until finally the last of the rope threads cuts through and his hands are once more his own. Glancing at the timer, he realises he has only a minute to vacate the building. He looks down at his feet and sees that they're cuffed. His eyes move quickly around his cell of flames, and it occurs to him that his captor hasn't been so benevolent as to leave the key.

Forty seconds.

Standing up, he barely registers the cramping pains shooting up and down his legs. Summoning the last of his strength, he glances once more at the timer.

Thirty-five seconds.

He jumps toward the edge of the ring of flames. As he reaches it, he closes his eyes, and, taking a deep breath, he throws himself towards the wall of flames and freedom on the other side. His desperate bid is accompanied by a loud whooshing sound in his ears.

His mind casts back to when he'd woken there and how he'd barely registered the fact he was wet. At the time he had been preoccupied with trying to take a breath. The realisation had come too late; he had been doused with petrol before he'd woken.

For a few moments he feels nothing. Then he can smell it: the stench of fat catching in a pan, the smell of human skin burning—his skin. As the flames continue to ravage his exterior, he falls face first onto the ground. His eyes are set, staring in the direction of the circle of fire. Behind his eyes, his mind races frantically in its last conscious moments.

His three minutes are up, and there was no big bang, no explosion of whiteness—just the gentle flames of his earlier incarceration starting to ebb away, and lying there in the waning light, he takes his last breath.

Chapter 1

The sunshine was bright behind the curtains as Gavin Rochdale stirred from his sleep; he had a nightmare task today.

He had a prospective client coming to inspect a council lock-up on the industrial estate. The place was a dump, having not been touched for the last two years. The previous tenants had played fast and loose with the regulations and had managed to knock through several supporting walls to create doorways. As it stood it was a death trap. In spite of this, Gavin still had to show round prospective renters. He couldn't understand why they couldn't wait until after the work was done to show people around, or at least have gotten the work done on it sooner. It could have been making the money for the last two years, but all the paperwork involved meant it had been put on the back burner. Until now, that is; now the council needed the extra revenue, and its unfortunate timing had meant that the burden had fallen squarely on Gavin's shoulders.

The woman he'd shown around last week had been the stereotypical wannabe business type. After wasting the best part of an hour, she finally left without so much as a backward glance. He had chalked that up to experience and made a note to see if she was still there twelve months down the line.

Sadly, Gavin had realised after just a five-minute conversation on the phone with the prospective renter earlier in the week that he was another wannabe and he really wasn't in the mood for another timewaster. He'd managed to get a cold over the weekend and didn't relish the idea of being anywhere other than in bed. He felt exhausted, and as his cold had made him fight for his breath all through the night, all he wanted to do now was roll over and get some much needed sleep.

As he was lying there contemplating calling in sick, the phone rang. Answering it, he wheezed a greeting and was met with a familiar voice.

"Hi hon, how you feeling?"

It was Rachel, his live-in girlfriend. She'd been a saint these last few days, but he knew her patience with him would start to wane within the next few. He was always such a grumpy bastard when he felt under the weather, and he knew it.

"Oh, I feel fantastic—my chest's tight and my head's so full of pressure and snot it might explode at any minute."

"Charming. Well, anyway, I was just ringing you to make sure you're up; you were breathing like a rhino when I got up this morning, I thought you might sleep through your alarm."

"Yeah, well, I was thinking I might ring in sick today—I feel like shit."

"Oh no you don't. You know my parents are coming round this evening and you're not crying off sick again. Now get yourself showered, shaved, and off to work."

Gavin grimaced; he'd completely forgotten about that. He might have known Rachel wouldn't tolerate him having a day off sick. She was a fitness fanatic, ignored colds until they went away, and generally was never rundown or tired. He'd always loved that about her, until now, that is. He always knew his choice of woman would backfire on him one day, and today appeared to be the day. And now he had his 'in-laws' to contend with this evening, too.

Forcing himself out of bed and into the shower, Gavin was ready and in his car on his way to the council unit twenty minutes later.

As Gavin pulled up by the council unit, it struck him how rundown this area must appear to prospective renters. There was a huge factory to the front of the units, but the units on either side had been rented out privately and were presently being used as warehouses or for storage. The lock-up to the left of the unit had a load of old mattresses dumped outside, and to the right there was a collection of old and decaying washing machines, fridges, and other household junk. No wonder he was having such trouble selling this place; the whole estate looked like a bomb had hit it, and it was obvious the council had just let the area slip further into decline. Also, judging by the tyre marks littering the road, it was a haunt of boy racers.

No self-respecting business would want this place fronting their operations.

And it smelt *rank* up here. What was that smell? It was faint, but it was there; even through his blocked nose there was a pungent, fetid odour. He looked around trying to locate its source, his eyes moving over to the collection of rubbish standing outside the unit next door. Only it didn't smell like household waste, rotted or otherwise; the only time he'd smelt anything remotely similar before was about ten years ago, when driving through the country. He'd been on his way to see a friend who lived in a village just five miles from town when a cloud of smoke moving over the road had temporarily blinded him. It had taken only seconds for the smell to work its way through the air vents of his car and then he'd gagged, pulled over, and been violently sick onto the grass verge. It had been during the foot and mouth crisis and a farmer had been burning his livelihood in a nearby field. Carcasses of cows had been piled up and then set alight. Gavin knew he never wanted to smell that again; it had taken him numerous showers and several days before he had believed he'd finally got the smell out of his nostrils. Sometimes he dreamt of it, all those animals discarded and destroyed so callously. Gavin had felt real remorse for the farmer, to stand and watch your livelihood literally go up in flames. Coming back to the present, he looked around to see if there was any smoke coming from anywhere. No, no smoke. As he started moving toward the unit, it seemed to get stronger, then receded as he made his way to the front door. Fishing the keys from his pocket, he opened the door and the smell hit him like a tidal wave. The next few minutes were a blur. In retrospect, he wouldn't be able to say exactly what it was that pushed him to move toward the smell instead of away from it. Maybe it was morbid curiousity. Maybe it was just because it was the first thing he'd smelt in the last three days and was curious to know what it was that could possibly have gotten through his blocked nose. He walked through toward the origin of the smell in the main warehouse. It took his brain a minute to register exactly what it was he was seeing. At first he thought it had been a mannequin, but then his nose came into line with what he was witnessing. It had been human at some point. Gavin turned and dashed back to the door.

Mr Roberts was driving up toward the council unit. Looking around the area, he sneered to himself.

Bloody council, oh so quick to claim all they're entitled to with the extortionate council tax, not so quick, however, to spend it. Building new offices? They really thought people were complete mugs.

He had to admit the rent on this unit was cheap. Although, the whole area was a dump—he'd have to get onto them about that, starting with Mr. Gavin Rochdale. He sounded like he could stand to be brought down a peg or two, and Mr. Roberts felt he was just the man to do it.

As he pulled in opposite the unit in question, he saw the door swing open and someone come crashing through. At first he thought it was a homeless person who'd broken into the unit to sleep; that would have been the icing on the cake as far as he was concerned, and he could feel his ardour rising. Getting out of the car and feeling his antagonistic characteristics jumping to the fore, he strode purposely toward the retreating intruder. As he came closer, though, he realised something wasn't sitting right: the person on their knees wasn't dressed in swathes of second-hand clothes; they were wearing a suit.

"Mr. Rochdale?" Mr. Roberts's voice was incredulous

Then he became aware of the smell and he, as Gavin had done not five minutes before, gagged.

"What's that smell?'"

"Body." Gavin replied whilst retrieving his phone from his pocket.

"What?" The response had thrown Mr. Roberts enough to allow Gavin time to dial. As Mr. Roberts went to speak again, Gavin held up his hand.

"Hello, police department, please—there's been a murder. Burnt body, address is Unit Four, Leicester Road Industrial state, Mannings Town. Yes, my names Gavin Rochdale, Ok, Thank you." Breaking the connection, he turned to Mr. Roberts.

"Showing's off today, sorry"

DI Holt and DC Henson drew up outside the council unit. The corpse had been discovered at nine thirty, but when the call had come in the operator hadn't been sure if it was genuine, and so had sent a couple of the young beat officers to investigate. They were still in shock, and a small pile of one of theirs partially digested breakfast served to illustrate as a reminder of that. DI Holt felt for the young lad; only twelve months out of training he was still wet behind the ears, and had been given a rude awakening into what kind of career he had chosen.

Dennis Grant, the coroner, was already there, pacing about, and upon spotting Holt he marched straight toward him.

"They lit him up like Christmas, and I *think* he was alive at the time, judging by the position of the body and the spread of the fire."

"Male or female?"

"Male, I'd say, between twenty and fifty, but other than that, there's not a lot more I can tell you until I've done the PM."

Holt walked past Dennis toward the unit. Looking around the area, he realised what a gift it was to the killer: there was no houses overlooking, no through traffic. The units on either side were rundown and looked as if they hadn't been touched in years. DC Henson, who had been brought in to assist Holt, was trailing behind, struggling with his jacket.

"So what do you see?"

"See, sir?"

"Yes, what can you tell me about the area?"

"Well, there are no neighbours, so it's a good choice for a killing room, especially given the fact that the fire would have created a lot of smoke."

"Precisely. Whoever did this must know the area, because no one would just 'happen' on this estate."

"And?"

"Well, this took organisation, and the killer must be local. Why do I feel this is going to get worse before it gets better?"

Chapter 2

The alarm resonated around the room. As Clare reached to switch it off, the pile of books sitting precariously on the edge of the bed fell, scattering themselves across the floor.

Clare made her way to the bathroom, carefully avoiding the books that were now strewn across the floor and getting into the shower began to plan her day.

She had work and then a meeting with Loretta, and at some point she had to go to her bank and try to reconcile her finances.

Loretta was a counselor she had originally contacted for some help with her psychology course. Loretta had been aware of how hard juggling work and study could be, and had agreed to help Clare whenever she had time. This meant that her meetings with Loretta were not as regular as Clare would like, but she appreciated it all the same.

Clare's decision to start studying again had been met with mixed reactions as her new routine had meant little time for socialising, something her friend Hannah had been quick to point out. Getting out of the shower and dressing, she grabbed her bag and headed for the door, stopping briefly to have a swig of lukewarm coffee.

As she made her way toward her car she noticed that one of her tyres was completely flat.

Knowing this was going to make her late for work, she decided to ring in. She knew this wasn't going to make her popular as the delivery of a new stock of perfume was due in this morning and she was supposed to be there to help with the display. Clare worked on the beauty counter at a large department store on the edge of Mannings Town, and although this had never been her career choice she enjoyed it when they got new lines in.

She pulled out her phone and scrolled to the stores office number.

"Can I help?"

The voice was so close Clare dropped her phone.

"Sorry, it's just that I noticed your tyre. I'm Dean by the way"

The man bent down to retrieve Clare's phone.

"Clare. Can you change tyres?"

He smiled at her and she was struck by how young he looked.

"Just open the boot for me."

Clare watched with interest as Dean methodically went to task.

"So what is it you do then?"

"Me? I work in a garage, can't you tell?"

He had a lop-sided grin that made Clare smile.

"In which case I'm sure this isn't offering you much of a challenge?"

"Not so much no."

"Is this going to make you late for work?"

"Possibly but I couldn't really walk past could I? No offence but you don't strike me as someone who'd know what they were doing with a tyre jack."

"And you'd be right there. Personally I would've just called the RAC."

After ten minutes, the car was ready to go. Dean hurriedly replaced all the tools he'd been using back into the boot.

"Can I give you a lift anywhere?"

"Nah, you're all right, I can catch the bus from here."

He pointed at the bus stop across the road.

"I've not made you miss your bus, have I?"

"There'll be another one along in a minute. See ya."

Clare waved her thanks and got into the car and switched the radio on.

'The charred remains of what is believed to be a man have been found on the Leicester Road industrial estate in Manning's Town this morning. The police have yet to make a statement regarding the identity of the victim, although it is believed he is not local to the area...'

Clare hit the search button and found a station playing 'non-stop hits.' Five minutes and five adverts later, she pulled into the car park singing along to 'Sound of the Underground.'

Aware she was already running a little late, Clare hurriedly dropped her bag in the staff room and went straight to her counter, where Hannah was already busy sorting through a new line of perfume that had come in. Hannah spotted her and smiled.

"All right, doll?"

"Yeah, yourself?"

"Uh-huh. You off to see Loretta tonight?"

"Half six. You want to come round later?"

"Sure. How are things going with her, anyway—she as good as her rep suggests? My sister in law swears by her, she's a modern day saint, and everyone who's met her says how fucking invaluable she is."

Clare could hear a hint of ill-disguised jealousy in her friend's voice and dismissed it.

"Well, it is good of her to help me; she doesn't have to."

"Yeah, modern day saint, like I said"

"Well, I can come over and talk behavioural psychology with you if you like, but I thought your strengths lay with your amazing ability to pick up random men in bars—"

Clare was baiting her, and Hannah knew it.

"Fair enough, point made. So lets move onto my strengths then. Are you coming out with me tonight or not?"

"Tonight? No, I can't do tonight; you know that. I've got too much work on at the moment."

"Tomorrow, then?"

"Hannah, I told you this weekend's not good for me."

"Bloody hell, Clare, you're turning into a hermit. One night off won't kill you; I might, though."

"Maybe next weekend."

"Remove the 'maybe.' "

"Ok, next weekend."

"Good. Ok, moving on: did you hear the news this morning?"

"The burnt body?"

"Yeah, they reckon it happened sometime last night."

"They don't know who it is, though, do they?"

"No, hope it's no one I know. It's a bit bloody worrying when it happens on your doorstep. I mean there haven't been any reports of missing people have there? And in a small town like this everyone pretty much knows everyone else's business."

"We'll have to check the news at lunch, see if the police have any more leads."

"Yeah, anyway, I've got to get to the stock room. If I take much longer Maggie will have my guts—she's still pissed off about the time I came in late. I mean, for God's sake, it was over a year ago, get over it."

"You mean when you were two hours late and hungover?"

"Yeah."

"And you threw up on her?"

"Uh-huh."

"I know what you mean, Hannah; some people really know how to hold a grudge."

Hannah smiled and wandered off in the direction of the stock room.

Clare checked her watch; if she wanted to get out in time to go to the bank, she was going to have to get the stock re-ordering done before lunch. Taking a deep breath, she began sorting through papers.

Clare was twenty minutes late when she eventually arrived at the bank. Red-faced and clearly flustered, she went straight up to the information desk and informed the teller she had an appointment to see the bank manager. After exhaling noisily, the teller begrudgingly swung her chair round and skulked off towards the back of the bank, presumably to find the manager.

As the teller came back into her line of sight, the manager was trailing behind.

"Ah, Miss Heathers, I'm Ian White. Glad to see you could make it." Clare decided to ignore the jibe, realising she probably deserved it.

"Would you just like to follow me through to my office?"

Clare smiled.

"Lead the way."

The office was sparse: it held only a computer, a desk, and a stand full of leaflets advertising all the new services they offered. As Clare took a seat, she wondered briefly how old the man-child in front of her was—he didn't look a day over eighteen. She had a horrible suspicion he was going to patronise her, and the days of her holding her tongue were long gone.

"Miss Heathers, the reason I wanted to see you is the fact that your account has been overdrawn several times in the last few months, pointing to the fact that you are having trouble managing it, which means your latest application for an extension on your overdraft facility has been declined. Sorry."

"So as you see that I'm a little overdrawn each month, you're not going to give me an additional extension on my overdraft facility, is that right?"

"Yes, I'm afraid that you have to show the account is stable for at least six months before we will consider extending your credit."

"So basically after six months, if I manage not to become overdrawn, you'll give me an extended overdraft facility?"

"Yes"

"But if I'm not overdrawn anymore, why would I need an extension on my overdraft facility?"

"Well, I'm sorry Miss Heathers, but that's bank policy, I'm afraid."

"Yes, well, forgive me for being a little cynical, but I can't help thinking I'm funding your Christmas parties. Every time I'm overdrawn by ten or twenty pounds, I get charged an additional fifteen pounds, and then I receive one of these thoroughly charming letters." Clare threw the bank letters on the table.

"Which not only informs me that I'm overdrawn, but also drops in the fact that you're charging me for writing to tell me about it."

"I'm sorry, Miss Heathers. If you'd like, we can meet up again in six months and do another review."

Recognising defeat, Clare scooped up her letters and jammed them back into her bag.

Mr. White sat back in his chair, watching Clare's retreating back, and released a long, low breath out. She may have been attractive, but he wouldn't fancy taking her out on a date—not with that temper, anyway.

Getting back into her car outside the bank, she allowed herself a moment of pity before starting the engine. Driving toward Loretta's office she almost missed the turn into the car park as her mind was still on her dwindling finances. She had known there had been little to no chance of the bank being able to help her. She decided to try and put it to the back of her mind as she parked up. Clare knew that Loretta wasn't going to be happy. Loretta had agreed to stay on later than she would usually to accommodate Clare's working patterns. As Clare walked into the office reception the receptionist looked up and smiled at her. Clare forced a smile back and the receptionist motioned her straight through to Loretta's office.

"Hi, Clare, how are you getting on with the course? Did you look up that case study I told you about?"

"Yeah, thanks for that, it was really useful, although I did want to ask you about something."

"Go on."

"Well, it's about something I read in a magazine. It was an article on a prison guard who worked in the paedophile wing in some prison, and it was so depressing. Did you know the majority of convicted paedophiles refuse help? I mean they can't or won't comprehend that they did something wrong."

Loretta nodded and sat back in her chair.

"You know, Clare, one of the best things about psychology can be the most frustrating. As in within traditional science, there are certain rules, the laws of physics, chemistry, and biology are irrefutable, and we know them to be true because we see them every day. With psychology there is no absolute truth; it deals with patterns, patterns of behaviour, patterns of thought. There are no absolutes. There are certain things we can look for, but if you expect to find a neat template that will fit every one of the seven billion people on Earth, you're going to come up short."

Loretta smiled.

"Now, have you heard of an experiment called 'gorilla in our midst?'"

An hour later Clare left Loretta's office feeling much better than she had going in. Her meeting with Loretta had gone so well in fact, that she'd almost forgotten how badly her day had been prior. Clare pulled her car back into the car park by her flat, noticing someone sitting on the wall opposite. There was nothing unusual in that; the local teenagers were always hanging about drinking, smoking and hurling obscenities at anyone who walked past. But this was different. For a start, there was only one person there, and she recognised him instantly. She grabbed her bag and got out of her car, slamming the door and locking it. She looked over at him.

"Hello again, what are you doing hanging about?"

"Waiting for you, as it happens."

"Really? And why's that?"

"I wanted to make sure that wheel was still attached," he said, gesturing towards the car tyre he had fitted that morning.

"Well, that's reassuring."

"To be honest, that wasn't the only reason. I was just wondering if you were doing anything Saturday."

Clare's eyebrows shot up.

"Are you asking me out?"

"Yeah, I guess I must be."

"Don't you think you'd be better off asking someone closer to your own age?"

Dean looked abashed for a second before regaining his composure.

"I'm asking you out for a drink, not proposing marriage."

"Fair point. Ok, then, why not?"

"I'll meet you here Saturday at eight."

Not waiting for a reply, he turned and left.

Clare watched him for a few moments before grabbing her bag and heading toward the door.

Her meeting with Dean had thrown her, and she was still smiling when Hannah arrived.

"All right, hon, what's got you smiling all of a sudden?"

"Nothing, just pleased to see you, is all."

Hannah wandered past her, looking somewhat unconvinced.

"I have a couple of bottles of wine, a takeaway, and *Dirty Dancing* on DVD—what more do you need for a perfect evening?"

Clare followed Hannah through to the kitchen.

"I stuck the oven on twenty minutes ago, so it should be warm enough. Stick the takeaway in and I'll grab us some glasses."

Clare wandered over to the cupboard to get the glasses. She considered telling Hannah about Dean, but given her knack for overreaction, she decided that it might be a good idea to keep the information to herself for now and see how Saturday panned out first.

Chapter 3

The front door to Matt's apartment was opened quickly and silently, the intruder slipped in and the door was closed once more. Moving swiftly and silently from room to room, the intruder checked for any signs of life. There shouldn't be—Matt's routines were just that: routine. He wouldn't be home until five, leaving more than enough time. Locating the packet of Temazepam in the bathroom cabinet, gloved hands quickly popped the tablets into a small plastic bag and using a can of deodorant crushed them. Taking the bag of ground temazepam into the kitchen, its contents were then emptied into the coffee machine filter. Scanning the surfaces to ensure no evidence remained, the intruder slipped silently out.

Three hours later the intruder returned, and, as expected, all was quiet. Walking through into the lounge, the figure noticed that Matt was slumped over the dining table, the coffee cup on the floor trailing the remains of coffee and Temazepam cocktail. Moving quickly, the intruder secured Matt to the chair he was in.

Forty-five minutes later, Matt awoke. Looking up, he saw the masked and cloaked figure staring back down at him.

Matt watched as the intruder moved slowly across the hard wood floor—*his* floor in *his* apartment, supposedly his haven. It felt far from a haven now. Looking around him, he wished he hadn't bothered working so hard to achieve the minimalist look because this clinical atmosphere he had created was far from comforting; it was like the intruder had chosen the room for its foreboding atmosphere.

The footfalls were loud on the bare floor, which brought Matt's attention back to his predicament.

When he had first woken up in his apartment and had found himself duct taped to one of his dining room chairs, he'd thought it was a prank, courtesy of one of his rugby mates. Then he had realised that he had no recollection of the last few hours after he had gotten home from work. He had come in, made himself a coffee, sat at the dining table to sort through the post, and that was it—after that he had nothing. And yet, here he was, bound, gagged, and sitting in his candle-lit lounge. He had been the one to put the candles out; he was going to propose to Helen tonight, but somehow he didn't think that would be happening now. Watching the intruder, his panicked mind flickered back to the news he'd heard earlier on his way back from work.

A body had been found. His mind grappled with the idea that the perpetrator might be the man in his apartment.

The intruder was watching Matt with interest as differing emotions flickered across Matt's face. The first victim's discovery had been the mainstay of all news reports for the day, and Matt was clearly wondering, and quite correctly, if he was to be victim number two.

The intruder turned and headed toward the bedroom door, Matt was still staring, finding it impossible to look anywhere else. The figure temporarily disappeared from sight into the bedroom. Matt shifted uneasily in his seat. Within minutes, the figure reappeared with a large box in hand. After a moment, Matt recognised it: his toolbox.

It had been in his bedroom for a while now. Helen had wanted some bookshelves putting up. It was a job he was continually putting off. Up until now, his avoidance of the toolbox had become a standing joke. Helen had taken to leaving it by the side of the bed in the belief that if he kept stubbing his toes on it, he would just get the shelves up, to save crippling himself every morning. Now, however, it couldn't be further from amusing; it looked dark and sinister in the half-light, casting long shadows across the floor that nearly touched his feet.

The intruder gently laid the box down on the floor in front of him, and he felt an icy cold hand clutching at his bowels. A bead of sweat released itself from the back of his neck and snaked its way down between his shoulder blades and into the crevice of his buttocks.

The intruder sensed his rising panic and started to move slower and more deliberately.

Looking sideways at Matt, the intruder stooped down and reached around inside the toolbox. Matt's eyes were glued to the figure, as he watched a gloved hand reached into the toolbox and pulled out an electric drill. A muffled squeal escaped Matt.

Eyes never moving from the drill, Matt began struggling with his bindings, causing the chair to sway.

"In a minute I shall untie you, and you will have five minutes to escape."

Matt suddenly felt a brief moment of relief; he knew that within thirty seconds of being released he could be out of his apartment and back in the safety of his car.

"Do you understand?"

Matt nodded.

"However," the voice continued.

"Perhaps I should mention that when—or should I say *if*—you make your escape, you'll be doing so with holes through both your ankles."

On cue, the drill screamed into life.

That was when Matt passed out.

Going through to the kitchen the intruder filled a glass with water and taking it back to the lounge threw the water in Matts face.

Coughing and spluttering Matt awoke. There was soft music playing in the background. Then reality crashed down on him as a familiar voice reached him from across the room

"Ok, Matt, I can see you'll need a little help, so I have generously decided to administer you a little anaesthetic to stop you passing out from the pain."

Matt wasn't sure what worried him more, the content of the statement, or the jovial, conversational tone that had been used.

All of a sudden, the intruder was upon him. Matt barely had chance to react, and the needle pushed easily through the flesh and found its mark. As the plunger was deployed, he felt the sickly, cold feeling of the condemned man.

The intruder headed back to the toolbox to collect the necessary instrument, and Matt started to feel a little light-headed. By the time he had returned, Matt had convinced himself that he wouldn't feel a thing, but as the drill sparked into life and made its way toward his right ankle, all he could think was that he'd never play rugby again. He briefly wondered if he'd live to see his unborn child—the child that had been the catalyst for his impromptu proposal.

As the drill ripped straight through the skin and hit the bone, he felt pain so acute he threw up. The gag prevented the vomit leaving the confines of his mouth, and he swallowed it back down. He willed himself to pass out. But the anaesthetic and adrenaline coursing through his veins was making it impossible for his body to switch off.

After what seemed like a lifetime of pain had been administered, the drill finally fell silent. Taking a penknife the intruder approached Matt once more and cut through the binds of his hands and what remained of the ones around his ankles. Somewhere in the back of his mind Matt was aware that the grinding had stopped, and he forced himself to look down. He instantly regretted the decision. Flesh and blood made up most of the floor space around him, and white flecks of bone shone within the blood. The intruder had set a little table in front of him, and on it was an alarm clock set for nine twenty-five—exactly five minutes from now.

"You have until the alarm sounds to escape."

Matt slumped onto the floor, painfully aware of the fact that his ankles could not even begin to support his weight. He glanced at his attacker, and upon doing so felt another surge of adrenaline pump through his body. He felt terror, but most of all anger. He was dully aware that at some point he must have soiled himself, as his trousers were wet and heavy, which only incensed his hatred. He slowly started to try and lean his weight forward onto his arms and upper torso and started dragging himself toward the hallway, the front door, and what he hoped would soon be safety.

His progress was painfully slow, but upon inspecting of the clock again he believed he could make it. His attacker was now sitting serenely on the opposite side of the room watching him. His breathing was coming in laboured gasps and his lower legs were screaming at him, but he continued to drag himself slowly across the floor. Again he was aware of the hard floor; it had become friendly once more. It was now aiding his escape, easing him across the floor, lubricated by his own blood.

Almost in the hallway now, there are only five feet between him and the front door—he was actually going to make it. From his position in the hall he could no longer see the clock, but assumed he must have about two minutes left. He felt relief that his door didn't have a Yale lock. Spurred on by the thought of imminent escape, he put in extra effort and suddenly found himself at the front door. Supporting himself on his right arm, he reached up with his left and found his mark.

From the shadows in the lounge, the tormentor

had watched Matt's progress with satisfied amusement. The vanity of the human condition was amazing. People honestly believed it could never happen to them; that these atrocities they heard about every day and didn't spare so much as a second's thought for couldn't ever happen to them, that they were somehow out of the circle. So really, the tormentor reasoned, that this was a public service, bringing people back in, making life *real* again. Because the cosseted world they'd surrounded themselves with had made them numb, numb to the pain they inflicted without empathy.

The intruder was brought back to Earth with the pulling of the door handle, back to the task at hand.

Matt pulled at the door handle a second time, nothing. It wasn't budging. It was locked. The realisation took exactly thirty seconds to filter through his conscious mind. Trapped.

"What's up, Matt? Door's locked? If only you'd thought to pick up your keys." Once more the intruder's voice was soft, almost lyrical, then it changed again, becoming hard and sharp, like a razor striking his face.

"But that's the problem with people like you, Matt, isn't it? You don't think, you just do, and to hell with the consequences. Well, finally the consequences of your actions have caught up with you."

Matt hadn't stopped to think that it would make absolutely no sense for his captor to release him, but now he knew for sure he was looking at his last day on this Earth. Surprisingly, he felt calmness spread through his body as he resigned himself to his fate.

He hoped it would be quick.

With that the intruder came striding toward him, electric drill in hand and a maniacal glint in his eye.

Once again the darkness came, and this time would be the last.

Chapter 4

At her front door, Clare was struggling to find her keys, rifling through the bottom of her bag. She heard the familiar jingling and made a grab, extracting her keys and opening the door.

Walking through her apartment, she flung her bags down on the sofa and went through to the kitchen to switch the kettle on.

It was only half past three; she had plenty of time before Dean arrived. She could have a cup of tea while waiting for the bath to run. Going through to the bathroom, she turned the taps on full. On her way back to retrieve her shopping bags she's interrupted by a banging at the door. Realising it could be Hannah she hurriedly stuffs the bags behind the sofa. If it was Hannah, she'd want to know why she'd been spending money on non-essentials when she consistently pleaded poverty. As she opened the front door, she realised she had been quite right to hide the bags.

"Hi hon, what brings you round?"

Hannah ignored the question, smiled a greeting, and strolled straight into the kitchen.

"Oh great, I'll have a cup, too, if you're making one."

With a sigh, Clare closed the door and followed Hannah back through.

Hannah had already got two cups out and was generously spooning sugar into one of them.

"So what are you up to this evening?"

"Oh, nothing much. I just thought I'd have a quiet night in, have a bath."

"Really? So why have you been out buying new clothes, then?"

"What? How did you know that?"

"I saw you in town earlier—you walked straight past me. Something on your mind?"

"No."

"Can I see what you bought?"

"Why?"

"Bloody hell, Clare, it's a simple enough question. Unless…" Hannah paused. A look of confusion being replaced with a look of amused shock.

"You're going on a date, aren't you?"

"Crying out loud, Hannah."

"You are, aren't you? Why didn't you say something before? I'd have come shopping with you; we could all go out together. I'm meeting up with Mike tonight."

"And this is exactly why I didn't say anything to you. I knew as soon as you knew you'd start trying to organise me. It's not serious."

"Thank you very much. Well, what's he like? Do I know him—does he live round here?"

"No, you don't know him, and yes, he lives quite close."

"What's his name?"

"Before I tell you, Hannah, you have to promise not to breathe a word of this to anyone."

"Brownie's honour."

"It's Dean Matthews."

"Dean Matthews? Why do I know that name?"

"Because he's Alice Matthews's brother."

"What, little Alice? Works in the store at the weekend? Jesus, Clare, how old is he? This is legal, isn't it?"

"I knew you'd react like this. He's nineteen, if you must know, and I've checked, it's perfectly legal, but thanks for the vote of confidence."

"Seriously, Clare, do you really think this is a good idea?"

"Well, I won't know 'til I've tried."

"Ok, well, I'll get out of your way then." Hannah finishing her tea put the cup in the sink and went to leave. Stopping briefly, she turned to Clare

"A word of advice before I leave."

Clare sighed.

"What?"

"Unless you're planning an indoor water feature, I'd turn the bath taps off if I were you."

Clare fled toward the bathroom.

Hannah shook her head and let herself out.

Luckily Clare made it to the bath in time, switching the taps off. She returned to say goodbye to Hannah, and was rewarded with an empty room. Grabbing the bags back out of their hiding place, she took them through into the bedroom, emptying the contents onto her bed and beginning to sort through them.

Three hours and numerous clothes changes later Clare was ready. She still had some time to kill, so she went back through into the kitchen and poured herself a glass of wine. By the time eight o'clock arrived, she was already pretty merry. Grabbing her bag, she went down to the car park to wait for Dean.

He was already waiting by the time she got there.

"You scrub up well," Clare said from across the car park.

"Yeah, well, you're not too bad yourself."

"Thanks. Right, where are we off to, then?"

"Well, I was thinking the Rose and Crown—it shouldn't be too busy and it's not too far to walk."

"Fair enough."

As Dean and Clare made their way into the Rose and Crown Dean asked her what she was drinking and Clare went off to find them a table. The pub was busy, but after a few moments she was able to find a table near the door. As Dean fought his way to the table with the drinks in hand she smiled at him.

Dean sat down and passed her her drink

"Thanks. So good day?"

"Not bad, got to help a damsel in distress this morning."

"Really? Well aren't you the knight in shining armour then?"

"I do my best. Anyway, do you come here often?"

"Not really, I've been quite busy recently. My mates always trying to get me to go out."

"So should I be feeling honoured that you agreed to come out with me tonight?"

"Yes I suppose you should really." She said, smiling at him.

After two hours Dean and Clare decided to leave, Dean had taken it upon himself to walk her home. Clare located her keys and opened the door, gesturing for Dean to go in first. Dean did as he was bid and proceeded to wait for Clare to close the door, before going further into the apartment. He had figured she'd had a few drinks before they met up and he had been right: she'd had three glasses of wine and was now steaming. Now, as he sat on the sofa, he could hear her stumbling around in the kitchen.

"Do you need any help?"

"No thanks, I have everything under control."

Just as she'd finished speaking, there was a crash.

"You don't take sugar, do you?"

"No."

"Good." She was laughing now, and he got up to investigate.

Clare was sitting on the kitchen floor, surrounded by glass and sugar. She looked up at him.

"Oops."

Looking at her hands, he noticed she'd obviously tried to clean the glass up and had cut herself. He strode over to her and helped her up, then steered her toward to the sink. He turned on the water, holding her hands under the faucets as he did. As he was cleaning the blood off of her she looked up at him

"I don't think you'll need stitches. Have you got a first aid box anywhere?"

"Plasters and savlon?"

"Yeah, that'll do."

"Over there, third drawer down."

Dean left her standing at the sink as he went over to the drawers. As he moved around, he noticed her starting to fall, and he rushed over, catching her and leaning her back up against the sink.

"Can you be trusted to stay there for just a minute?"

Clare looked up at him and smiled her affirmative.

After retrieving the required items, he moved back toward her again.

Working quickly, he dried her cuts smeared on the savlon and applied the plasters. Picking her up, he took her through into her bedroom and laid her down on the bed. She opened her eyes briefly.

"Blimey, you don't hang around, do you?"

"Funny fucker, just get some sleep."

He removed her shoes, and after deciding against undressing her, he pulled the duvet over her and quietly left the room.

He went back into the living room and sat back down on the sofa. Should he stay? She clearly wasn't in any fit state to be on her own tonight. He took his shoes off and lay back down on the sofa.

In the darkness of her bedroom Clare's eyes snapped open. She made a grab for her phone. Three o'clock. She cast her mind back to the evening before.

Her head started to scream at her, and when she rubbed her head with her hands, she felt something on them. Switching her bedside light on she saw her hands were covered in plasters and then pulling the covers back, she was relieved to find herself still fully dressed

She decided to go and get some water from the

kitchen and as she opened the fridge door a snippet of memory came back to her: she'd been making coffee, something had happened. She looked down at her hands once more and saw that the sugar jar was missing; she could make a guess as to what had happened. Swallowing a couple of aspirin, she decided to watch some TV as the pills took effect. As she opened her living room and switched the light on, she let out a quiet exclamation. There, spread on her sofa, was an unconscious Dean. The light had woken him and he stirred, and wiping the sleep from his eyes, turned to look at her.

"Oh, you're up and about again, are you?"

"What are you doing here?"

"Well, it didn't feel right leaving you here on your own."

"Umm, right, thanks, and sorry about last night."

"It's fine. You're quite amusing steaming drunk."

"Oh God, what did I do?"

"Well, you started with a little bit of karaoke— "

"I didn't know they had a karaoke machine"

"They don't."

Clare started to redden as Dean continued.

"You followed up the Rocky Horror medley with a little dancing...on the table."

"I didn't? I'm amazed you're still here. I'm *so* sorry. I don't suppose you'll want to go out again."

"Why not? You're a dream date."

Clare looked at him, bemused.

"What are you on about?"

"I got you into bed on the first date and I ended the evening better off than when I started it."

Clare looked confused.

"Yeah, your table top exploits earned me a few quid." His lopsided grin was back, and Clare had to laugh.

"You bastard." Smiling, Clare picked up a cushion and threw it at him.

Chapter 5

When the news of the second body came through to the station, Holt hadn't been surprised. Judging by what he had seen at the first crime scene, their perpetrator was organised and meticulous. Having both the bodies discovered within hours of each other showed a level of control that was making Holt uncomfortable, and he knew he would need to bring in outside help. The victim's heavily pregnant girlfriend had discovered the body. She'd had to be taken straight to hospital after the shock had brought her labour on. Luckily she'd gone on to have a healthy baby boy; unfortunately, it would also mean that one day she'd have to explain to her son the demise of his father and the fact that his birthday fell on the same date. Already the reach of these crimes was moving into the next generation. There hadn't been a murder in the town in over thirty years, and the last one had been a mugging that had gotten out of hand. These crimes weren't opportunistic.

For the first time in his career, DI Holt was scared. He had no idea how to deal with the nightmare unfurling before him. Now that he had made the decision to go and see this Loretta Armstrong he felt a little calmer, despite the knowledge that she had been instrumental to his own divorce. He thought about the first time he'd heard her name; it had been shortly before his wife had finally walked out on him. His wife Helen; had been going to see Loretta to talk through some 'personal issues' she'd been having at the time. As it had turned out these 'personal issues' had been that she'd had enough of her marriage. Holt let out a derisory snort as he cast his mind back to the final conversation he'd had with his then wife. She'd had the affront to accuse him of being 'emotionally retarded'. When she'd said it to him he'd laughed in her face, before reminding her it had been she who had sought out the advice of a perfect stranger to discuss the intricacies of their marriage. With her doctorate, she could—and probably would—make him feel very nervous. But he knew he'd need a head start on this case, and maybe she could shed some light on the type of person they were looking for. And going by what he'd witnessed in the last twenty-four hours, it wasn't a rational mind he was looking for. He leant forward, cradling his head in his hands, and attempted to rub the sleep away from his eyes and force his mind to wake again. He stared back down at the photos in front of him. He just hoped Dr. Armstrong was as good as her reputation suggested, because he had a feeling he was going to need all the additional help he could get.

Grabbing his jacket from the back of his chair, he called for DS Henson, and the two men headed for the car park.

Holt pulled the car into the car park outside Dr. Armstrong's office and the two men got out. Harry

Henson was practically giddy. His first *real* murder case, and he had not just one, but two mutilated bodies.

Not so much bullied as ignored by fellow classmates growing up, his choice of job ensured that people would take him seriously, and, more importantly, would get him noticed. Whereas most of his peers were respected within the community, Henson had systematically put everyone's back up. Holt had only agreed to bringing Henson in on the case due to Henson's persistent nagging. He had an almost desperate need to be constantly reassured and patted on the head, which made him nauseating in the extreme. That, coupled with the fact that he would stitch any one up in an effort to make himself look better, ensured that no one else would work with him.

Harry had subscribed to the idea a long time ago that to appear better to others, the quickest and often simplest route was to make everyone else look worse by comparison.

This case was a defining moment in his career. At the age of thirty he was still young, and here he was, accompanying DI Holt on what was potentially the biggest murder case in recent history.

Detective Inspector Jimmy Holt was the antithesis of Harry; he was a slightly rotund man with greying hair and a ruddy face. He had the look of a weatherworn man, and was well liked at his station. He had also been blessed with the patience of a saint and, as such, had been prepared to bring the young DC Henson in on this case with him. Painfully aware of how much the other officers disliked the young lad, he had seen fit to try and let him prove himself to his peers. He had not foreseen how trying that might be on a potentially long case. He had hoped the brutality of the murders might have sobered the young DC to the horrors that policing could hold, but unfortunately it had just seemed to fan the flames. So now, just forty-eight hours into the investigation, the DI was seriously starting to regret his decision to bring him in on the case. He was practically preening himself for the cameras; a few of his officers had already been snickering about how his face seemed to be getting more tanned by the day.

Pulling himself from his thoughts, the DI stopped to look at the front of the building. He didn't agree with the idea of criminal profiling; he didn't understand it. When he had started his career been he had been taught to find the clues and piece the puzzle together as simply as possible.

Now, though, the police force required an in depth analysis of who it was they were looking for. How these people were supposed to know that he had no idea; he could never know someone until he had met them, and yet these people claimed to be able to read the psyche of someone they had probably never seen before in their lives.

But for all the DI's gruff exterior and disbelief, psychiatrists and counsellors made him nervous. For the most part he was a private man, kept himself to himself, and that suited him just fine. The idea of someone poking round inside his head unsettled him more than he cared to mention.

He read the sign on the door: 'Dr. Loretta

Armstrong, PHD,' and exhaled loudly, turning to see if Henson was still with him, he was.

Walking through the reception area to the front desk, DI Holt was happy to see that it looked relatively normal, relaxed even. The walls were a pale sage colour; there were lots of large leafy plants around, and a small child's play area. The child area troubled him briefly, as he wondered why a child might need to see a psychiatrist, but he dismissed it as a sign of the times. He felt that children today as a whole were over sensitized and under disciplined. The parents couldn't control them anymore, as any physical disciplining could resort in a court case, and so the first taste of discipline a lot of kids would encounter would be at the hands of him or one of his officers.

He thought back to when he was growing up; societies young had always created groups. Little niches where they were free to express their individuality by dressing the same and appreciating the same core ideals. The vast percentage of children these days were born with silver spoons in their mouths, and, God help him, sometimes he wished they'd fall flat on their faces and choke on the damn thing.

As DI Holt approached the office door of Dr. Armstrong, he took a deep breath. He needed to remain calm; the last thing he needed was this woman knowing he felt nervous in her presence. Motioning for DC Henson to follow him, he knocked on the door.

Within her office Loretta was busy tidying her desk, it was an unconscious behaviour brought about by how nervous she was now feeling. She'd never seen a detective before, at least not in this sense. What if he wanted information on her patients? She knew realistically he couldn't—and probably wouldn't—ask. A sharp knock on the door signalled his arrival.

"Come in."

As if on cue, the door opened and DI Holt strode in, closely followed by that bumbling idiot of a DC she'd seen on the evening news the previous night. Resembling the colour of a tangerine, he'd spoken at length about nothing that seemed of any real significance, and he was even so bold as to make a suggestion as to the sort of man they were looking for. That was the problem these days—everyone was an amateur psychologist. What was his name, anyway? As if answering her thoughts, DI Holt spoke.

"Dr. Armstrong, I'm DI Holt, and this is DC Henson. Thank you for seeing us on such short notice. I appreciate that you must be busy."

"No problem, officers, anything I can do to help you with this case that's within my power I will do."

"Well, we'd certainly appreciate that. Oh, and just to let you know, we're here off the record."

"Off the record? How do you mean?"

"Well, the only people who know we're consulting you are the three of us in the confines of these four walls, and maybe your receptionist. We'd appreciate it if you'd let her know the situation and instruct her to keep the information to herself."

"Well, consider it done. Michelle is not at liberty

to discuss anyone who comes into my office. But may I ask why all the secrecy?"

"Well, a number of reasons, really. As you've probably seen, the murders have generated a lot of media attention recently, but we're trying to keep the cases as closed as possible, and for two reasons. Firstly, we don't want the severity of the situation getting out to Joe Public. And secondly, we *do not* want tomorrow's front-page headline to read 'Clueless' above a photo DC Henson and myself. So let me tell you what we know for sure: we have two brutally disfigured bodies, no real motives, no witnesses, and not even a realistic list of prospective suspects."

"So let me get this straight, Detective Inspector Holt, is it?" Holt nodded his confirmation and gestured for her to continue.

"You have no motives for these crimes? None whatsoever?"

Holt looking suitably embarrassed and avoided direct eye contact, nodding his affirmative once more.

"Are the two murders linked?"

"Well, the methods used are not even remotely similar; however, there are certain circumstantial similarities."

"Go on."

"Well, there's the fact that the last murder to happen in Manning's Town was over thirty years ago. And both of these victims were very brutally murdered—not just killed, but maimed. Also, both crime scenes were 'clean.'"

"Clean?"

"Yes, no prints, no hair, nothing to go on, and also both murders took place within forty-eight hours, so an awful lot of planning would have had to have gone into it."

"Any similarities between the victims?"

"Matt Reynolds, the second victim, was in his early thirties, white male. As for the first victim, all we know so far was that he was white male, possibly older than Matt; we're pretty sure he wasn't local, though."

"What makes you say that?"

"No one's been reported missing. We don't even have an ID on him yet.'

"Interesting."

"What? What's interesting?"

"Well, your killer's age and gender specification is within the range that most serial killers are in when they have their killing spree."

"Serial killer? You think this is the work of a serial killer?" Holt was shocked. It wasn't a term he'd even considered in connection with the case; the term 'serial killer' didn't belong in his little town. The subject of many books and films, it certainly didn't fit here in his small town.

"Yes, don't you?"

"Well, I hadn't really considered it"

"As you said, Detective, there hasn't been a murder here in over thirty years. And I imagine it wasn't anything as elaborate as the recent murders."

"True, true." Holt was lost in thought. A serial killer; he'd never had to consider such a prospect in all his years on the force, and now here he was, in the winter of his career having to contemplate facing a possible serial killer.

If he'd been worried about coming to see Dr. Armstrong, it wasn't anything compared to what he was feeling now.

"Inspector?'"

Holt broke from his thoughts.

"Are you sure we're looking for a serial killer?"

"I can't be *sure* of anything, but you shouldn't dismiss the idea just because you're uncomfortable with it, impending retirement or not."

Holt stood stock-still. This woman had just read his mind. He was shocked, but for the most part, he was angry. How dare this woman question his ability to do his job properly.

"With all due respect, Dr. Armstrong, whatever I may or may not feel about these two murders has absolutely nothing to do with my impending retirement, or, for that matter, anything to do with you."

"I'm sorry if I offended you just now, but I really don't see how I can help you."

"You really can't see how you can help us?" Henson's voice was incredulous.

"We have two bodies show up within forty-eight hours, one hideously burnt, the other with so many cuts and drill holes he could have been a stand in for a Black and Decker work mate, and you honestly can't see how you could be of use to us?" Henson was warming to his theme.

"You have the low down and inside track on every nut and loony in the area—you could point us in the direction of some probable suspects. There's a lunatic on the loose somewhere out there, Dr.

Armstrong. Do you want to be the next victim tonight as you're walking to your car?"

"I don't appreciate your tone, DC Henson."

"I'm just saying what everyone else is thinking: anyone could be next—you, me, the inspector."

"So you're asking me to break the doctor patient confidentiality oath? You'd happily send my career into the gutter while advancing your own?"

"Well, no, of course not." Henson's argument was starting to wane.

Holt, sensing his young colleague floundering, stepped in.

"But Dr. Armstrong—Loretta—could you sleep at night, knowing you could be concealing a possible suspect?"

"Compelling argument, DI Holt, and I appreciate what you're saying. Still, without any firm evidence or even a possible suspect, I don't see how I could assist you. Now, if one of my patients were to come in tomorrow and confess to the murders, you can rest assured you would be the first people I'd call. However—"

"You can't see that happening." Holt looked deflated, and Loretta felt for him. He seemed a genuinely nice man, albeit one who was lost. Catching his eye, she smiled softly at him.

"What I can do if you're interested is set about working a profile about the psychological make-up of the type of person you're looking for. This would take a little time though, if you'd like to come back and see me another day."

"Ok, well, thank you for your time." Holt and Henson were moving toward the door.

"No problem. Oh, and before you go, DC Henson, going back to you what you said earlier, I very much doubt I'll be the next victim."

"What makes you so sure of that?"

"If it is in fact a serial killer in operation, they tend to stick to the same gender, and this one seems to have decided on the male of the species. Good evening, gentlemen."

Loretta closed the door behind them.

"What do you think, sir, is she going to be of any use?"

"Maybe. Let's get back to the station—who knows, maybe we'll get lucky and some witnesses have turned up. Or, failing that, a lead on the first victim."

Chapter 6

As Loretta picked up the phone to dial, she wondered if her decision to do so would come back to haunt her. Ever since DI Holt had come to her office to ask for assistance, she had felt guilty about the way she had handled the situation. She had already decided that they were going to put her in an awkward situation and she'd jumped down their throats before she'd even had chance to offer them a coffee. She had felt particularly annoyed with herself at her treatment of DI Holt; he looked like a kindly man, and she had used her profession to cause him unnecessary discomfiture. In short, she felt that she'd behaved like a child. She had known, however, why she'd done it: people always came to see her for her help, but they didn't usually have badges. Badges made her like most—nervous; they were a symbol of authority. But as DI Holt had informed her straight away, they were there off the record, not in an official capacity. Had there not been so much media attention surrounding the cases, maybe she wouldn't have felt so intimidated by the two police officials standing in her office. Since the first body had been discovered, both detectives had been on the TV each night trying to answer increasingly demanding questions. Seeing Holt struggling she had felt genuine pity for him. But that young wannabe he'd been lumbered with for the case had really gotten to Loretta, trying to be

Dick Tracey and Kojak rolled into one, with his glistening insights into the type of guy they were looking for.

It made him sound like he was auditioning for *NYPD Blue*.

When the two detectives had turned up together, Loretta had found herself in a quandary. One of the detectives she could imagine herself liking, and the other was someone she'd like to beat with a blunt object. Finally she'd settled on antagonism.

Now she had to make amends. She wanted to help DI Holt with his enquiries; from what had been said earlier, she knew that he needed her.

Dialling the number, she waited nervously for an answer; she didn't have to wait long.

"Oh, hello, would it be possible to speak to DI Holt, please?" As Loretta held the line, waiting for the officer to locate Holt, she started to bite her fingernails, a nervous gesture she had not been prone to since childhood.

"Hello, DI Holt, it's Dr. Armstrong here. I just wanted to apologise for earlier and offer any assistance you might need. I appreciate you're a busy man, but if you'd like to have a proper talk about the matter, we can."

Holt was in his office on the other side of town with the phone tucked under his chin, sorting through paperwork. He started rubbing at his brow, an unconscious movement that let anyone who knew him know that he was under stress. He didn't want to go back to her office; aside from the fact the last meeting there had been a disaster, he didn't like the overall feel of the place. With its sage walls and leafy plants, it was like the whole building was trying to be something it wasn't.

"That would be appreciated, Dr. Armstrong, and in relation to earlier, I fear Detective Constable Henson and myself were equally to blame. Although to be honest, I'd prefer it if we could meet elsewhere to discuss matters. I'd rather it didn't get back to the press that we're consulting an outsider."

"That's understandable. You're welcome to nominate a more suitable place."

"Well, it can't really be a public place, I'm afraid."

"Well, I could suggest my apartment, or would that not be allowed? It's just that it's quiet there and I live alone, so there's no chance of someone walking in and overhearing something they shouldn't."

Holt wondered briefly if his anxiety was somehow communicating itself to her through the line, then, trying to keep his voice as relaxed as possible, he spoke.

"Well, that would be perfect, as long as you wouldn't find it too much of an intrusion."

"Not at all, but I must make one insistence."

"Yes?"

"Could you come alone, please? That young DC really gets my back up."

Holt had to laugh out loud at that.

"You're certainly not the first person to say that. He can be a little, how should I say, overbearing at times."

"When do you want to come round?"

"Whenever it's most convenient for you. You're

the one helping us, remember?" He was smiling now.

Well, you can come round tonight if you're not busy."

"That would be great, as long as you're sure."

"Yes, I'm sure. Shall we say seven?"

"Great, and I promise I'll make sure DC Henson's safely back home first."

"Thank you. See you at seven, then. Bye."

"Bye." Holt broke the connection and then stared into the receiver. If someone had told him that this would be the outcome of the afternoon, he'd have laughed in his or her face.

Chapter 7

Clare had just gotten in from work, and after putting the kettle on, she wandered through into the lounge and slumped down on the sofa.

Clare's phone rung to life, and when she answered it, she was met by a familiar voice.

"Hey gorgeous, we still on for later?"

"Yeah, of course, be here around seven."

"Will do. Anyway, how's your day been?"

Clare rolled her eyes. Dean was a lovely guy, but he was becoming a little suffocating; this was the third phone call today. They'd gone on several dates since the first and each date resulted in him becoming more clingy. Every time they went out seemed to result in more phone calls the following day. And if she were being honest with herself, she didn't want him becoming too attached, something which was already apparent.

"Fine, thanks. Nothing much has happened in the last two hours since I spoke to you."

"All right, all right, sorry."

Clare reddened.

"No, I'm sorry. I've had a shit day work-wise, that's all."

"Well, I guess you've got stuff to do, so I'll see you later."

"See you later."

As he rang off, Clare threw her phone down. Simultaneously, the doorbell rang. Opening the front door, she found a flustered-looking Hannah weighed down with shopping bags. Passing some of the bags to Clare, Hannah strode straight through and turned the TV on.

"And hello to you, too." Struggling with bags, Clare managed to close the door and followed Hannah into the living room.

Hannah had the news on and was watching intensely.

"Hannah, what's this all about?"

"Be quiet a minute and watch."

Clare watched as the news report recanted its main story: two bodies found in Manning's Town. They both watched in silence, and as the report finished, Clare turned to Hannah.

"Yeah Hannah, I heard about it on the news this morning. Have you only just heard?"

"No, I knew they'd been another body, what I didn't know though is that I knew him."

"What?"

Clare watched Hannah for a moment; she seemed lost in thought.

"Hannah what's wrong?"

Hannah looked at Clare, her eyes welling up.

"Clare, the second body was Matt's."

"Oh my God. Hannah, I'm so sorry."

"It's fine. I mean, it's just that I don't know how to feel about it. It's weird, but a small part of me feels relieved. That sounds awful, doesn't it?"

Clare was well aware of Matt; Hannah had started seeing him five years ago, before Clare had known her. He had been a very jealous and insecure man, and he'd spent months running her down emotionally. He had repeatedly cheated on her, and eventually he'd started to physically abuse her. Luckily for Hannah, she had had a strong network of family and friends around her and she had managed to get away from him after the first time he'd hit her. Though his next partner hadn't been so lucky; after one particularly savage attack, she'd been knocked unconscious. The girl's parents had picked her up from the hospital and taken her away. Matt had been given the opportunity to get professional help to deal with his anger management issues. He had accepted the help, and of late Hannah had heard he had been doing quite well —he had a partner, she was pregnant, and there had been no ugly episodes. Although Hannah hadn't really believed he had been capable of change, she had hoped he was, if just for the sake of his latest partner.

"No, honey, it doesn't sound weird. Is that what's upsetting you? You feel guilty because of that? Just because you wasted enough tears on him when he was alive doesn't mean he deserves your tears now."

Hannah was wiping her tears away and nodding.

"Look, Hannah, I've got to go to an appointment, but feel free to stay here; there's some wine in the fridge, and when I get back we can get wrecked and have a proper chat if you feel you need it."

Hannah was picking up her bags again.

"No, doll, I'll be OK anyway; I've got frozen stuff in here. I might bell you later, if that's all right?"

"Yeah, course."

Clare opened the door for Hannah once more and watched her leave. Closing the door behind her, Clare turned and slumped against her front door briefly before heading back in the direction of the kitchen.

She had twenty minutes to kill before she had to leave for Loretta's office—just long enough for some tea and toast.

She really appreciated the encouragement Loretta had been giving her since she'd started her course. Clare smiled to herself as she thought of all the people who would have cut off their right arm to have someone of Loretta's calibre mentoring them. Although, if she were being honest with herself, she wasn't spending as much time on her studies as she should. Unfortunately, with work, Hannah, and Dean all making demands on her time, the studying was coming along slower than she'd hoped.

Finishing her tea, she grabbed her bag and headed back out the door again.

As Clare pulled into the car park outside Loretta's office, she checked her watch: it was a quarter past one. Loretta was going to be pissed; she was fifteen minutes late. As she grabbed her bag from the passenger seat, she pulled her keys from the ignition and practically ran to the door, taking the steps two at a time as she went. Ignoring the peevish looking secretary, she strolled straight through and gingerly knocked on the door of Loretta's office. Upon hearing the command to enter, she walked in and sat down opposite Loretta.

"Sorry I'm late."

"It's fine. I had some paperwork that I had to catch up on, anyway." Putting the paperwork away Loretta looked up at Clare.

"Clare, is there something bothering you?"

"Actually yes, yes there is. I'm assuming you've heard they've found another body?"

"I don't think there's anyone that hasn't heard."

"Hannah knew him, she went out with him for a bit. He was awful to her, but now she knows he's dead, she's really upset about it."

"That's understandable, she did have an emotional connection to him. And you're good friends with Hannah, I'm surprised it hasn't affected you."

"Oh, I have no sympathy for him, he had it coming, but Hannah, well, I guess I didn't think it'd affect her so much." Clare had started biting her fingernails.

"Clare, what do you know about Matt?"

"I know he set about trying to control Hannah's life, and when that failed, he moved on to his next victim."

"Victim? Clare, you didn't tell me about anyone else."

"No. I didn't want you to become too involved; you've helped me enough as it is. And as for Matt's next victim, he left her with a permanent reminder of him: he convinced her to try suicide with a rusty blade. She spent weeks in hospital recovering from that and blood poisoning."

Loretta's eyes darkened.

"Don't worry, though, he got help—anger management classes. Can you believe that? He systematically sets about destroying people and he's the one who gets help. People like him are incapable of change."

"Everybody's capable of change, Clare, remember that. Matt's paid for whatever sins he may have committed in this life, so I think now it's probably best left alone."

Clare was staring at the floor.

"Clare, do you hear me? Walk away."

"What, before someone gets hurt? I think it's too late for that."

Chapter 8

"Hi, gorgeous."

Dean thrust a bunch of flowers into Clare's hands and kissed her on the cheek.

Clare forced a smile.

"I've made lasagne—is that ok with you?"

Since she had made the decision to split up with Dean, she had been feeling more and more tense, and, if she was honest, she was irritated by his presence. She knew she was being irrational, but a small part of her wanted him to pick up on her decision without it being spoken so she wouldn't have to explain her reasons. Or see rejection on his face.

"Lovely, it smells fantastic." He wandered past Clare and toward the kitchen. Clare followed him through and started rustling around in the cupboard, trying to locate a vase.

"It's been so long since I've had flowers I may have to wash the cobwebs out first."

The small talk was forced, and she glanced over at Dean, trying to detect whether he had picked up on it. He seemed completely oblivious, and she bit back her irritation at him for not being mature enough to pick up on undertones. His youth, which had initially attracted her, was becoming more and more tedious.

Pulling the vase out, she started to wash it.

"What time's the food going to be ready?"

"Oh, another fifteen minutes or so. You want a drink?"

"Yeah, what've you got?"

"There's some wine in the fridge, or there's beer, ribena, milk?"

She said the last two quietly, but Dean had heard. He watched her quizzically for a moment before dismissing it.

"I think I'll just stick with beer, if it's all the same to you."

"Well, you know where the fridge is."

Clare started arranging the flowers and Dean grabbed a can from the fridge. Clare took the vase through to the living room and placed it in the middle of the table. Returning to the kitchen, she found Dean looking pensive. Relieved he might be thinking of splitting up with her, she sat down opposite him.

"What's wrong? You look stressed."

"I'm fine. Clare, I've got something to ask you."

"Ok."

"Do you think—and don't jump down my throat—we could possibly try living together?" Clare felt like she'd been struck in the face. Whatever she'd been expecting, it hadn't been that.

"Living together? Dean, we've only been seeing each other for a couple of weeks."

"I know, but you have to admit we are good together."

"*Two weeks.*"

"Ok, ok, but the thing is, I think I'm falling for you."

"What? You think you're falling in love with me?

I'm ten years older than you, you're not even out of your teens yet—do you even know what love is?"

"Wow, that's a new one. So let me see if I've got this straight: I'm old enough to sleep with you, but not old enough to fall in love. That's a great double standard you've got going there. Anything else I should know about what I can and can't feel?"

Clare was watching Dean closely; he was obviously hurting, and somewhere she deep down she knew she should feel sorry for him, but she couldn't. They'd been together two weeks, and now he wanted them to live together.

"Live together?"

Clare started laughing, a light, bitter laugh.

"And where do you suggest we live? Here, I suppose? You would move into my flat and bleed me dry? Well no thank you, I've played the role of babysitter long enough."

As she finished, she looked to meet his eyes. His eyes were full for a moment, then he blinked and his gaze hardened. Without saying a word, he grabbed his jacket, walked out, and slammed the door.

She let out a sigh of relief and sat down at the table, reaching for her phone.

"Hannah? It's me; I think Dean and I are over."

Hannah's voice was sympathetic on the line.

"Oh, hon, I'm sorry, is there anything I can do?"

"Well, you could come and eat some lasagne with me."

In a little under fifteen minutes Clare opened the door to a dishevelled Hannah.

"Jesus hon, you could have dried your hair before

leaving the house."

"When your best friend rings you to tell you her relationships over, it's your duty to be there for her straight away."

As Hannah said this she stopped at the mirror in Clare's hall.

"Oh my God, I look ridiculous."

Clare burst out laughing.

"Come on, let's have something to eat and then we can do something about the toilet brush masquerading as your hair."

Clare had already set the table and the two sat down to eat.

As the two women finished eating Clare cleared the plates and Hannah started to wash up. Clare topped up both of their wine glasses and took Hannah's over to her. Hannah smiled her thanks.

"So what's the plan then? Are you going to leave it a few days and then ring him?"

"There's no point, really, we both want different things."

"But you said you liked him."

"I do like him, he's a sweet lad, but there's a big difference between liking someone and being in love with them. If we continued to keep seeing each other, it wouldn't have been fair to him. I'm not up to scarring someone emotionally, not even with my track record."

"So what now, then?"

"Well, now I guess I'll have more time to study."

"Ah yes, The Study. How's it going?"

"Ok, thanks. It's odd having to discipline myself again."

"I bet. I'm bad enough at taking the bins out on the right day."

"So how are things going with Mike, anyway? It's been three weeks, Hannah—that's got to be a record for you. He proposed yet?" Clare had deliberately designed the question to get Hannah off the subject of her study, and as Hannah snorted into her glass of wine, Clare knew it had worked.

"Oh, give me a break. No one's tying me down. Actually, we're not even seeing each other anymore."

"You're kidding. You split up?"

"Yes, last night, actually."

"Why?"

"Got bored."

"Bored? You're right, Hannah, you certainly aren't the settling down type."

"Look who's talking; poor Dean, the little lad's heartbroken."

"Could you stop, please, I feel bad enough as it is."

"For crying out loud, he'll be over it by the end of the summer holidays."

"Enough already."

"Do you want to go out tonight? I've heard the Rose and Crown's had a makeover."

"Can't, you know I've been barred."

"Oh, haven't you heard? It's under new management."

"In that case then, yes, why not."

"Right, go and get changed."

Clare made a move toward the bedroom, Hannah turned to look at her.

"And no jeans please."
"Fair enough."

Clare and Hannah turned up at the Rose and Crown at ten past eight. The whole bar was heaving.

"Hannah?"

"Yes?"

"This place is packed; can't we go somewhere quieter?"

"Why? Look, this is just what you need, hon, a bit of noise, a complete change from what you're used to."

"Ok, then, but I don't want to stay long."

"Message heard and understood. I'll go and get the drinks, and you try and grab us a table. Do you want your usual?"

"Please."

Hannah turned away and began wading toward the bar. Clare spotted a small table in the corner and started fighting her way across the room.

Ten minutes later, Hannah appeared with two wine glasses.

"Found a spot, then. Well done."

"Thanks." Clare gratefully relieved Hannah of one of the glasses.

Suddenly Clare felt eyes on her. Looking up, her eyes were met by a man standing at the bar. He looked to be in his mid thirties, tanned and very self-assured. Around him were a few other men that Clare assumed must be his friends and they were dressed almost identically. One of them had has his head turned away from Clare and was quite obviously whispering into his friend's ear.

She didn't know who they were, but they were making her feel uncomfortable. Looking back at Hannah, who appeared not to have noticed, Clare gestured toward her.

"Do you know those guys at the bar?"

Hannah turned to look.

"No. I don't *know* them but I've seen them around town a few times. The one staring at you has got a bit of a reputation, fancies himself as a playboy. His name's Adam. They seem harmless enough, never really spoken to them."

Before Hannah could say anything else, Adam was heading for their table.

"Hi, could I buy you two a drink?"

The question had been aimed at Clare, but before she had a chance to respond, Hannah accepted. Adam headed back to the bar to order two more glasses of wine.

"What the hell do you think you're doing? I've just split up with Dean, and here you are setting me up again?"

"I'm not setting you up with anyone—it's just a drink, Clare; nothing more, nothing less. Relax a little, would you?"

"How can I relax? You've just accepted drinks from a complete stranger. Those guys will want something in return—blokes like that always do."

"You don't have to marry them, you know, it's just a bit of fun."

"And I suppose now we'll have to talk to them?"

"Yes, I imagine we will, is that so bad?"

"Yes. I thought we were just coming out for a

drink, you know, two girls having a chat, and then you bring in a gang of morons. Thanks, Hannah, thanks a lot."

"Oh, for God's sake, have you no idea how social etiquette works? You don't have to have a huge in-depth discussion every time you converse with someone, you know. Occasionally it's nice just to talk about insignificant things, like what happened in *EastEnders* last night and what you're doing at the weekend. You know, just normal chat."

"I don't watch *EastEnders* and I'll be working at the weekend—there, topics covered. Can we go now? Preferably before Hugh Hefner and his cronies come back."

As Clare finished, she looked up and realised she was already too late; Adam was on his way back to the table. Luckily, it seemed two of his mates had gone. Clare wasn't sure if that was by accident or design, but she wasn't happy. Now there was a potential coupling off.

Clare stared daggers at Hannah, who returned it with a smile. Turning the smile onto Adam, she motioned towards the empty seat. Adam smiled his thanks and placed the two wine glasses on the table. Clare uttered her thanks through clenched teeth and a false smile.

Three drinks later, Clare was considerably happier and considerably drunk. She had hated Hannah at first for the forced socialising, but now she was grateful. For the last forty-five minutes, she'd been talking with Adam, and quite contrary to what she'd first thought, he was remarkably easy to talk to. He had done a lot of charity work thanks to the fact he only had to work part time; his parents owned a successful business that he had been promised when they retired. His kind of wealth would usually irritate Clare, but he was remarkably humble. He knew how much he owed to his parents. It was amazing how much else they had in common. They liked the same films, had a similar taste in music, and Adam had even been thinking about doing some home study. Clare smiled across at Hannah, who seemed to be having just as much fun with Tom. Tom was clearly as close to Adam as she was to Hannah. Adam and Tom, as if of one mind, got up and moved toward the bar. Hannah looked over at Clare.

"Forgiven me yet?"

"Just about. They're really nice guys; I wasn't expecting that."

"Well, there you go, just goes to show it doesn't do to judge a book by its cover."

On the other side of the bar Adam was relaying his order to the barman handing over the money he then turned back to Tom.

"How's it going with your one?"

"Putty in my hands, mate, and you?"

"Bit prickly at first, but I just turned up the charm."

"Charm—you? Bloody hell, now I've heard everything."

"Laugh it up, but I'm getting laid tonight."

"Well, I shouldn't have any trouble, either; she's all over me."

"Yeah, but yours was hardly a challenge. Yours drops her knickers in a heartbeat, but mine—"

"All right, all right, next time I get first pick, though."

Adam pushed his chest out, grabbed the drinks, and started to make his way back to the table.

Clare and Hannah were deep in discussion when Adam returned.

"Not interrupting anything, are we?"

"Don't be daft. Sit down."

"Tom and I were saying at the bar that it seems mad to stay here; we can barely hear each other speak, so why don't we all go back round to mine? I've got some drinks in."

Clare looked over at Hannah.

"Well, what do you think?"

"I'm game if you are."

"Well, in that case we'll finish these drinks and make a move."

"Great."

The two girls went back to chatting, not noticing the exchange of glances between Adam and Tom.

Chapter 9

As DI Holt approached Loretta's front door, he wondered if he should just turn about and go back to his car. This woman wasn't officially police, and he was about to discuss particularly sensitive issues with her. He knew it would be, at the very least, frowned upon, but he needed her assistance. How many times had he told himself that in the last three days? Besides, it wasn't like he was discussing the case in the local watering hole with a good percentage of the town's loose-lipped community. Dr. Armstrong was a respected member of the community whose job was basically to keep secrets and help people who were incapable of helping themselves. And anyway, if this did get back to the station and it wasn't well received, he'd be retired, and considering that's what he was planning to do at the end of this case, he didn't feel he had a lot to lose.

Standing in front of the door, he took a deep breath, as was fast becoming the tradition when meeting this woman. He knocked on the door. He was just starting to get second thoughts again when the front door swung open.

"DI Holt, I'm glad you came. I was wondering if you might have had second thoughts."

Inwardly Holt shuddered; this woman had an uncanny knack for getting him spot on every time.

"No, not at all; I said I'd be here, and here I am."

Smiling, she opened the door wider and gestured him inside.

"Well anyway, it's good to see you again in more informal surroundings. If you'd like to go through to the living room, I'll bring us in some coffee and we can get started." Noticing the confusion on his face, she pointed in the direction of the living room and disappeared through a door on his right.

"I'll rather have tea, actually, if that's ok," Holt called through the door at her retreating back. He wanted to stay in control of at least one part of this meeting, and if that was beverage choice, then so be it. Trying to appear relaxed, he started to walk in the direction of the living room. Once inside and alone, he started to relax. He saw the room for what it was: a haven. In hindsight, it was hard for him to say what he'd expected, but he was sure it didn't resemble this. The place was painted a rich blue colour, which should have made the room feel cold, or at least small, but the high ceilings and large windows prevented that. The heavy deep blue curtains that framed the window should have looked chintzy, but somehow they didn't. The sofa was big, obviously expensive, but had a lived in look, as if the owner might fall asleep in it occasionally. There was a blanket thrown haphazardly across the back of it that fitted in with that purpose. Occupying the far corner of the room was a small office area. Papers littered the desk, and although a small set of bookshelves stood next to it, most of the books had found their way onto the floor around the chair, stacked neatly in little piles. On the wooden floorboards rugs of varying sizes and styles gave the room a warm, comforting feel. There were two armchairs on either side of the sofa, angled around an antique oak coffee table. As he was trying to work out which was the most uncomfortable looking seating area—he didn't want to sit in the chair Loretta classed as 'her chair'—Loretta walked in with a tray.

"Take a seat, Mr. Holt." Smiling, she placed the tray down on the coffee table and sat down.

"Thanks, and please call me Jimmy." Just as Holt sat down, Loretta jumped back up again.

"Forgot the biscuits. I always have to have coffee and biscuits when I get back from work—it's one of my little rituals. Won't be a minute."

Holt allowed himself a little smile, he'd never had pegged Dr. Armstrong as a biscuit lover; it didn't fit in with her lifestyle at all.

Loretta came back into the room and offered him a biscuit. Jimmy declined and watched as she ensconced herself back in the armchair opposite him and proceeded to dunk a biscuit into her coffee. She noticed him watching her.

"Oh, sorry, another habit of mine; it doesn't bother you, does it?"

"Heavens no, I used to do that myself, but my wife hated it. My ex-wife," Holt corrected.

"Oh, I know your ex-wife, don't I? Sorry, I wasn't trying to pry, it's just—'

"No, no, it's ok. I wondered if it would come up. Actually, one of the reasons I chose to come and see you was because of what she'd said about you."

"Oh yes, and what exactly did she say about me?" Loretta's voice was light and jovial, trying to diffuse any tension.

"She just said you're very good at what you do."

"Well, that's good. Now, let's get started. I already know a little about the cases."

"You do?"

"Yes, the cases are being followed quite closely by the media, Jimmy. Have you brought any photos of the crime scenes with you?"

"Yes, but Loretta—it's ok if I call you Loretta, isn't it?"

"Yes, of course, please continue."

"Well, before I show them to you, you must realise that I'm taking a huge risk in doing so. The atrocities performed on these poor souls are brutal even to the most hardened of people."

"It's ok. I attended medical school and have some experience working in the A&E department. Trust me, I've seen my fair share of mutilated bodies." She said this in a conversational tone, but the underlying weight of the statement hung in the air.

Jimmy reached to the folder he had laid on the coffee table earlier.

He pulled a wad of large, glossy photographs from the folder and handed them to Loretta. Taking the photographs from him, she started carefully looking through holding them carefully, almost gently, as if she was afraid that leaving her fingerprints on their surface would inflict further humiliation and pain to the victims. He saw a look of disgust cross her face briefly. After a few minutes of perusing the photos, she stopped on one particular print, leaning forward toward Jimmy and showing him the photograph.

"What's that?" He recognised the photo straight away. It was from the first murder scene. It was a photograph that showed where the ring of flames had been on the warehouse floor. Loretta was pointing toward the back of the photo within the ring; there was a box with a digital clock sitting on top of it. He had to admit that that particular find had stumped him, too. Especially when he'd looked inside the box. It had contained the keys to the handcuffs that had been used on the man's ankles. It had been a very odd find.

"It's a box with a clock on top of it," he answered, not sure if he should mention anything else. The fact that it had had keys in it had not been released to the press, and he wasn't sure if he should tell her about that.

"Did the box contain anything?"

Why did this woman always seem to know what was going on in his head before he did?

After a pause, Loretta spoke again.

"If you're serious about me helping you with this case, don't you think a good place to start would be for you to be straight with me? I know there was something in the box, Jimmy."

"Why would you assume that?" Jimmy's voice was high and strained all of a sudden; he was alarmed that she'd seen through him once more.

"Well, two reasons, really. The first is that you took too long answering me when I asked a direct question that you should have already known the answer to, indicating you were thinking about your answer, a little inner conflict, maybe?" She paused then, looking at him sideways, eyebrows arched and a small smile on her lips.

"And secondly, when you finally did respond, your voice was all squeaky and defensive. My God, it's a good job you joined the police force—you'd make a terrible crook."

Jimmy laughed.

"Ok, you caught me. Yes, there was something in the box."

"May I hazard a guess as to what you found?"

"By all means."

"A key?"

Jimmy's jaw dropped open.

"How did you know that?"

"Well, it was just an educated guess, really."

"Educated guess? Where did you get the information to make this guess?"

"These photos." She picked them up and handed them back to him.

"What do you notice about the pattern of scorched ground?"

"It's a circle, and…?"

"And the victim, we all agree, started out in the middle of the circle and lost his life trying to escape it."

"Yes."

"And the victim must have been soaked in petrol."

"Yes."

"And the circle was made with petrol."

"Yes, what's your point?"

"Think about it: put yourself in the deceased's position. You're in a warehouse, in a circle of flames, soaked to the skin in petrol, you've managed to cut through the binds on your hands, but your ankles are handcuffed. What are your options?"

"I'd look around the area to see if there was anything that could help me escape—the keys for the handcuffs for example. And being in a warehouse would mean a flat concrete floor, so the petrol must have been the source of the flames surrounding you."

"Yes, and what do we know about petrol?"

"It's highly combustible."

"Exactly, which means it will burn out quickly, so…"

"Why didn't he just wait until after the flames had burnt out to make his escape?"

"Now, all these photos show the scene as it was found, yes?"

"Yes."

"So the box was unopened when it was found?"

"And?"

"If you're in that predicament, where you can't wait for the flames to burn out, you'd look around first to see if there was anything around to help aid your escape, but he didn't look in the box, which was the only thing in the ring with him. If that had been me, the box would have been the first place I would have looked, personally."

"Yes, but when you find yourself in a ring of flames, I'm sure you probably aren't thinking straight."

"Good point, however, it wouldn't take long for the survival instinct to kick in. You'd be surprised how resilient and resourceful the mind can be under the extreme pressure to carry on living."

Jimmy took a large drink of his tea and winced. Coffee. Drinking it down quickly, he put his cup back down and turned back to Loretta.

"Ok, so why didn't he look inside the box?"

"Well, why wouldn't you look inside the box in his position?"

"I don't know. I guess if I thought opening it would make my situation worse."

"Exactly. Now consider what was found on top of the box."

"A clock.'"

"Yes, now, considering everything else, why do you suppose he didn't open the box?"

Reassessing all the new ideas, it didn't take Jimmy long to work it out.

"He believed there was a bomb in it? That's the reason he didn't wait for the flames to die down or open the box? But why leave the keys in the box? Did the killer want him to escape?" Jimmy's face was agog.

"I wouldn't think so. Maybe they wanted you to believe the victim had a chance, but in reality, he didn't. It's an incredibly elaborate plot; I don't think these two murders are going to be isolated."

"Meaning?" Holt was almost afraid to ask.

"Meaning, given the amount of time taken to execute them and how close together they were…"

Loretta paused for a moment and looked Holt in the eye.

"You are looking for a serial killer, a highly organised individual. The only thing you can be completely sure of, Inspector Holt, is that there will be more bodies. How many more is up to the killer."

"And us," Holt amended.

Loretta got up and went to pick up Holt's cup.

"I'll get you a refill" Holt, still lost in thought, brought his hand down on top of Loretta's to stop her.

"No, it's ok, thank you. I've got to get going now anyway."

Realising his hand was still covering Loretta's, he quickly removed it and gathered up all the photos that now littered the table. Getting up, he turned to Loretta.

"Well, thank you for your time, but I really ought to get back to the station."

Holt wasn't sure why, but he suddenly felt embarrassed. His need to leave the confines of Loretta's apartment made him suddenly clumsy. As he reached the living room doorway, his jacket caught on the door handle. Acutely aware of his faux pas, he started quickly down the hall toward the front door when his foot found the underside of the hall runner rug. He fell face first, and the photos spewed across the floor. He heard Loretta coming up behind him, and he quickly started gathering the photos up. She knelt down next to him to help. As she did, she paused to look over the photos of the second murder scene. She stared at them for a moment before handing them back to him.

"Did you want to leave those photos here so I can look over the second murder properly?"

"I appreciate the offer, but I can't, I'm afraid; they shouldn't really have left the station."

"Ok, then." Getting up with him, Loretta walked him to the door.

"Well, thanks again. Would it be ok to come round again at some point?"

"Of course, glad to be of service." She grinned then, and the act made her look childlike. She opened the door for him and he walked out.

"Take care of yourself, Jimmy."

"Will do; you, too." He smiled at her as she closed the door, and then he leant back against outside wall of the apartment.

What the hell was that?

He hadn't behaved like that in female company since he was fifteen. There was no denying Loretta was an attractive woman, but to lose his nerve so quickly? All he'd done was touch her hand. He could see why strangers would find themselves opening up to her. She had the rarest of qualities; an authoritative presence coupled with a gentle manner. And her eyes, she had the eyes of a long lost friend, someone you may not have seen in a lifetime but you feel entirely comfortable pouring your soul out to.

Putting his behaviour down to lack of food and rest, he turned and made his way to the lifts.

Chapter 10

Clare woke up feeling terrible; she knew she'd thrown up at some point, as she still had an acrid taste in her mouth. In the dim light she stared around her, nothing was familiar. Sitting bolt upright in the bed she felt something moving next to her and grabbing the duvet she pulled it back to reveal a half-naked Hannah

"Hannah, wake up." Clare's voice was hushed, but the urgency in it roused Hannah.

"What the hell?" Hannah was stirring, and her mind was clearly going through the same questions Clare's had not minutes before.

"What happened last night?"

"I'm not sure; we were at the pub with those guys, we went round to Adam's flat… I don't know, it all goes hazy after the pub."

"Oh God, Hannah, where are we? Where are they? Why can't I remember anything?"

"I don't know—let's just get dressed and go."

"We can't leave yet; I need to know what happened."

Hannah swung around to face her friend.

"Clare, we are half-naked in a bed, in a place we don't know, not able to remember anything. What do you think went on?"

Clare's face was confused and then the confusion was replaced with horror.

Don't say anything, Clare. Please, let's just go."

"Go where? The police?"

"The police? Are you kidding?"

"Hannah, we've been drugged and assaulted—we have to report it."

"Why, do you really want everyone knowing about this? Even if by some miracle it went to court, what then? Nearly all rape cases get thrown out."

"We have to do something."

"We will."

"What?"

"Go home and never speak of this again."

Hannah finished dressing herself and made for the bedroom door.

"Wait for me." Clare was hurriedly putting her shoes on.

Both girls were silent the entire walk back to Clare's apartment.

Once they were inside Clare's flat, something seemed to snap in Hannah.

"I don't want to think or speak of this ever again. I'm going to make us a cup of tea."

Clare sat down. She'd never felt so low before. She started thinking back to all the times in her life when she'd believed things couldn't possibly have been worse None came even remotely close to how she was feeling now. She felt sick to the pit of her stomach, and all she wanted to do was fill the bath with bleach and submerge herself in it until she felt clean again. She could feel tears stinging her eyes, but she held them back.

Hannah returned to the living room with two cups of tea.

Clare took one from her.

"Do you want something to eat?"
"No thanks."
The two sat in silence, both in their own hells, both wishing there was some way they could turn back the clock.

Chapter 11

Henson bowled up to Holt's desk.

"How'd it go with Loretta the other evening, then?"

"*Dr. Armstrong* had some insightful thoughts on the case, actually, and I'd appreciate it if you didn't announce it to the whole station, thanks."

"Ok, ok, sorry. I didn't want to step on anyone's toes."

Holt looked up briefly, eyebrows raised.

"Was there anything else?"

"Well, I was wondering if you were going to share any of these glimmering insights with me?"

"Of course, but not now, I'm meeting someone for lunch." Gathering up his papers, he shoved them unceremoniously into his briefcase.

"Oh yes? Anyone I know?" Henson ventured.

"I doubt it. Now, while I'm out, I want you to find out everything there is to know about Matt Reynolds, family, friends, ex-girlfriends—anything. Somebody must know something."

Holt strode up the corridor in the direction of Loretta's apartment. Damn that bloody idiot Henson; he was such a cocky little sod. He seemed to be constantly surrounded by reporters and didn't seem to have learnt the standard police reply for such situations: 'No comment.'

He was thriving on his newfound celebrity status,

and it hadn't yet dawned on him that the sooner this case was solved, which Henson himself wanted to happen, his enraptured audience would disappear, along with any 'glory' that had accompanied it. Henson would be back at the bottom of the pecking order, but this time instead of being disliked by his peers, he would be ridiculed. Henson was starting to act as if he was the star in his very own detective show. Well, he was going to have to start realising sooner rather than later that television dramas were not a mirror to the real world. As far as Holt was concerned, this story was going to end, and it *wasn't* going to get a second season.

Loretta opened the door to a very weary-looking Jimmy Holt.

"Jimmy, come in."

Holt did as he was bid.

"Have you had any news on the first victim's identity yet?"

"No, I've got people trawling through the missing persons file as we speak."

"What about Matt Reynolds? Do you know why he was targeted?"

"Well, not really; all we know is that he had a slightly chequered past as far as his relationships were concerned. He had been arrested for domestic abuse; we spoke to an ex of his, and apparently he was, shall we say, a difficult man to live with."

Loretta nodded at this. She still wasn't sure how much she could trust Holt as far as her patient files were concerned, and as he'd found out about Matt's questionable personal life, she didn't feel she needed to break a confidence.

"Although…" Holt leant towards Loretta for emphasis.

"We think his past may have had something to do with his selection."

"What makes you say that?" Loretta rose to the bait as was expected.

"Part of his heart had been removed."

"I didn't read about that in the papers."

"Well, you wouldn't; we didn't release it. The press are hysterical enough at the moment."

"What do you mean 'part' of the heart?"

"Well, whoever did it certainly wasn't an expert. It had been hacked at using whatever tools they'd found in the toolbox."

"Was the heart removed from the scene? Is it a trophy?"

"No, it was found a bin in the corner of the room, in the chest cavity where it had been there was a note, the note read 'heartless'. According to Dennis Grant—that's our coroner—Matt had been dispatched with the drill and the heart had been removed post mortem.'

Loretta looked amazed for a moment.

"Heartless. The killer felt that as he hadn't used it during his life, he had no need for it in the next."

"And again, the scene was set to make it look as if escape had been a possibility. There was an alarm clock on the table next to the chair that Matt had been taped to. The door keys were found just behind it, obscured from view of whoever was in the chair. While Matt was secured in the chair, it appears he had two holes drilled through his ankles. The tape had then been deliberately cut away, and he had attempted to drag himself to the door. He made it, as well; his fingerprints along with his blood were found on the door handle. But the door was locked, and I imagine that's when his time was up. The alarm was set for nine thirty, and that pretty much sits exactly in the estimated time of death bracket."

Loretta took a minute to digest what had been said.

"You know, I'm not so sure about the 'possibility of escape' thing. I think it may go deeper than we think."

"How do you mean?"

"Well, it's a bit tenuous, isn't it? Almost as if it's been thrown in."

"I thought we agreed that the killer was organised."

"Yes, but I don't know. It's starting to feel a little like it's been put in to distract us—sorry, I mean you."

"But you're the one who brought it to my attention."

"Yes, but now I'm not so sure. It's quite clumsy, and I'm starting to think the whole idea of a possible escape may not be a part of the ritual of the kill, but the psychology behind it that is being called into question."

"What?" Holt was starting to feel annoyed. How was he supposed to catch this person if the goal posts were continually moving?

"I think the idea of escape isn't to ridicule the victim as much as it's ridiculing psychology in general. The killer's not trying to help the victims; instead the killer is showing us that some people can't—or more likely *choose* not to—be helped. Hold on.'

Loretta got up and started rustling through papers on her desk.

"Here it is."

Passing a crumpled piece of paper to Holt, she sat back down to give him time to read it.

It was an article on paedophiles in the prison system. Holt scanned the page and looked back up at Loretta.

"It says here that ninety percent refuse counseling for their crimes when they go in. Is that true?"

"Near enough. The thing is they don't recognise their actions are wrong, only that society deems them wrong. And how can you rehabilitate someone who refuses to acknowledge they were wrong to start?"

"You don't, I suppose."

"Exactly, so they sit in there and serve their time, all the while in the company of like-minded people, until their release date."

"But at least they are registered, then."

"Yes, but I imagine that's cold comfort to the families who live near them."

"So what you're saying is that the victims may have been offered professional help at some point in their lives, more than likely due to unsavoury actions on their part."

"Possibly, although it may just be an insult aimed at the justice system as a whole."

Holt looked deflated.

"Look, have you eaten yet?"

"No, I was just going to grab a sandwich on the

way back to the station."

"Well that settles it, then, you can stay here. I've got a casserole in the oven, and it should be ready about now."

"I can't, really, I've already annoyed Henson…" Holt paused and thought for a moment.

"On second thought, the little snot deserves it. Yes, I'd love to stay, thank you."

Loretta smiled and went to the kitchen to sort out the food. Holt took the chance to reflect back on what Loretta had said. The country, as Holt had seen it, had been in the midst of a swing towards civil liberties for the last fifty years, and now it was time for the backlash. And the backlash here in his quiet little town was a maniac with a vendetta.

When Loretta came in and started laying out food on the little dining table next to him, he barely registered her presence.

"You look lost in thought." Looking at her as if seeing her for the first time, he moved his elbows off the table to allow her to put the placemats down.

"Oh, I hope you're not going to extra trouble for me."

"Trouble? No, no trouble, I always eat at the dinner table." She finished laying out the serviettes and walked back into the kitchen. Holt watched as Loretta brought a casserole dish in and placed it on the table. Since the divorce he had lived alone, surviving on little more than take-aways and foodstuffs that came in a can. *If* he sat down to eat the meal, it would be a miracle if it were served on a plate, let alone accompanied with placemats and serviettes.

"How much would you like?" Loretta's voice drifted through into his consciousness.

"Sorry?"

"Casserole—how hungry are you?"

"How it comes would be fine, thank you."

Loretta plated the food up carefully and wiped the edge of his plate with a clean napkin when she'd finished, placing his plate in front of him. Looking down, he noticed he'd left the photo of the late Tom Reynolds in full view on the table. Quickly he scooped it up and put it back in his briefcase, but luckily Loretta didn't appear to have noticed. She continued to plate up her own meal and Holt waited until she had finished before he started his own food. He did not want to appear uncouth to Loretta; she already managed to make him feel like a dinosaur, as it was.

When they had both finished their meals, Holt went to pick up the plates and clear the table.

"Oh no, you don't. You're a guest here. Go and make yourself comfortable while I take this out. Would you like anything to drink?"

"A cup of coffee would be great, thanks."

"Ok, I'll be two minutes."

Holt sighed contentedly before getting up and making his way back over to the armchair. This wasn't something he'd be telling Henson about; he was hard work at the best of times, but if he found out Holt had had a meal, there he'd be, ribbing him all the time.

Loretta came back into the room with two mugs of coffee, and Holt grabbed a couple of coasters and placed them on the coffee table. He was starting to understand this woman a little more now, or at least he liked to think he was.

"I can't tell you what a relief it is to have some decent food for a change. I can't remember the last time I had a home cooked meal."

"You are more than welcome." Loretta smiled at Holt.

"It's also nice to have someone intelligent to talk to."

"What about DC Henson?"

"Are you kidding me?"

Loretta chuckled.

"Yes, he is a little overzealous at times, isn't he? Not a great thing, considering the sensitivity of the case."

"You're telling me. Anyway, I'd better get back to the station. Thanks again for everything, especially the lunch—it's been a while since I've eaten that well."

"It was my pleasure; it was nice not to be eating alone again." As Loretta opened the door for him, he paused briefly and turned to look at her.

"Have a good afternoon."

Loretta stood for a minute watching his retreating back. As Holt walked away from Loretta's apartment he found himself deep in thought.

Had Matt Reynolds attended anger management classes?

Holt grabbed his phone from his pocket and quickly punched in a number.

"Hi, it's DI Holt. Is there any way of finding out if Matt Reynolds had any counseling or anger management classes?"

Holt went quiet as the desk PC pulled up the file.

"There's nothing on here that I can see. Hold on, DC Henson's just come in."

Holt waited patiently as the officer on the line spoke with Henson. Then Henson came on the line.

"Hello, sir, I've just gotten back from speaking with Matt Reynolds's ex, Rebecca Lowes, or, rather, her family. It's strange that you would ask about the counseling thing; apparently he was offered it after he was arrested for being violent towards her. He agreed, went twice, and never went back."

"OK Henson, I'm just heading back now."

Without waiting for a response Holt hung up.

Chapter 12

Dean woke up and lifted his head gingerly, as if any sudden movement might cause it to explode. He looked down at his crumpled shirt and found it covered in dried vomit. After Clare and he had split up, he hadn't spent a single night in. His mate from the garage, Pete, had ensured that.

Last night had been no different; he and Pete had gone out, and judging by the state of his clothes, they had gotten absolutely hammered. He thought he'd enjoyed it at the time, but now, covered in his own sick and with the mother of all hangovers, he wished he hadn't bothered. But the biggest regret Dean was having at the moment was not being able to call Clare. He looked over at his alarm clock and realised he'd forgotten to set it. Realising he was going to be late for work again he jumped out of bed and headed to the bathroom. Peeling last night's clothes off and dumping them on the floor, he got into the shower. As he stood under the shower his mind his mind crept back to Clare. Why had she dumped him so fast? She had completely freaked out when he'd suggested that they move in together. He tried to force his mind back to last night. There had been women there, but he hadn't been interested.

Getting out of the shower he dried himself off quickly and dressed. In his bedroom his phone started to ring, running into his room he grabbed the phone from his bed. Seeing it was Pete, he allowed himself a moment of disappointment before answering.

"Hi, Pete, what's up?"

"All right, mate, you coming in to work today?"

"Yeah, I'm on my way; tell Jon I'll be in within the hour."

"You better get here quicker than that, he's going ballistic."

"All right, all right, I'll see you in a half hour." Dean hung up his phone. Dashing down the stairs he grabbed his jacket. Charging out of the door he ran to the bus stop and managed to get there just as the bus arrived.

Dean arrived at the garage within the thirty minutes he had promised.

Pete wandered over to Dean when he arrived.

"Jon still doing his nut?"

"Nah, he's calmed down now, had a phone call from the missus."

"Real or slag?"

"Slag, of course, his real missus hasn't so much as coaxed a smile from him in years."

"Are you coming out later? I'm going down the Rose and Crown later to enjoy my last hour or so of freedom before the weekend."

"Yeah, all right, haven't got anything else planned."

"You never do these days, you've got to get yourself a woman, Dean, someone closer to your own age this time."

"Give it a rest, Pete. I've told you, I'm all right as I am. You fancy going and putting a few bets on

Saturday?"

"I'd love to, but Collette's got me retiling the bathroom Saturday."

"What about Sunday, then?"

"Nah, I've got to put the lino down, and once the bathroom's finished I think she's targeting the living room. At this rate I won't have a weekend free for the next six months."

"One chat with you and you could put most men off women for life."

"It feels like I've got a life sentence sometimes. Bloody hell, maybe I should bump her off; at least I could get parole at some point."

Dean started to laugh.

"Still, I shouldn't moan, she's not a bad old girl, really, and there are compensations."

"So I've heard."

As Dean spoke a Mini Cooper pulled into the forecourt.

"Ok, this is mine." Dean motioned for the driver to bring the car straight into the garage. As the driver vacated her vehicle she passed the keys to Dean and Dean explained the work should be completed within an hour.

Dean got into the Mini, parked it over the inspection pit and started work. Fifty minutes later Dean dropped the bonnet and jumped in to take it over to the collection bay. As he parked, he noticed Pete coming toward him, coat in hand. Dean dropped the keys back in the office and the two started toward the pub.

"I've only got until six. Collette's actually cooking from scratch tonight, and God only knows I don't want to be late for that."

"She's got you well trained."

"So she thinks, but I've been out with you most nights recently. Really this is just a strategic move to ensure my clothes aren't on fire in the front garden tomorrow. Besides, she's quite a good little cook when she puts her mind to it."

As they neared the entrance to the pub, they noticed a group of lads loitering around outside. The Rose and Crown had benches outside for smokers. A couple of lads were sitting on the benches. As Pete and Dean walked past them, Dean nodded slightly in their direction. As soon as they were inside, Pete spoke up.

"Friends of yours?"

"Kind of, I know them from school."

"Well, if I were you I'd keep your distance; right little fuckers, the lot of them. Remember I told you about all the smash and grab car incidents up round mine? Well, I heard it was down to them lot."

"Come on, mate, you don't know that."

"I'm telling you, and they deal."

"Deal?"

"Yeah, coke, heroin, skunk, whatever they can lay their hands on—my sister won't take her kids down the park anymore cause there's always some crack addict milling about. Take it from me: stay away from them, they're bad news."

Dean thought back to his school days; they had been the reason he'd been kicked out of school. He'd been caught with half a dozen ecstasy tablets on him. Funnily enough, the school wasn't keen on having a drug dealer as a pupil, and he'd been shown the door.

Getting their drinks, the pair moved towards the pool table.

After three games of pool and several pints, both Pete and Dean were a little worse for wear.

"Your missus is going to do her nut when you roll in."

"Nah, she'll be all right, she's good as gold, really." Pete was busy trying to fit both his arms into the same sleeve of his coat, and Dean got up to give him a hand.

"You staying here for a bit?"

"Yeah, might as well finish my drink; I haven't got anybody cracking the whip."

"Collette's not cracking the whip; there's only one person wears the trousers in my house."

"Yeah, that's true, and at least she can work the zip on hers properly."

Pete looked down and hurriedly did himself up.

"Well, I guess I'll see you Monday, then, me old mate."

"Yeah, will do." Dean escorted Pete to the door. As he opened it for him, one of the lads who had been sitting outside walked in. After watching to make sure Pete navigated the road safely, Dean went back to retrieve his pint.

"Still whipped, then?" The voice was loud in the bar.

Swinging round to see where it had originated from, Dean recognised the culprit immediately: Mark Prime. Mark had always been the leader of the group, and now here he was, calling him out.

Dean smiled, and taking the remnants of his pint, strolled toward him.

"All right, Mark, mate, long time no see."

"You ain't kidding, Deano, how's that bird of yours, then? Last thing I heard, she was wearing your balls as earrings."

"If you mean Clare, we split up, and for the record I was never whipped."

"Well you knocked the old dope on the head for her, and the party powder. I heard you'd become a real hermit."

"It was fuck all to do with her; I guess I just grew out of all that shit."

"In two weeks? Fucking hell, you're breaking me heart here. I thought you were one of us?"

"Ah, sorry mate, but you know what I mean."

"No, but fuck it; what you drinking?"

"Stella, but I was just going."

"Bollocks, you're coming outside and having a beer and a toke, see some of your old mates."

Before Dean could object again, Mark had grabbed the pints and was heading for the door.

On the other side of town, Lauren Matthews, Dean's mother, was in the middle of a stand up shout down row.

"For the last time, Alice, you're only fifteen; you are not going to a sleepover at a boy's house."

"But his older sister's going to be there."

"Oh great, a seventeen-year-old girl's holding the fort. Why didn't you mention this before? What do you want to take, vodka or whiskey?"

"Nothing's going to happen—why won't you

trust me?"

"You're not the one I have the trust issue with, it's the twenty or so other people who'll be there."

"But you know Cathy, she'll be there."

"Really? Her parents are ok with this, then?"

Sensing she may have chanced an arm too far, Alice tried to change tack.

"You let Dean stay out all night when he was fifteen."

"Yeah, and look what happened to him—he ended up hanging about with those losers and got kicked out of school. I'm sorry, Alice, but the answer's still no."

"It's because he's a boy, isn't it? This isn't fair. I thought there was supposed to be equality now."

"Well, I'm sorry to hear you feel as if you're a victim of sexual discrimination, but until boys can carry a baby to full term, the answer to every fifteen-year-old girl who wants to go to a boy's sleepover is going to be no."

"Oh, so that's why I can't go. You think I'd be stupid enough to get pregnant. I'm not you."

"I know you're upset about not going, so I'm going to pretend I didn't hear that."

"Mum, please."

"No, and what's more I'm going to give Cathy's parents a call, see if they know what's going on."

Alice turned on her heel and stormed out the kitchen. Dean, who was just getting in, was almost knocked sideways as his sister stomped past him and flew up the stairs. Dean sauntered through into the kitchen.

"Bloody hell, Mum, what's up with her? She

almost knocked me off my feet just now."

"Oh, the usual. She wants to go to a sleepover and I've said no, so now I'm the tyrannical bitch sent to make her life miserable."

"Fair enough. What's for tea?" Dean knew better than to get involved.

"Well, Alice and I had shepherd's pie; you could have had, too, if you'd been here three hours earlier. Where've you been, anyway?"

"Just out with some mates."

"Pete from the garage again?"

Thinking about her reaction if she knew who he'd really just spent the last couple of hours with; Dean decided to go along with her guess.

"Yeah."

"He's a nice guy, that Pete, a lot better than that other lot you used to hang around with."

"Yeah, he's a nice guy, all right."

"I saw that Mark and his cronies outside Tesco the other day, hanging about by the cash point and hurling obscenities about. He looks like he hasn't had a good scrub in weeks. Is he still dealing?"

"How the hell should I know, Mum? I'm not his fucking keeper."

"Watch your tongue. If you're going to start talking to me like that, you can just fuck off and find a new address. God knows I have enough to put up with from that moody little mare upstairs."

"Sorry. I've just been having a rough few weeks."

Lauren stopped and regarded her eldest.

"You've had a hard few weeks? You wait 'til you're out in the real world, you're gonna get the shock of your life."

"Oh Christ, am I due for a verse of 'the rising costs of living,' rounded off with a chorus of 'you'll never make it on your own.'"

Lauren cracked a smile at this and cuffed him round the head.

"All right, you cheeky sod, what do you want to eat?"

Chapter 13

It had been a week since Clare and Hannah's fateful night, and both women had managed to avoid speaking of it. Clare had invited Hannah around and had brought in a bottle of vodka to help keep them numb. Hannah was bringing a film, and the two of them hoped to get back to a place where they could just enjoy each other's company once more. Both women hated to admit it, but they were well aware of how much they reminded each other of that night.

A knock at the door heralded the arrival of her friend, and Clare went to answer it. Prior to the assault she hadn't kept her door locked, never fearing for her safety in her own town before. But after last weekend, she now never answered the door without the chain firmly on.

Clare checked it was Hannah, and, satisfied, she released the chain and let her in.

"How have you been?"

Both women knew just how ridiculous the question was, but Clare played along regardless.

"Oh, great, thanks. What film did you bring?"

"*Texas Chainsaw Massacre.*"

Clare laughed, releasing tension.

"In the mood for a bit of mindless violence, are we?"

"Aren't you?"

"These days? Always. Thought you might have

had enough of that from the local newspaper."

Clare walked through to the kitchen, got two glasses out, and started pouring the vodka before returning to the living room and setting up the DVD player. An hour into the film, both Clare and Hannah seemed a little more relaxed, the vodka having taking the edge off. Clare's mobile suddenly sprang to life, making both of them jump. Clare grabbed it from the table and checked to see who it was.

"Who is it?"

"I don't know, I don't recognise the number."

"What's it say?"

"It's a text but all it contains is a web address. Hold on, I'll find out."

Clare scrolled to the address and clicked on it. The phone became busy once more as it tried to locate the page. As the screen started to load, Clare's mouth dropped open with a look of absolute shock. Hannah watched as her friends face drained of all colour.

"What, Clare—what the hell's wrong?"

At that moment Hannah's phone started to vibrate, informing her of an incoming message. Hannah retrieved her mobile from her bag and opened the message just as her friend had done not a minute before.

Hannah took one look and knew why her friend seemed so horrified. On the screen in front of her, clearly illustrated, was herself in a very compromising position, with whom she knew instantly had to be Tom Webber. His face had been scrambled in a bid to protect his identity, something he hadn't bothered doing for Hannah. Hannah grabbed her stomach and ran toward the bathroom, and in the background Clare could hear her throwing up. Within two minutes Hannah was back, her head in her hands.

"Oh God, Clare. What are we going to do?" Hannah clasped her hands and turned to face her.

All the colour in Clare's face had drained

"To be honest, I've absolutely no idea."

Adam Woodacre and Tom Webber were still riding high. They'd just sent the text messages to Hannah and Clare, and the lines of coke they taken a few minutes before were doing their job.

"Can you imagine the look on their faces?"

"I know they must be shitting bricks now, stupid bitches."

"Serves them fucking right, didn't they listen to their mothers? Never go off with strange men."

Tom howled with laughter at this.

"Well, they don't get much stranger than you, me old mate."

Grabbing another can of beer from the table, Adam chucked it at Tom.

"Cheers. Look, Ad, you sure they won't go to the old bill?"

"Course they won't, would you? Besides, the rohypnols out of their systems by now, so we're home and dry."

"Yeah, and I suppose the coppers have got enough to deal what with all the murders."

"Yeah, I'd love to have seen the last one; apparently he was killed with an electric drill. Get pictures of that on the web—can you imagine how many hits it'd get?"

"Mind you, I reckon our photos should get a good few hits themselves. That was a stroke of genius, mate, setting up that website."

"Well, now we've got it set up, there's no reason why we can't make a bit of a business from it. I've made sure other people can post things, too."

"Nice one. I'll drink to that."

Chapter 14

Lauren Matthews was concerned. She'd thought she'd finally managed to get both her children on an even keel. For the last fifteen years it had felt like her life had been a continual balancing act, trying to divide her time equally between her job and her kids. But ever since they could walk, Dean and Alice had seemed to act as a tag team as far as trouble was concerned. Dean had come off the rails at school and Alice although less trouble, seemed to rally whole-heartedly against any decisions she made as a mother. She knew in her heart that they were good kids, and in a lot of ways they could have been a lot worse, but being a single mum had meant she had to deal with every tantrum and bump in the road on her own, and it was tiring. Now, just as Alice's obsession with sleepovers was starting to wane, Dean had become unpredictable again. He was out until the early hours every night, he was argumentative, and had been late for work every day in the last week. He was on drugs again—Lauren knew that for a fact—and she wasn't sure if she was strong enough to go through it all with him again.

As Lauren sat at the kitchen table nursing a cup of tea, she heard the front door open and close. She regarded the clock: ten past three; it would be Dean. As if on cue, Dean stumbled into the kitchen, and when he saw his mum he gave a small smile.

"Why are you still up?"

"I was waiting for you."

Ignoring her, he went to the fridge and grabbed the milk, taking the lid off and swigging it back. Replacing the top, he put the milk back in the fridge. He turned to his mother.

"Not going to bollock me for not using a glass?"

"Didn't think I'd bother."

"Good." Dean turned to leave.

"Dean, I think we need to talk."

"Really, about what?"

"Your behaviour. What've you been taking?"

"Tonight? Alcohol, good old legal alcohol."

"And what about last night, and the night before, and the one before that? You're hanging around with Mark again, aren't you?"

"What's it to you?"

"Oh nothing, nothing. That's fine, become a loser again, why not?"

"Give it a rest, Mum."

"Don't you take that tone with me. If you think I'm going through all that shit again, you're mistaken. You've got a roof over your head, a family that loves you, a job with good prospects, and you just want to piss it all away."

"I'm not pissing anything away."

"Yes, you are, you've started using this place as a doss hole again, ducking in and out at all hours. And as for your job—well, I say 'your job,' that's if you've still got one."

Dean became more alert at this.

"What do you mean by that?"

"I've had Jon Hamilton on the phone today."

"Jon from the garage?"

"Do you know any other Jon Hamilton's? And he told me you've been late every day this week, apart from today, when you didn't show up at all. He says when you are in, you're surly and uncooperative, and that on Wednesday he had to send you home 'cause you were drunk. Drunk while working in a garage—honestly, Dean, I didn't realise I was capable of raising such an idiot. It's an eye-opener, it really is."

Dean started moving toward the kitchen door.

"And where do you think you're going?"

"To bed."

Lauren sat and watched her son leave. She stared forlornly into her teacup. Getting up, she put the cup into the sink and reached up to retrieve a tumbler from the top shelf of the cupboard. Then, squatting down, she started rattling around at the back of the condiments cupboard, stretching her arm right to the back of the cupboard and finally locating what she was after. Pulling the vodka bottle out of its hiding place, she regarded its contents. There was only enough for a couple in there; she'd have to grab another bottle tomorrow. Emptying the remaining contents of the bottle into the glass, she took a swig.

Jesus, that's harsh.

Wincing, she took another mouthful. She didn't enjoy the taste, but it was the only thing that could guarantee her sleep at the moment. Once she'd finished, she washed the glass up and returned it to its rightful place. Then, taking the empty vodka bottle, she quietly let herself out the back door and pushed it down into the wheelie bin, making sure it was out of sight. Content it wouldn't be noticed, she went back inside and got ready for bed.

Dean managed to get into work by half past eight; considering he was supposed to start at seven, he was greeted with a scowl by most of his work colleagues. Pete bowled up to him

"For fuck's sake, mate, I told you Jon was baying for your blood. What time do you call this?"

"Give it a rest, Pete, where is the fat bastard, anyway?"

"In his office. He's on the phone at the moment, so give him a couple."

"You want a cup of tea?"

"No, and I don't think you should, either. That Astra needs a new set of spark plugs; if I were you, I'd get busy." Pete handed Dean the spark plugs and returned to the inspection pit.

Dean had just opened the car bonnet when Jon stuck his head out of the office.

"Was that Dean I just saw stroll in?"

"Yep, he's sorting the Astra out." Pete pointed over to the other side of the workshop.

"Send him in, would you?" Jon closed the office door again.

"Dean, Jon wants to see you," Pete shouted across to Dean.

Dean looked up and started toward the office.

"Good luck," Pete offered as Dean opened the office door.

Jon was sat back in his chair.

"Sit down."

Dean did as he was told.

"I want to talk to you about your attitude over the last week."

"And I want to talk to you about ringing my house and worrying my mum."

"Well, what could I do? You're hardly ever here; your mates have tried talking to you—"

"Oh, you put them up to that, did you?"

"And you're getting worse. Now, I like to think I'm a patient man, but your attitude is taking the piss."

"Well here's an idea: why don't you, and all those pricks out there, take this job and stick it up your collective arses."

Dean got up and slammed out of the office, walking past Pete to retrieve his jacket. As he walked out, he gave Pete the finger.

Dean wandered round to the pub and rang Mark. Within twenty minutes, Mark had arrived, and by the time they were on their third chaser, they'd come up with a plan.

"I'm telling you, mate, it won't be a problem. I've got the brake fluid back at mine, you know where he lives—it's a piece of piss."

"All right, then, let's do it tonight. Meet you back down here at eight."

After necking the remains of their drinks, they left.

By the time Dean arrived back home, Lauren was furious. She'd had four vodkas since Jon had rung and told her what had happened, and she was fit to maim.

"I've had Jon on the phone again. He told me you've walked out of your job."

"And?"

"You had a really good opportunity at that place, Dean."

"We've done all this before, Mum."

"You little fucker, don't you take that attitude with me. You can't carry on living here if you don't pull your weight; even your little sister's got a Saturday job, and I can't support you forever. You're nineteen now, Dean. Grow some balls, for fuck's sake."

Dean glanced over at the kitchen table and noticed the vodka bottle.

"Isn't it you who's always saying intoxicants don't solve anything?"

"Don't get smart with me—that's cause of you, that is; it's just easier than going to the doctor's and getting sedatives."

"Guilt trip now, eh? That's a new tactic."

"Guilt trip? That'd imply you've got a conscience, which you obviously haven't. If you did, you wouldn't be hanging around with that fucking Mark."

"What?"

"Oh, don't play the innocent with me; I know you're hanging round with those losers again. Are you dealing drugs again? You're not a minor anymore, so if you get nicked, you'll be going to the big boys' prison."

Ignoring her protests, Dean disappeared up to his room.

Chapter 15

"Hi Loretta, sorry it's so late."

"No problem, come on in." Loretta opened the door wider to let Holt in.

"I'll get the coffee on."

Loretta went through into the kitchen as Holt made his way through to the lounge.

"I can't sleep; I keep going over the crimes again and again."

Holt spilt the contents of his folder onto the table.

Loretta came through from the kitchen holding two mugs, and placing coasters on the table, she slid one mug toward Holt. Holt was staring at each of the photos in turn, a look of incomprehension drawing across his face.

"Jimmy? Are you ok?"

"Yeah, it's just seeing them—I mean, I must have spent most of the day poring over these photos, and they still shock me. Who could do these things to another human being? I thought I was a jaded old copper who couldn't be shaken by anything, but here I am, wondering if the world has gone completely mad."

"Well, take comfort in the fact that there are always patterns to find. Rarely do people commit these kinds of acts without there being a trigger point in their lives. Find that, and you'll find the killer."

"But what constitutes a trigger point? We all start

out with a clean slate—what goes on to turn a person's mind from an ordinary, functioning human to a demonic force of nature? Sometimes I imagine catching this guy and looking deep into his eyes, and do you know what I see? Nothing. No emotion, no soul, no empathy."

"You have to remember this killer was once human; we need to find out what happened to make the switch. What did they see or hear to change them? Most serial killers tick quite a few of the same boxes: broken home, bullied as a child—"

Holt snorted at this.

"Sorry, I'm not trying to be rude, but you've just described nearly everyone's childhood there."

"Well, let's try getting more specific. Serial killers are usually narcissistic, completely convinced the world exists purely to serve them."

"And that's every teenager I've ever met, myself included."

Loretta smiled briefly.

"Ok, they are usually sociopathic as an extension of the narcissism. A sociopath is someone who is completely amoral, and although recognising that laws aren't supposed to be broken, have no qualms about breaking them to achieve their objectives. Unfortunately they can blend effortlessly into society, making them difficult to apprehend."

Picking up his coffee, Holt sat back in the chair for a moment, cradling the cup. Loretta watched him for a few moments.

"Right, lets get back to basics. Most serial killers are between the age of eighteen and fifty years old when they perpetrate their crimes. Over ninety per cent are male. They've usually already been the victim themselves as children either mentally, physically or sexually and this will have occurred at the hands of someone they should be able to trust; close family friends, family members maybe a parent. Many will have spent some time in institutions as children, they may have been abused or bullied during their time and this will have only served to isolate them further."

"I suppose, if he had been institutionalised as a child, that may be why he feels the system's failing. And that's why he's decided to try and—for want of a better word, rectify the situation himself."

"That would make sense, but at the moment this is all conjecture. Have you found any potential links between the victims yet?"

"No, we're still working on it."

"How about the first victim? Have you managed to identify him yet?"

"No, we thought we had for just for the briefest moment this morning. A hysterical woman rang in to say her boyfriend was missing—turns out he'd been missing since last night, coincidentally at around the same time he'd gone down to the pub with his mates."

Loretta leaned back in her chair for a moment and spotting the two empty coffee mugs, picked them up.

"I get the impression this is going to be a long night. Top up?"

Holt gave her a weary smile.

"Please."

Chapter 16

As soon as Clare was safely inside her flat, she put the shopping away quickly. She grabbed a glass and poured herself a generous measure of Bacardi. Her week seemed to be getting worse each day; the main reason was her growing paranoia. Since she and Hannah had received the messages on their phones, neither woman had slept properly. Clare hadn't done any studying in weeks, and she was drinking heavily every night. A little part of her wanted Dean to ring, but they'd cut all contact since they'd split; all she kept doing was thinking how much simpler her life had been with him in it. She knew it was an over simplistic way of looking at things, but in her head Dean represented the part of her life before the assault. The only person Clare had told about the assault was Loretta, and Loretta had warned her about the need to cling on to any part of her 'old' life just to feel normal again. Loretta had also said how detrimental that would be in the long term. Clare knew Loretta was right but it didn't stop her longing for her perception of 'normality'.

As Clare went to retrieve the bottle of Bacardi, her landline rang, and thinking it would be Hannah, she answered without thinking.

"Hello?"

"Hi, Clare."

"Dean?"

"Yeah, I was just wondering how you've been."

Clare became defensive.

Did he know? Had he seen the website?

"Yeah, I'm fine, why do you ask?"

"Maybe 'cause I haven't seen you around in a while."

"Well, we did split up, Dean."

"Yes, I know."

"Why are you ringing me, anyway?"

"Like I said, to see how you are."

"I'm fine, thanks, so I'll see you around."

"So we can't even be mates now? I thought women liked to try and stay mates with a bloke once they'd broken his heart."

"Dean, we went out for three fucking weeks, and anyway, we've nothing in common."

"Fine, well, fuck you, then."

Across town Dean was pacing in his room, hanging up his phone he pushed it into his pocket. Taking the stairs two at a time he grabbed his jacket and slammed out of the house.

Well, that was it. Jon's car was going to get properly done over now. Dean had made a promise to himself: if he could have had the choice between going to see Clare or going to meet up with Mark, Clare would have won. But seeing as she was being a complete bitch, he knew exactly what he could take his anger out on.

Dean saw Mark waiting for him in his car at the end of the street.

"I thought we were meeting back at the pub?"

"Nah, thought it'd be better if I met you here; we

don't need anyone overhearing us."

"What have you brought?"

"Spray paint and brake fluid."

"Right, let's go."

Dean jumped into the car and the two men set off toward Jon's house.

As Dean and Mark pulled up outside Jon's house, Dean saw that he had predictably left his car on the street—something he always did to allow his wife to use the driveway, and also to ensure her car couldn't trap his in.

Getting out of the car, the two men circled the Bentley and set to work on it.

Five minutes later, satisfied that the car's paintwork was ruined, they got back into Johnny's beat-up Peugeot.

Jon was furious; he'd just gotten back home from a particularly arduous shopping trip with Joanne to buy his son, Harry's, birthday present. They had been sniping at each other the entire time, including the hour-long round car trip it had taken to get there and back. Harry had wanted a new flat screen TV for his room, and they'd finally found the particular model Harry had had his eye on. When Jon had mentioned the model that Harry wanted and pointed it out to his wife in Dixon's, Joanne had retorted,

"Are you talking about the TV or the shop assistant?" At that point, the pretty young girl who'd been serving them retreated, blushing furiously, and the manager had come over and finished the transaction. And that had pretty much set the tone for the rest of the evening.

They had decided to go in Joanne's car upon her insistence that she thought he drove like a lunatic. As she had pulled her car back into the driveway, Jon's eyes had moved to his Bentley. When he noticed his paintwork bubbling, his stomach dropped. Getting out of the car, he moved gingerly toward his Bentley, in absolute shock. He knew instantaneously who had done it; now, though, he knew he had the uncertain task of figuring out what to do about it. As he was appraising the paintwork, Joanne moved up behind him.

"Spurned lover?" She could barely contain the humour in her voice, and Jon's rage boiled over.

"Oh, shut up, you old bitch."

Joanne's smile was replaced by a sneer.

"Sorry, I forgot, you don't have spurned lovers, do you? Just disappointed ones."

Satisfied she had achieved the KO she was hoping for, she returned to her own car, locked it, and went into the house.

Reaching into the inside pocket of his jacket, Jon opened his phone and scrolled down to the number under Dean's. Hitting 'call,' he waited for the recipient to answer. He was rewarded on the third ring.

"Hi, Lauren, is there any chance I could pop over?"

Lauren was confused, and, if truth were told, a little worried.

"Yeah, that's fine, is there something wrong?"

"I think it'd be better if we spoke in person. I'll be there in five."

Jon hung up the call and crept quietly into the

house. He could hear Joanne banging pots and pans around in the kitchen. Spotting Joanne's car keys, he picked them up and quietly closed the door behind him. In the kitchen, Joanne heard her car engine spark to life once more, and rushing into the hallway, she saw that her car keys were missing. Absolutely furious, she returned to the kitchen and continued to peel the potatoes.

"Tea or coffee? Or do you need something stronger?"' Lauren could see the stress etched into his face.

"Well, I could use something stronger, but I'd better not; I've got Joanne's car, and she's annoyed at me enough at the moment without me wrecking her car, as well."

"Well, if this is about Dean, and I'm judging it must be, I'm going to have a vodka."

"Don't let me stop you." Jon watched as Lauren poured herself a generous measure into a mug.

"I didn't know you drank."

"Well, there's a lot you don't know, Jon.' Jon took the verbal slap and sat down.

"So what's the little shit been up to now?"

"He's poured paint stripper over my car."

"Really."

"You don't sound very surprised."

"Well, I'm not. He's been hanging round with Mark again."

"Mark? Who's Mark?"

"Sorry, I forgot you have absolutely no knowledge of the first eighteen years of your firstborn's life."

"Is this going to descend into a slanging match? Because I've just come from one of those, and I could do without another."

Lauren sat back and finished her drink. Waiting for Jon to continue, she emptied the rest of the bottle into her glass.

"I was young—what did you want me to do? Drop out of uni and work in a dead end job for the rest of my life? At least this way I can give you decent money for him."

"It's all about fucking money with you, isn't it? I had to drop out of school; how many fucking options did you leave me?"

"All right, well, if that's how it's going to be, I'll go."

"Sit down." Lauren's voice was resigned

Reluctantly, Jon sat back down.

"I don't know what to do anymore, Jon. That boy's run me ragged recently, ducking in and out of here at all hours, fighting with his sister—I know he's dealing again."

"Dealing? How do you know?"

"Because it's not the first time."

"He's dealt before?"

Lauren bit her tongue and nodded.

"So what do you want me to do about your car?"

"Look, don't worry about it, the insurance can cover it." Getting up, Jon felt in his pocket to make sure he had his keys.

Lauren was nursing her mug of vodka in both hands and was watching Jon with interest. He'd hardly changed since they had first met; he had been 24 and absolutely stunning. When Dean had turned out to be the double of his father, Lauren was unsure how to feel about it. She loved Dean, but he was truly his father's son, and Jon had hurt her. If it had been love she'd once felt for Jon, then none of it remained; all she now had was the bitterness she felt whenever she saw Joanne out with her children.

"What are you going to tell Joanne?"

"I'll just say it was a disgruntled customer—not that it'll matter she's already decided it was a woman."

"So who is your newest bit of skirt, then?"

Jon was caught completely off-guard.

"How do you know?"

"You'll never change, Jon, all the time you've a hole in your arse." Lauren said this with a smile, and just for a moment Jon saw the sixteen-year-old girl he'd fallen for all those years before.

Lost in their memories, neither one had heard the front door open. Dean, recognising Jon's voice, crept toward the kitchen door.

"To be honest with you, Lauren, I think I've fallen in love."

"I know you probably want to talk to someone about this, but I really would prefer it if you could choose anyone other than me."

"Sorry, that was insensitive."

"No, Jon, insensitive was when you dumped me and your child for another, more respectable, woman. Trying to make small talk to me about your most recent upgrade is tactless."

As Dean listened just outside the door his stomach suddenly dropped.

Still reeling, he took a deep breath, calmed

himself, and walked into the kitchen.

Jon and Lauren stopped abruptly and shot each other worried looks.

Dean could feel his mother and Jon's discomfiture and realised he was enjoying it. He moved slowly and deliberately across the kitchen to the kettle, all the while feeling their eyes flickering between him and each other. Suddenly he became aware of the situation: here he was, in the kitchen with his mum and dad. 'Dad'—now there was a word he hadn't had much use for during the last nineteen years. The thought made him laugh.

Lauren had finished her drink and was now watching her son with keen interest. His brief snigger had alarmed her. It wasn't his normal natural laugh; it was gruffer, and somehow more malicious. She knew at that minute that he had heard. That was why he was here in the kitchen now; he had needed her to know he'd heard them. She wondered briefly if Jon had worked it out, as well. Glancing at him, she assumed he hadn't; he was also watching Dean, but with a mixture of confusion and annoyance.

Dean had started filling the kettle.

"Anyone else want a drink?"

Deans back was still towards hem, and neither replied. Dean turned to face them.

"Mum, would you like a cup of tea? Oh no, of course you've already got a drink."

Lauren watched her son's lip curl into a sneer. She hated this; she'd been finding it harder and harder to get through to him of late. Now she realised that the last vestige of any respect he might still have had for her had disappeared along with the vodka from the bottle in front of her.

"And what about you, *Jon*?" Dean had deliberately emphasised his name, and Jon stared back at him.

"Is that all you've got to say?" Jon's voice was incredulous.

"Why? What do you want me to say?" Dean's voice was steady, monotonous even, as he held Jon's stare.

"I know it was you, you cocky little bastard. You trashed my car tonight, didn't you? You're lucky I haven't rung the police—you've got your mum to thank for that."

"Bastard. How appropriate, because, Jon, you see, I am a bastard, but I can't really be blamed for that; some lowlife piece of shit knocked my mum up and fucked off. Yeah, I know, it's amazing, isn't it? The amount of shit some men can do and get away with." Dean was leaning back against the worktop with his arms folded; he looked relaxed. This was only serving to rile Jon up more as he watched his eldest calmly make a cup of tea. Jon couldn't believe the bravado of this boy who had caused thousands of pounds of damage to his car just hours earlier. Jon could see a younger version of himself; he was unequivocally attractive, slim but muscular, his hair falling around his unlined face. Jon felt a moment of jealousy; he had let himself go early. With the first flush of success in his business, he had believed in rewarding himself by eating lavish food, drinking the most prestigious scotch, and only smoking the very best cigars. As he worked so hard at work, he didn't see why he should have to work at home, and exercise came under the heading of work, as far as he was concerned. Dean had inherited his mother's frame, and as such was blessed with a fine metabolism and musculature passed to him by his maternal grandfather. Dean would fill out, but only with muscle. Jon knew, having met Lauren's father before, that the man was predisposed to put on muscle, but he seemed completely incapable of putting on an ounce of fat. Jon looked his son up and down and felt a mixture of pride and jealousy. As far as Dean would be concerned, the middle age spread was just going to be something that happened to other people.

"I haven't got time for this shit. You want to grow up, mate, before you come unstuck."

Jon was standing in front of Dean now and jabbed him in the chest with his finger.

Dean snorted and shook his head.

"Why don't you just fuck off, old man, go and see your latest jump." Dean hadn't bothered to conceal the contempt in his voice.

Jon grabbed his jacket and stormed out.

Walking back to the car, Jon thought about the exchange. He unlocked the door and threw his jacket into the backseat. Starting the engine, he started to drive back home, but not for one moment was his mind on the drive. He kept thinking about what Dean had said to him just before he left: he had called him an old man. Or had he called him 'old man?' Did he know he was his father? Was the 'old man' a dig at him? Well, either way it didn't matter; if he had overheard and wanted to confront him about it, he'd have done it then, while his mother was present. Jon tried to force his mind off of the subject. Only another two weeks and he'd be out of it, at least for the weekend. A smile crossed his face as he pulled the car into his driveway.

He could see the light was still on in the kitchen; he let himself into the house and went through to the kitchen where Joanne was still busy cooking. Jon mumbled a brief apology to Joanne, she shrugged and he picked up the paper and took his leave into the living room to relax before dinner.

Chapter 17

Jon smiled as he looked over his Bentley; the bodywork garage had done a good job, the car looked as good as new, and the inside had been valeted, as well. Jon praised himself for insuring the car so heavily; it was for moments like this that he didn't begrudge his inflated premiums. Had he gone for the basic, it would be a toss up as to what would come first, the insurance pay out or the Second Coming.

It had been three days since the altercation with Dean, and Jon had all but forgotten it. He had reasoned that if the boy had wanted to use the information, he would have made a move by now. Jon was convinced that the tempestuous nature of youth would have made it impossible for Dean to play the long game with such information. Jon had other things to occupy him that were infinitely more gratifying than dealing with estranged offspring. Her name was Sarah, and Jon was absolutely infatuated. He'd been seeing Sarah for the best part of four weeks now, and he enjoyed the time he spent with her and her kids. Her apartment had become a haven for him, but he had to admit to himself he was really looking forward to this weekend—a whole weekend, just him and Sarah. This time next week he'd be cosily ensconced in bed with Sarah in a nice quiet hotel somewhere in the country. They'd decided earlier not to contact each other in the previous week so as not to arouse suspicion at home. Of course he was aware that his wife Joanne must suspect anyway—he'd been doing it for years—but it was his son, Harry's, birthday soon, and they agreed the lad didn't need his mother becoming any more neurotic leading up to it.

He had spoken to Sarah earlier and she had sounded happy; she had said she had something to tell him. He had worried at first that the weekend away was just a ruse to soften the blow when she told him she was growing tired of him, but after further probing, he was satisfied that the news must be good news. She had said it was exciting, and he was glad, as he had some good news himself: he'd come to the decision that he was going to divorce his wife so he could be with Sarah full time.

His wife, Joanne, was not a bad woman; she had always kept a nice house and brought up both his children exceptionally well, but over time he had fallen out of love with her. Being aware of this, Joanne had always dealt with Jon's various indiscretions over the years with a quiet air of dignity. She'd come to terms with the knowledge that he was going to have them with or without her blessing, so she resolved to turn a blind eye and accept that fact along with all the other duties expected of a wife and mother. Now, though, he felt a little guilty; he'd fallen in love this time, and he'd fallen hard. He wished his wife would 'find out' and go mad at him, shouting and swearing and throwing things so he was left with no other option than to walk out. He would become the injured party and not have to feel guilty about leaving her, but he knew that would never happen. He also knew that when he did tell her she'd cry, making him feel terrible. Women crying sat uneasily with Jon ever since childhood, when he'd have to comfort his mother after his father had stumbled in drunk, smelling of some old tart's perfume. If he was honest, he secretly felt that his wife had somehow cheated him out of his youth and into the family home. He had started to resent any time he had to spend with her and her aging body—it made him feel old. He'd lost interest in his marriage, and the end result was a self-perpetuating cycle of dislike, which had turned into hate after the first few years.

Sarah was different—she made him feel young whenever he was around her. To his mind, she made him a better version of himself, more alive, more fun to be around. Most would had seen her for what she was at twenty paces, but Jon had relished the excitement of spending time with this younger woman. He almost liked himself around her, and that was where all his insecurities had stemmed from, his own self-loathing. Now he had found reassurance in his own self worth by having an affair with a woman half his age, who, in most people's eyes, would be viewed as no better than a common tart.

He had stopped by the new bar in town, Andre's. It was populated generally by the more youthful contingency of the town, and he had actively avoided the place. Now, though, as he sipped at his pint, he felt quite at home here. He noticed several young women eyeing him up, and he couldn't help smiling to himself. He intrigued them; he couldn't believe it had taken him so long to work out the simple truth that young girls *preferred* older men. They were more experienced with life, they treated them better than their younger counterparts, wining and dining—women liked that, and that was something his younger counterparts never seemed to be able to get their heads around. Women, for all their harping on about being equal to men, still wanted to be treated like ladies occasionally. But the biggest advantage that he as an older man had over the younger male generation was conversation. All the young lads at his garage only had two topics of conversation, the first of which was football, and the second, women. Neither of these topics interested the average woman; surprisingly enough, hearing the latest play of their boyfriend's latest infatuation, be it their favourite football player or the front page of this month's FHM, turned them off completely. The lads couldn't seem to understand that these pseudo gods and goddesses that bewitched them so made their partners feel somewhat less than perfect.

He, however, was feeling invincible. He had the woman he deserved and he could see the pair of them going away on holidays together, visiting his kids at the weekend, and starting off a whole new chapter of his life. The pretty young things sitting at the bar giving him the come- on could forget it. From now on he was a one-woman man, and that idea, knowing he was now a far better version of himself, pleased him immeasurably. As he finished his pint, he nodded at the young lads, who were steadily advancing toward the women at the bar, as he made his exit. Walking out into the car park, he held up the remote for his car and pressed the button twice, and he was rewarded with the familiar *beep-beep* as the car responded to the command. He walked swiftly over to the other side of the car park to where the sound had originated, spotted his car, and quickly got inside. Although it was summer, it had been quite a cool day, and there was a slight chill in the air. Putting the key in the ignition, he turned it and felt relief as the fans started blowing warm air at his face. Relaxing for a second to enjoy the warmth and happiness growing within him, he relaxed his head back against the headrest. Simultaneously he felt something cold being pressed against his neck. Slowly opening his eyes, he carefully tilted his head back and moved his eyes up to look in the rear view mirror, his eyes coming to rest on the reflection in it. He froze briefly at the sight of the small, cherubic face staring back at him. Already anticipating his movement, the locks on the doors clicked back on.

"What do you want? Money?" Already knowing the answer to the question, Jon looked back at the pale face.

"No, I don't want your money."

"So what do you want? You can have anything. Just say it and it's yours—anything." Jon knew he was babbling, but he didn't know what else to do.

"Drive." The voice was stronger this time.

"What?"

"I said fucking DRIVE!"

Jon started to whimper.

"Please, I think you've got the wrong person…"

"No, Mr. Hamilton, I think I've got just the right person. Now drive before I pull this blade across your neck and watch you bleed out."

Not daring to question again, Jon flicked the ignition and the engine roared to life. Steering the car very carefully, he proceeded to drive the Bentley toward the exit of the car park.

Sarah Lester was ecstatic. She had managed to find a babysitter for this weekend, and she had made the reservations for the Swan Inn. She'd booked two nights away, away from the kids and the drudgery of her non-existent life. Things had been better for her lately; she had met Jon at her local pub, when she'd been out with her mates one Saturday night four months ago. He was tall, funny, and handsome in a scruffy kind of way. At forty-three he was twenty-two years her senior, but that hadn't bothered her; the older ones were always more attentive anyway. He was married, like the fathers of her two children had been; she had always had a penchant for rich, older, married men. They lavished gifts on her, treated her well, and then scuttled back to the wives to get their tea and their laundry done. The idea of getting married and saddling herself with the same mug for the rest of her life had held little appeal as far as Sarah was concerned. She liked it better this way, when she got the best of them, and when she was bored she'd just move on. The fathers of her children still popped by every now and again to see their kids and have a bit of 'fun,' as they termed it. It was a win-win situation, as far as she was concerned. She had everything she could want, from the plush three-bedroom apartment to the brand new car, the men got to see their kids, and, most importantly, their wives didn't. Sarah had this gig stitched up, and now she was pregnant again, with Jon's baby this time. She'd wanted a bigger place for a while now and she could just see herself in one of those big detached houses on the edge of town.

It was thirty degrees outside and Sarah was beginning to feel tired. She'd bumped into some old friends earlier while out shopping and had stopped to have a few drinks with them. She didn't usually drink during the day, and as the first few flashes of pain streaked across her forehead, she was reminded why. She knew she should really be thinking about packing for the weekend, but decided she could leave it until tomorrow. Her mouth was starting to feel dry from the alcohol. Getting up and going through to the kitchen, she decided to get a cold drink, but changed her mind when she remembered how sick it had made her feel last time she'd felt a little drunk. Putting the glass she'd just gotten out back again, she went to the freezer. She'd started making the kids ice-lollies every day; it gave them something to shut them up and was a damn sight cheaper than the ice cream van. She'd actually bought the trays from Pound Land and they'd turned out to be one of the best investments she'd ever made. Taking the tray out now, she saw there was only one left, and she pulled it out of its plastic case and shoved it in her mouth. Savouring the coolness against her tongue, she grabbed the rest of the plastic cases, stuck them in the sink, and vowed to have them washed up and back in the freezer again within the next twenty minutes.

Sauntering through to the living room, she kicked off her shoes and sprawled herself across the leather sofa; it felt wonderfully cool under her warm legs. She rested a minute; flashes of pain still warning of a potential hangover. She looked slowly around her, quietly sucking away at the lolly. If she were to move, she would need a whole new living room suite; this modern look certainly wouldn't work in a detached property in the suburbs. It would need to be more classic; she had always liked the more classic style, but in a modern purpose built apartment it would have looked chintzy.

After staring round her living room for a few minutes, Sarah decided she really should try and work out what clothes she should take away with her this weekend. The warning flashes of pain across her forehead had ceased, and she thought she might just get away with moving around again now.

She'd recently bought a new gypsy top, and teamed with jeans it would be the perfect casual outfit. She prided herself on being well turned out but still casual, approachable. She relied on this look heavily, as it had won her most of her men. She was the opposite of their wives, casual, comfortable, and young enough to get away with it. She knew her relaxed attitude was what initially drew them to her, and she exploited this in the clothes she wore. Even after two children she was still very comfortable with her body, and it showed. She secretly laughed at the women these men were married to, all pompous and trying desperately to appear happy with their perfect house, perfect children, and apparently perfect husband. But their neatly manicured lawns, nails, and perfectly-coiffed hair didn't fool Sarah, it just showed their marriages for what they were: loveless. Any woman who had time to trim the garden borders or spend hours in a beauty salon getting their hair, nails, and face done obviously had no time for their husband, or, sadder still, the husband had no time for them. So these vanities became their way of filling their sad, wasted little lives. Trying so hard outwardly to project the right image ended up doing just the opposite: they were obviously trying to hide something that was far from perfect.

Sarah knew all this because she had met both her men's wives at one point or another during the relationships. She enjoyed turning up at the same restaurant as them occasionally, introducing herself as a work colleague, watching the fear on her lover's face as she did so. Then she'd spend a good long time chatting to the wives, enjoying the way they would look her up and down, as if to ascertain if she was a threat, and then talking down to her about how she should find a good decent man, settle down, and have kids. Sarah would happily nod along, knowing she did have a good decent man, she had *their* good decent man, his kid, and, oh yes, she was the reason the wives family could only go on holiday once a year. This had rankled with both wives. They could never understand where all their husbands' wages went. That was usually Sarah's cue to laugh jovially and suggest that maybe he had a mistress on the go, to which both wives had had similar reactions.

"Him? What young girl would want to saddle themselves with him?" And both women had laughed raucously as they continued discussing the merits of men, or rather the lack of. As far as the wives were concerned, she had found a kindred spirit, but little did she know the biggest threat to her marriage, as she would have seen it, was sitting right there in front of her, laughing at her jokes and drinking her wine.

And this behaviour would serve two purposes: firstly, it put Sarah out of the frame as far as a potential threat to the marriages were concerned. Secondly, it made the husband feel angry with his wife for showing him up, and consequently he would forget that Sarah had been the one who had created the scenario in the first place.

Sarah hauled herself up out of the chair and walked through into her bedroom, holding the ice-lolly between her teeth. She reached up and grabbed the overnight case she kept up there for her weekends away. Throwing it onto her bed, she walked back through to the kitchen. If she didn't get the ice-lolly tray refilled and back into the freezer soon, there'd be hell to pay when the kids got back. Once again placing the lolly between her teeth, she started running the hot water to wash them up, and as she was doing this her teeth started to slide through the ice. Aware she might drop it, she quickly dried off her hands and went to catch it before it fell. But no hurry was needed—her teeth had gone through the ice and had found something, something hard but strangely soft, like perished rubber. She spat the remains of the ice-lolly out into the hot water of the sink, and it only took a few seconds in warm water for it to become apparent what she had had in her mouth. As the ice melted, she rubbed at her eyes. For a moment she thought she was hallucinating, a strange hallucination brought on by pregnancy and the alcohol she had consumed earlier. But no matter how hard she rubbed, it was still there. First she thought it was one of those rubber fingers that you can buy from joke shops, and that one of the kids must have done it as a joke. But what she noticed next told her irrefutably that what she was looking at was no child's prank: at the base of the finger there was a ring, a wedding ring, and she knew who its previous owner had been—Jon.

The scream rang round the large building, and within half an hour the police were there.

Dean had left numerous messages on Clare's phone since finding out about his paternity, hoping it might prompt her to phone him. Since then, a week had passed, and he had given up trying, and the only call he was anticipating was Mark's.

They were going to a party tonight. Mark thought they could get rid of the fifty ecstasy tablets Mark had acquired at the weekend. Rustling round in his pockets, Dean found the slip of paper Mark had given him earlier—it was the web address of a new porn site. Apparently Mark knew someone who knew the guy who'd set it up. Turning the computer on, Dean waited for the screen to load and typed in the web address. As the computer located the required site, Dean leaned back in his chair, taking a swig of his lager. The screen took only a few seconds to load, but when he saw what was on the screen, Dean's heart missed a beat. Nearly choking on his lager, he spat it out, spraying the computer as he did. His eyes were fixed on the screen, which displayed the woman he still loved for the entire world to see. His face hardened. She was taking the piss out of him, her and that prick in the picture with her. They were taking him for a mug. As he watched, a dribble of his beer and spit snaked down the screen and between her breasts. He snapped, sweeping his arm across the computer table and sending the monitor crashing to the ground. Grabbing his jacket, he decided he was going to go and find Mark and find out exactly who the man on the website was.

Grabbing his mobile from his pocket, he found Mark's number and hit 'call.'

"Mark? Where are you?"

Mark's voice was loud on the line.

"I'm just getting in my car on my way to you, why?"

"Meet me down at the Tin Whistle."

Five minutes later, Mark arrived at the pub. Scanning the room, he saw that Dean sat in the corner, and he seemed on edge. Mark ordered two pints and went over to join him.

"So what's up, then, mate?"

"Who told you about that website?"

"What website?"

"You know what website."

"What, the porno one? Yeah, a bloke I met in

here told me about it—why?"

"No reason. Is he in tonight?"

Mark looked around the bar once more.

"Nah. Look, are you going to tell me what all this is about?"

"I knew someone on the site."

"Male or female?"

"Female." Dean's voice was low. Mark knew this was his cue to leave the subject, but his natural curiosity couldn't let the subject drop.

"An ex?"

"Can you just fucking drop it? All you need to know is that I want the name of the guy who runs the site and the guy who's boning the girl on the home page."

"Ok, give me a couple of days."

"Good."

The conversation fell flat as both men went back to their pints.

Chapter 18

Clare sat staring at the papers in front of her. When she had signed up for the psychology course, she hadn't realised how hard finding the time to study would be. However, if she was honest with herself, it wasn't the time management that was giving her the most trouble as far as her study was concerned; she found it unbelievably hard to concentrate on anything these days. Ever since she and Hannah had been assaulted, her life had changed beyond all recognition, and she longed for the days when her life had been normal. Normal to her, like most people, meant boring. Not anymore, though; her mind was continually racing lately and she wished it could just stagnate for a bit. As she got up to make herself another cup of tea, her mobile rang. Checking the number, she saw it was Dean again, and sighing loudly, she answered it.

"What do you want?" Clare's voice sounded bored and that just served to incense Dean's anger further.

"Well, I was just wondering what your going rate was?" Clare's stomach dropped. He must have seen the website.

"I mean, if I had known I was going out with the local porn star, I'd have gotten my money's worth."

Clare hit the 'end call' button and threw her phone on the sofa. She went through into the kitchen in shock. If Dean knew, then how many others knew, as well? Ignoring the kettle, she grabbed the bottle of Bacardi she always kept now and poured herself a cupful. Knocking it back, she could hear her phone ringing loudly in the living room, each ring seeming to get louder and more aggressive. Picking up the Bacardi bottle, she went back through to the living room, and grabbing her phone from the sofa, she switched it off.

Dean stood staring at his mobile. The last time he'd tried ringing, it had cut him off. Dialling her number again, he listened to see whether or not it would ring. Clare's phone rang straight through to her voicemail.
'Fine then, don't talk to me. I'll just leave a message, and seeing as you won't listen to this, I'll have to make sure you get my message another way.'
Dean ended the call and grabbed the spray paint from his bag.

Twenty miles away, in a derelict farmhouse, Jon regained consciousness. Even with the gaping holes in the building, he could smell the stench of charred flesh. He looked down at his left hand and winced. When he'd first realised he was being abducted, he'd thought it had been for money; he had laughingly tried to bribe his abductor with fifty thousand pounds on the journey.

His businesses had been doing great recently. Originally making his money out of the organic industry boom, he had branched out into other areas. A little over a year ago, Jon had decided to take early retirement. Unfortunately the dream of retirement and the reality bore little resemblance when he found himself spending a lot more time with his wife, Joanne. Before the first week of his retirement was up, he'd purchased a new business, but it was a business he knew nothing about. He'd bought a small garage, and it already had a full employee quota complete with manager. Joanne, who knew little of his business dealings, believed he was putting full time hours in once more, whereas in reality he could pop in and out of the garage if and when he chose. Luckily they were all good lads, and had covered for him a few times. It had even meant he could attempt to make amends to his eldest son, the son he'd ran out on nineteen years ago. The garage had a booming business, so all the little extras he liked to spend on his extra-curricular activities didn't raise too many questions at home. All in all, it was one of the best investments he'd made. It also meant that whatever his abductor demanded of him, he should easily be able to afford it.

When he'd seen where his abductor was taking him, he'd thought it had been for a cooling off period before they decided what amount of money they thought they could get out of him. When his abductor had produced a cigar cutter, he wasn't sure if he should laugh or cry. He'd seen them used in certain gangster films before to relieve the victims of their digits; he had thought it was a sick, depraved joke. His abductor had taped him to the chair that he was now sitting in, and halfway through the removal of his ring finger, the pain had become too much and he'd passed out. Looking at the bloody, blackened stub he now sported, he could make an educated guess at what had happened afterwards: the abductor had cauterised the wound. And judging by the lack of surgical equipment around, he assumed they had used the cigarette lighter from his car. Oddly enough, that thought calmed him a little; if they'd bothered to stop the bleeding then maybe they didn't want to kill him after all. Or at least they wanted something more from him; either way it bought him more time.

Staring around the dilapidated room he was sitting in, he noticed something he hadn't noticed before: on the wall opposite him there hung a clock that certainly hadn't been there earlier. The abductor must have left it for him. According to the clock, he must have been here for at least five hours. As he sat there waiting, he noticed the first rays of light from the new days sun stretch across the room. Where the hell was his captor, where had they gone, why had they gone? Had they gone to collect the next instrument for this sadistic game?

Jon started to drift in and out of consciousness and dreams started blurring with reality, the most painful of which was where he woke up in the bed at Sarah's apartment. She'd come in with two cups of tea, two cigarettes, and an ashtray. They would stay in bed most of the morning, debating the merits of various mundane things—in this particular case, tea-cosies—and then Jon would wake once more and find himself still incarcerated.

That part became harder every time.

Fitful sleep and a restless mind ensured Jon was

far from being in a sound mental state when the persecutor arrived back at the building a full twenty-four hours later.

The persecutor strode straight up to Jon and ripped off his gag.

"Wake up. *Wake up*."

Jon's head slowly rotated up in the direction the command was coming from. He felt dazed, as if someone had been consistently hitting the back of his head with a rubber mallet for the last two hours. He decided to ask once more what they wanted, and looking them directly in the eye and summoning as much strength as he could muster he spoke steadily, in a voice that sounded much stronger than he felt.

"What do you want with me?"

"You're thinking of leaving your wife, aren't you?"

No answer. Sighing inwardly, the voice spoke again.

"Jon, as a supposedly intelligent man, I'd have thought you'd have known that if someone asks you a question, it is good manners to answer them."

As Jon listened to the voice, he noticed it had an almost lyrical quality to it, quite at odds with the voice that had threatened to slit his throat the previous evening.

"No, I'm not *thinking* of leaving my wife; I *am* leaving my wife. Now if you've quite finished with the twenty questions, can you just get on with whatever it is you plan to do, because I'm bloody sick of *waiting*!"

"Ah, you're sick of waiting, are you? I imagine a busy man like *you* hates waiting, people wasting your time—I know I don't like the idea of five minutes of wasted time, so can you imagine how it'd feel to waste *seventeen years* of your life? Stuck with the same ungrateful bastard every day, all the time knowing he's off having sordid little affairs with any two-bit scrubber that came along, and then after *seventeen years* of raising *his* children, keeping *his* house, and forfeiting any life of her own in a bid to keep *him* happy and at home, he suddenly decides to up and leave? Can you imagine how that'd feel, Jon*? Can you?*" The calm, lyrical voice had disappeared, and in its place was an almost hysterical scream. The last two words practically slapped Jon across the face.

"Well, hopefully you will understand a little more soon, Jon, 'cause you'll have plenty of time to think about it." The soft voice was back once more and the cherubic face stared down at Jon as the gag was refastened.

"I may not be able to give you seventeen years, Jon, but you'll be amazed how long time can stretch when you're in desperate need of something, whether it's love, caring, understanding, or…"

The voice became low and malicious.

"…food and water."

With that, his persecutor turned and started to head once more toward the exit.

The abductor could hear the muffled protests turning to desperate anguished grunts in the background.

"Bye, Jon."

Chapter 19

Clare woke with a start. Her head was pounding, and she started to go through the previous evening's events. After Dean's barrage of calls, she ended up drinking herself into oblivion. Getting up, she retrieved her phone and rang Loretta's number.

"Hi, sorry to call you at home at the weekend, but is there any chance I could see you soon?"

In her office Loretta leaned back in her chair and frowned; Clare had been anything but forthcoming the last few sessions they'd had. She had agreed to help Clare's study, but Clare had seemed disinterested recently. Loretta had asked her what was wrong and Clare had assured there was nothing, so Loretta could only assume she'd lost interest in the course and Loretta had no time for half measures. She had considered calling time on the whole tutoring aspect; if someone didn't give their all, then she didn't see why she should have to give up her free time. Jimmy Holt had earmarked enough of that for himself lately, although she didn't begrudge that; in fact, she admitted, she enjoyed his company. But this girl, she wasn't being straight with her, and although technically Loretta was 'off-duty' with her, it was still a principle of her profession never to force any issues.

"Well, I'm going into the office later anyway to sort out some paper work. I can meet you there at three if you like."

On the other end of the line, Clare's face broke into a rare smile.

"That'd be great, thank you. I'll see you then."

Loretta hung up the phone. She made the decision to give Clare one last chance. She just hoped this meeting would be more productive than the last few.

Clare had finally managed to kick her hangover. She had been so relieved when Loretta had suggested meeting in the afternoon. Clare knew she'd been sailing close to the wind with

Loretta lately and that Loretta was becoming impatient with her attitude, so Clare had made the decision to come clean with her and let her know about the whole mess. Once the decision had been made she had felt lighter, as though she didn't have to face it on her own anymore. She knew she had Hannah, but Hannah had been keeping her distance recently and Clare couldn't blame her; they had both become reminders of that night to each other.

Clare stepped into the shower and enjoyed the feeling as the warm water washed over her, making her clean again. If only memories were so easily washed away. Ever since the attack Clare had stopped spending time on her appearance, so within ten minutes she was ready to go. She never used to be able to get ready so quickly, but now she felt that the less attractive she was, the safer she was. Grabbing her car keys, she slammed out of the flat, feeling lighter than she had in weeks. She chose to take the stairs down to the ground floor and the car park. Bursting out of the door into the car park, she spotted her car and suddenly stopped dead.

Her car was sat in its usual position, but the deep blue paintwork was scribbled with bright pink profanities. Drawing closer, she could begin to make out the words: "whore," "slag," "bitch."

Clare stood stunned for a moment, watching her own car as if waiting for its next trick. Then breaking her stare she rushed to it and got in, sparking the engine to life she drove quickly to Loretta's office. Parking her car in its usual space Clare made her way inside.

Loretta was already waiting in her office and Clare went in and sat down. Loretta didn't bother looking up.

"Hi Clare, I'll be with you in a minute. I've just got to finish this."

"There's no rush." Clare's voice broke and she started to sob uncontrollably.

Loretta put her paperwork down and gave Clare her full attention.

"Whatever's the matter?"

"It's hard to know where to start."

"I often find the beginning as good a place as any."

With that, Clare poured out all the events in detail, occasionally stopping to draw breath. Loretta sat solemnly, listening until Clare ran out of steam.

"Clare, what on Earth prompted you to keep all this to yourself?"

"Well, because it's not just me who's been affected, Hannah didn't want anyone else to know, and I couldn't go behind her back."

"Did you report this to the police?"

"No, we think they used rohypnol, and by the time we realised what had happened, the drug was out of our systems. Besides, neither of us wanted to have to go through it all again."

"And that is exactly why these attacks continue—the offenders rely on their victims' humiliation to keep them quiet."

"Well, it works." Clare dissolved into sobbing once more.

"All too well, it would appear. Now, where's your car?"

"Parked just outside the door—why?"

"Because I want you to take my car home; I'll get yours sorted out and drop it back to you during the week. In the meantime, I'll see about getting that website closed down."

"How?"

"I know someone who's good with computers."

"It's not the police, is it?"

"No. Look, I don't want you worrying about it, just get home and get some rest, OK?"

Loretta pushed her keys across the desk toward Clare.

"Um, ok, as long as you're sure…' Clare went to hand Loretta her keys and then stopped.

"I really appreciate this, you know."

Loretta's hand was out for the keys and she replied without looking up.

"I know."

Clare retrieved Loretta's keys from the desk muttering her thanks once more she left.

Loretta watched out of her window as Clare got into her car and drove away. Clare had finally started being honest with her again and this gave Loretta a sense of relief. Picking up the phone, she started the first stage of the clean up process: getting Clare's car picked up for re-spray. As Loretta dialled the number she wondered if she should mention this afternoon's episode to Jimmy Holt. Technically this Adam Woodacre who Clare had named as the ringleader of this website had broken the law, so she could report him in good conscience. However that would mean she'd be breaking a promise to Clare, and even though she wasn't Clare's counsellor, she felt honour bound to uphold her professional principles. When the phone was answered on the other end of the line, she had made her decision: she wouldn't report it to Jimmy.

Chapter 20

Joanne was shattered; she'd spent all morning cleaning the windows. She finished them off and walked back through into the kitchen, filling the kettle and putting it on to boil. She went over to the kitchen table and started sorting through bills. All but one was addressed to Jon. Where was her estranged husband staying? And more importantly, why hadn't he called to tell her he'd be away so long? It was their eldest, Harry's, sixteenth birthday on Monday, just two days away, and Jon hadn't made any attempts to contact her about arrangements. He really was a selfish bastard at times. She could cope with her own embarrassment that her husband's dubious reputation allowed her, but he had always been an outstanding dad for the most part. Joanne was used to him disappearing for days or even weeks at a time with his latest squeeze, dressing it up as a "business trip." Part of her hoped he realised she was aware of the indiscretions and that she wasn't just completely stupid. But then again, if he knew that she knew and didn't care, that would be worse, wouldn't it? Joanne tried not to dwell on these things too much; neither answer would please her.

She thought about how simple the whole 'marriage' idea had appeared when she was a little girl. It had all seemed so very easy: find a nice man, marry him, and everything else would just fall into place. Home, kids, then grandchildren. She had had no comprehension of the hard work that a marriage entailed—continual, unrelenting work. She had also falsely assumed that the man you married was the one you spent your married life with. Again, not so; men were rarely as attentive once they had the ring on. It was like the wedding ring held special powers; once upon its owner's finger, it was the key to the unlocking of civilisation within the home. Joanne knew that marriages required effort from both sides—her married friends had seen fit to tell her on her hen night. They had been quick to mention their own husbands' shortcomings: praising their own gas, believing that wet towels lived on the bathroom floor, and that toenail clippings on the side of the bath constituted interior design. And at the wedding reception she'd heard from the husbands about their wives commonly held misconception: that they could "change" them. The most common way to approach this was to verbally beat the man into submission. Nagging seemed to be universally considered the wives' number one weapon of choice in the war of the genders arsenal. One man had commented to Joanne, 'I'll rip my ears off if I have to hear about tile grouting anymore.'

    Joanne had smiled politely at this. But even so, her friends marriages still remained strong, even now, seventeen years later, whereas hers had started to slip after the second year. Not helped by the fact that there was usually a third wheel. And she reluctantly had to admit, that third wheel was usually her.

She resigned herself to the fact that her husband was slipping even further away from the family home and opened the only piece of mail addressed to them as husband and wife—the joint bank account statement. Yanking the thick wad of papers that made up the complete statement out of the envelope, she started reading through it, and what she saw sent a chill of fear down her spine. A week and a half ago he'd made a transaction of fifty thousand pounds to an estate agent; he'd put a deposit down on a house.

The bank statement confirmed what she had feared: he was leaving her.

Caught up in her own woes, she failed to notice that he'd made no transactions within the last week.

Chapter 21

Richard stared at the computer screen in rapt enthusiasm. It made him look peculiar; enthusiasm was not an expression often found on Richard's face. He usually wore a look of indifference, or, worse still, arrogance—the arrogance of youth, coupled with the belief that he held all the answers to the mysteries of life

Richard was a goth. The usual belief of immortality that most teenagers subscribed to was compounded by the goths' love of all things macabre. The idea that even if death were to come it would somehow merely see him as one of its own and move on.

Richard loved the way people would cross the street to avoid him; it made him feel important, almost akin to a reputation that a gangster would possess, the only difference being that it was his appearance that alarmed people. He had long, straggly black hair that hadn't met with shampoo in at least three months. His face was naturally quite long, and after a few heavy nights of drinking and taking drugs he took on the pale, gaunt look of the living dead. He still lived at home, to his own annoyance, and his mother would continually berate him about not washing often enough and how he was 'throwing his life away'. He just ignored her, like he did everyone. She should just accept him for what he was.

The reason, however, for this sudden change in Richard's expression, was the chat he'd been having in a goth chat room to a girl who called herself "Queen of the Damned."

Richard was obsessed with the film by the same name, and from the replies he was getting, this girl seemed just as into him.

He allowed himself a little smile—something that would have been previously unheard—to grace his lips. She told him to meet her at eight o'clock outside The Tin Whistle.

Richard started to get ready; he had only half an hour to get ready and get there in time. He turned to the mirror in his room and began the ritual of applying his makeup. Richard always used the same 'mask' whenever going out: white face paint, black lipstick, and heavily lined lids that accentuated his paleness. Noticing his nail varnish was chipped, he filled it in quickly with a permanent black marker he kept in his bedroom for emergencies. Lastly, he grabbed the small plastic bag full of mushrooms and headed for the door. His mother walked into the hall as the front door slammed closed behind him.

Richard arrived outside The Tin Whistle at eight o'clock precisely and was met by a small girl with a pale face, dark red lips, and short, spiky black hair. He couldn't believe his luck. She introduced herself as Katy and they went in. It was as always hot and sticky inside. Richard fought his way to the bar while Katy went to find a table. Richard had already decided that the situation called for spirits and had ordered double tequilas for them both, paying the barmen he found Katy sat at a table at the back of the bar.

The conversation had started pretty much where they left off; they had discussed most of their favourite films by eleven o'clock. Both of them were drunk and after another double helping of tequila they were both ready to leave. When Richard had shown Katy the mushrooms, she had laughed and invited him to a party she was going on to after. The party was happening at a house that was only a fifteen-minute walk from the pub. Richard stopped at the gents' before leaving, where he took a couple of handfuls of mushrooms. Twenty minutes later he was out of his head. Katy, having grown tired of his continual giggling, had given him the address and relieved him of the mushrooms before going on ahead. He staggered out of the pub onto the street in his, propping himself up against the side of the building he stared up and then down the street, trying to remember the directions. After a few minutes, and still none the wiser, he decided that going right seemed to be the best idea. Turning he started down the street.

When the car pulled up next to him, he didn't notice it at first. Someone got out of the car and came straight up to him.

"It's Richard, isn't it?"

"Yeah," he replied, grinning wildly. Richard couldn't be sure if what he was seeing was real or not, but it looked like this guy was wearing a mask. He decided it didn't matter; it was probably the mushrooms.

"Are you going to the party?"

"Yeah, can't remember where it is, though." He

started to laugh again.

"I can give you a lift if you like—jump in."

"Cheers." And with that he got in the car, happy in the knowledge he no longer had to worry about finding directions. He could relax and was free to gaze out at the shadows being cast by the streetlights as they streaked past. Richard could feel his eyelids getting heavy, he slowly turned his head to look at the driver who'd been kind enough to offer him a lift. He was mildly surprised to find the driver looking back at him.

When Richard woke, he felt terrible. He'd thrown up all down himself, but worse than that, he realised he was still coming down.

Christ! It smells like shit in here. He couldn't pinpoint the smell, but it kept making him gag. He stared wildly around him, trying to make sense of where he was, but it wasn't anywhere he recognised. He had woken up in questionable places before, but he'd always known whose house he was at or at least there would be someone he knew next to him.

This time, though, was different; there were no familiar sights, sounds, or, for that matter, people. He was alone. He tried to move and couldn't, and he looked down to see what was preventing his departure. He was alarmed to find he was duct taped to a wheelchair. As his mind tried to adjust to process the incoming information, he started to panic. Only a little at first, but as he properly ingested the information that he was helpless, the panic started to rise.

Then he had a thought: maybe this wasn't real;

maybe it was a cruel prank that his mates had decided to pull at the last minute. Or maybe he was dreaming, stuck in a maddening nightmare. Then he threw up again. Well, that confirmed he wasn't in a nightmare. He started to try to work out where he was. It seemed that he was in some sort of derelict barn; the wind was blowing through, chilling him to the bone. And yet even with the strong wind he could still smell that nauseating stench—it wasn't dissipating. He was starting to feel sick and was becoming increasingly paranoid; his mind seemed to have turned against him, coming up with all sorts of scary scenarios to tease and torment him. He decided the best course of action, seeing as there was no alternative, was to sit and wait.

After what seemed like an age, someone came into the room he was seemingly incarcerated in. Hearing the footsteps, Richard decided to call out.

"Listen, I don't know what the fuck you think you're doing, but you better get your arse over here and untie me right *fucking* now!"

Richards's anger bubbled over as he continued.

"I don't know who put you up to this, but let me tell you something. Once my mates and I have finished with you, you're gonna wish you'd never set eyes on me."

The stranger quietly walked up behind Richard then stepped in front of him so he could see his captor properly.

Richard took a sharp breath in. Standing in front of him was a cloaked figure. But that wasn't what had taken his breath away.

The figure had a pale cherubic face, which

obviously a mask; it was completely white but for a few homemade amendments. The lips were black, looking like a gash in an otherwise perfectly angelic face. As his eyes travelled up the contours of the face they stopped as he noticed another, obviously intentional, flaw. On one cheek of the mask, crudely painted on, was a single tear. It was a cruel parody of his own tears, which were now flowing freely down his face.

The mask spoke.

"Why are you crying?"

"Why do you think, you *freak*? You're the one who's been tearing people up all over town aren't you? I don't want to die—please, please let me go. I won't tell anyone, I swear."

Richard's voice was pleading between sobs.

"Begging Richard? That doesn't exactly fit with the hardened, indifferent image you strive so hard to achieve. Anyway, I intend to teach.'

"Teach? What do you want to teach me?"

"I'd like to teach you about death."

"Why?"

"Why not? I mean, you seem obsessed with it, and you study it almost religiously, if you'd excuse the turn of phrase. Now Richard, you spend all this time emulating death, and I want to help you, so I'm going to teach you all about death."

The mask moved out of his line of sight once more, and all of a sudden he was moving swiftly, and in what seemed to be one fluid movement, he was facing the opposite side of the room. His eyes were drawn to something on the floor, and in a sudden, violent instant, he knew what the smell had been.

Unable to control himself, his body tried to evacuate. When he'd finally managed to get a grip on himself, he forced his eyes to travel back to the body once more. He recognised it instantly as that of the man who'd gone missing over a week ago.

What was his name? Jon. Jon something or other. Jon…

"Jon Hamilton." As if reading his mind, the mask spoke.

"Is he…is he…?"

"Dead? Yes. I really thought you'd have known that, though." The voice had a chastising quality to it.

"It seems you still have a lot to learn about death. Well, why put off 'til tomorrow what you can do today? That's what my mother always said, anyway." With that, the mask leaned over him, clamping a damp rag over his nose and mouth. With his arms bound, there was nothing Richard could do.

He tried to hold his breath, but the masked man had anticipated this, and a gloved hand stroked his face as the stranger's gentle voice started to speak.

"Try to relax, Richard; it'll all be over soon."

Knowing there was nothing he could do, his lungs screaming at him, he took a few gasps of air.

Sometime later, Richard stirred once again. He could feel pressure all across the front of his body, and he was lying on the cold floor. His arms had been tied round something in front of him, and something cold and spongy was on top of him. As he slowly opened his eyes, he let out a high-pitched, primal scream. Directly in front of him, Jon Hamilton's glazed, milky eyes stared back at his. Up close he could see the discolouration on his face; it looked as if someone had prised his mouth open after death had got hold of him, and now there was a fetid smell emanating As Richard tried to kick out and push the body away he realised he was tied to a pole, which was thwarting any efforts he made. But as he moved, a soft, rasping breath escaped the dead body on top of him. This was the last straw, as far as Richard was concerned, and he threw up again and started to cry.

The cloaked figure watched Richard from the other side of the room, once Richard was spent the figure moved slowly toward him. Richard cried out, trying in vain to sound angered as opposed to frightened, but unfortunately the wavering in his voice gave him away.

"You freak! Let me up from here right now, right fucking now…"

His voice trailed off as another gasp of air escaped Mr. Hamilton.

"Please, please, let me go, I won't tell anyone—who'd believe me anyway?"

"Oh, dear Richard, we're missing the point, aren't we? I'm doing this for your own good. You'll learn everything you need to know about death within the next few hours, days, weeks, hell, I'm not even sure how long this will take." The last bit was said jovially as if this was some kind of bizarre experiment that was to culminate in an exciting discovery.

"Why me? What did I ever do to you?"

"It's not what you did to me, Richard. There are so many reasons you're here now, none of which I particularly care to share with you."

"But why *me*?" His voice regained a little strength.

"Why you? Well, why anyone, really? So many people have such little say in what happens to them in their lives. People lose people they love every day through disease and accidents that they had no control over. And to them death is something to be respected. They have a personal insight into what death holds; it's not something to be emulated and mocked by people like you who've never felt the pain of loss. You and your ilk pass drugs around, introducing them to the most vulnerable people in society without any concern for the consequences. People get hurt—or sometimes worse—by your actions, but still you don't care, still the indifference."

"So you're teaching me that lesson by strapping me to *this*?" Richard nodded toward the body on top of him.

"Yes, I'm afraid I can't take credit for the ingenuity of it, though—I got the idea from the Etruscans."

"*Who*?"

"The Etruscans. Really, Richard, for one so arrogant you really are painfully stupid."

Ordinarily Richard would have had a row with anyone who dared to call him stupid, but now he feared that perhaps his abductor had a point. He had, after all, gotten willingly into the car.

"The Etruscans were in Rome before the Romans.

They were pirates, basically, for want of a better word. They did this to their own when they stepped out of line, the idea being that one may inhale death from a dead body. Personally, I can't see how it would work, I suppose no food or water *and* a dead body strapped to you; I imagine it's a pretty nasty way to die, but I suppose time will tell."

And with that, the masked stranger turned and walked away, Richard's screams of protest and disgust punctuating the night air.

Chapter 22

As the two uniformed policemen pulled up outside Joanne Hamilton's house, they gave each other a sideways glance; neither of them relished the thought of what they had to do now. They had agreed this was definitely the worst part of their job. Letting out synchronised sighs, they got out of the car and made their way up the path to the front door, ringing the doorbell. They straightened themselves up as they waited for the door to be opened.

This was the young PC Bannerman's thirteenth month on the job, and from what he'd seen in the last twenty-eight days, he was starting to wonder if it might be his last. Nothing they'd taught him during training had prepared him for what he'd seen in that disused council lockup on the industrial estate four weeks ago. He still felt ill whenever he thought back to it, and he'd not had one decent night's sleep since. Now here he was, on the doorstep of another potential victim's house, and he was about to tell some poor woman that one of her husband's digits had been found in an ice-lolly at her husband's mistress's house.

Again, no training for that, either; he'd received training in how to break the news of death to relatives, but what body did they have? A finger. A finger doesn't necessarily mean that the man was dead, so what were they going to say?

"Hi, Mrs. Hamilton, I'm afraid we have some bad news. Someone's relieved your husband of a finger and we were wondering if you could formally identify it? We have a positive ID from his mistress, who incidentally found it an ice-lolly she'd been sucking on at the time. No, I'm afraid we can't be sure if the rest of him is dead or not, but once the police examiners have finished with the finger, we will release it back to you and if we find the rest of him, we'll be sure to let you know."

No, this was all wrong, this wasn't why he'd joined the force—so some sick creep could play games with him.

P.C Bannerman was brought soundly back to Earth by the sound of a key in the door in front of them. As the door slowly opened, his eyes met the pale, drawn face of a lady who had clearly been very attractive in her day but had obviously let herself go. There were dark rings around her eyes, her dark blonde hair, streaked with grey, was lying limply round her face, and she was still in a dressing gown.

"How can I help you, Officer?" Her voice was strong, despite her appearance. PC Bannerman spoke then.

"Mrs Joanne Hamilton?" She nodded her response.

"I'm afraid we have some news concerning your husband—would it be possible to come in for a minute?"

"Yes, yes, he's not here, though, never is these days. I haven't seen him in over a week; he even missed Harry's birthday."

"Harry?" PC Bannerman queried.

"Oh, sorry, Harry's our son. Sixteen he is now. Would you like a cup of tea?"

"No thank you, Mrs Hamilton. About your husband, I think it might be best if you sat down."

As if hearing him for the first time, Joanne swung about to face him.

"Listen, Constable, I believe my husband's left me; I always knew the day would come, but I'm still in shock, so unless he's dead I have no interest in anything he's done, whether past, present, or future. He hasn't been my husband for a very long time, always running around with any bit of skirt that caught his eye, but he crossed the line when he missed his son's birthday. I know he's been seeing someone else and I also know that he's left me—of course the coward couldn't tell me to my face, he wanted me to find out for myself."

The verbal tirade stunned Bannerman, and he mentally cursed the forces that had brought him into the middle of this shit storm. He stared calmly back at her and spoke gently.

"So he didn't tell you he was leaving you?"

"No."

"How do you know he left you, then?"

"'Cause I found out he's put a deposit down on a house, and I know it's not for us, because he never mentioned moving. So come on, out with it, what has my dearest gone and done, anyway?"

"Well, I'm afraid it's not anything he's done. Earlier on today we had a call from a distraught woman saying she'd found something that belonged to your husband at her apartment."

"Yes? So what does that have to do with me, or, indeed, you, for that matter? Obviously that's my husband's newest bit of skirt—what was it she'd found? His morals in a bin bag?"

"Actually, it was his wedding ring."

"Aha! The dirty bastard didn't even have the decency to give it back to me in person." Knowing there was no easy way of doing this, PC Bannerman blurted out,

"Complete with his finger."

Joanne had drawn a breath, readying for a long line of expletives, when she stopped dead.

"What did you say?"

"I'm afraid the wedding ring was still on his finger when it was discovered."

"So you mean to tell me someone cut his finger off?"

"Yes."

"I want to see him." Her voice changed suddenly; the hostility was gone and she now sounded quiet and concerned.

"I'm sorry?" Bannerman replied.

"Take me to him—he's still my husband and the father of my children. I need to see him."

As she was talking, she moved around, locating her handbag and checking that she had her keys in there. Then she slipped off her slippers, went into the hall, and came back with a scruffy pair of shoes. As she started putting them on, Bannerman once more looked at his colleague and, practically pleading with his eyes, gently spoke.

"I'm afraid I can't do that, Mrs Hamilton."

She stopped what she was doing and looked the

young PC straight in the eye.

"What do you mean? Why can't I see my own husband?"

"I'm afraid we haven't been able to locate his whereabouts as yet."

Joanne dropped to the floor in front of the PC. PC Bannerman watched her as she dissolved into sobs in front of him. Then almost as quickly as she had started to sob she stopped. Getting up she walked through into the kitchen. The PC followed her. She put the kettle on and then going over to the dresser she opened the top drawer and retrieved an envelope. Grabbing the contents of it she laid it out on the table in front of her. PC Bannerman walked up behind her and glanced over her shoulder.

Sensing the PC's presence Joanne spoke.

"It looks like he hasn't made any transactions for over a week."

As Bannerman reviewed the statement, the other PC gently took Joanne by the arm and led her back into the living room and sat her down on the sofa. Returning to the kitchen he made the tea.

Joanne sat in the interview room at the police station. She'd never been inside a police station, let alone been in an interview room before. And she decided she didn't like it. She didn't like being made to feel like a criminal. She'd been questioned about Jon's behaviour leading up to his disappearance and asked the obligatory question about if there were any problems within their marriage. That had almost made her laugh—she couldn't think of a time when they hadn't had problems. Not that that would have had any bearing on the facts. So, resolutely, she had continued to play the doting wife and said that everything was fine.

Although she had been reassured that she wasn't a suspect, it hadn't stopped her feeling guilty. It was as if these sparse rooms were designed to make you believe the worst of yourself.

She'd left the kids at home alone, and even though they were old enough to be there unsupervised, she still didn't like it, especially not with the way things stood at the moment. No one had seen hide nor hair of Jon in well over a week; well, discounting the sudden appearance of his ring finger. She was also unaware of exactly how she should feel about the news. So far the thing troubling her most was the thought of explaining it to the kids, and then there was the question of life insurance. She was sure they needed to produce a whole body before the insurance company would cough up. Typical bloody Jon; he'd been disappearing most of their married life, and now it looked as if his disappearing act would yet again leave her bereft, but financially this time. Then, of course, she'd felt guilty for being so callous about a man she had once loved who was the father of her children. The Police had told Joanne that they had questioned the mistress about Jon's whereabouts leading up to his disappearance, but apparently she hadn't seen him for a week prior. But then she was probably lying; her type always did, especially when in a tight spot. It was after all the tart stock and trade: lying, cheating, causing pain to people they'd probably never met before in their lives.

A WPC broke into her thoughts by walking into the interview room.

"Ok Mrs Hamilton, we're finished for tonight. We can give you a lift home if you'd like."

As the WPC had walked through she'd been taken aback by the broken shadow of a woman sitting in front of her; it looked as if she'd had all the fight drained from her. The irony of what had been found in Sarah Lester's apartment earlier had not been lost on her. She'd been brought up in a household where it had been practically expected for her father to stay out at his mistresses' houses at least one night a week. She'd watched her mum go through all the stages. Anger, belligerence, and denial, until finally her father had worn her down from the proud, formidable woman he had married to a doormat.

Now she felt she was looking at her mother, only twenty years younger and with a more permanent absentee husband. The WPC couldn't shake the feeling she was having about the killer—he seemed almost vigilante in his choice of victims. Although the police still weren't sure about the identity of the first victim, the second victim, Matt Reynolds, was rumoured to have been a drunken, abusive partner. Their enquiries had led them to a girl called Rebecca, an ex of the late Matt Reynolds, and although they had split up years ago, she was still a shadow of a woman. The WPC had stood there, practically agog, as Rebecca's mother had recanted the miserable affair of her daughter and Matt Reynolds's abortive relationship. She had seen all the scarring up the girl's arms and wondered how one person could be allowed so much control over another. As soon as Rebecca had heard about his demise, she had run off upstairs, sobbing. According to her friends and family, she'd been lively and outgoing—that was, until she'd fallen under the spell of Matt.

And now there was Mr Hamilton. The killer must have been feeling more confident now, as it had been quite a daring stunt to pull off. To have the wedding finger complete with ring frozen inside an ice-lolly, where it was discovered several hours later by the adulterers' mistress must've taken some planning.

Joanne spoke up then.

"Are you going to question her more?"

"Miss Lester? No, there's nothing tying her to your husband's disappearance."

"But she was his mistress, wasn't she? She must have a clue to his whereabouts. She managed to keep their relationship a secret, lying and cheating; what makes you think she's telling you the truth now?"

"She has a watertight alibi."

"Fine, well, if it's all the same to you, I would like to go home now, please; I've got kids at home who I've yet to tell the news to."

With that, Joanne got up and strode to the door. The WPC opened it for her and followed her out back into the reception area.

"Would you like a lift back home, Mrs Hamilton?"

"Please."

"Ok, just wait here, I'll get a car sent round to you."

Joanne watched as the WPC disappeared back into the station. Realising it may take a while Joanne sat down once more on one of the hard plastic seats located in the reception area and stared around at all the various posters and paraphernalia littering the walls—this truly was a depressing place. Joanne was aware that her circumstances for being there were less than ideal, but she got the distinct impression it would still be just as depressing to the casual observer. Leaning her head back against the wall, she stared up at the ceiling. She was absolutely shattered. As soon as she got in, she was going for a hot bath then straight to bed. Her gaze fell back towards the desk in the reception; it was deserted. And then, in her peripheral vision, there was movement—the door she had just come through was opening. People were talking.

"I'm sorry I couldn't help more, Officer."

The voice had a whiny, childish quality to it.

"That's ok Miss Lester, I'll send a car straight round to pick you up."

"Thank you, Officer."

Joanne heard the door swing again as the officer went to sort out an available car.

Joanne knew she shouldn't look; she knew she didn't really want to see, but she already knew who it was: Sarah Lester. She'd met her before; she'd shown up at the restaurant when her and Jon had been out about three weeks ago on their wedding anniversary—one of the few times of the year he actually took her out.

Sarah had introduced herself as an ex-employee, and even though she could have sworn she'd seen a flicker of annoyance cross Jon's face, she had naïvely put that down to the fact that he hadn't wanted to be disturbed. Now, though, she knew differently. Joanne had taken an instant liking to the girl, who had seemed young enough to be their daughter and had invited her to join them. Now, as she fixed Sarah with a steady gaze, everything suddenly made sense. That little bitch had not only been sharing her husband, she'd had the audacity to befriend her. Whether part of a power trip or just to see the look on Jon's face, it didn't matter—the humiliation was still there whatever spin was put on it. She looked at Sarah now, tight clothes and makeup smeared down her face, and she knew that if her husband were here, he would still want her. Even with her hair a mess and panda eyes, and that hurt—really hurt. Joanne's look hardened as she stared at the pathetic girl and she felt nothing but burning, seething hatred. She knew it was unfair; Jon was as much—if not more—to blame for the affair, but he wasn't here now, and this young tramp was, still laughing at her and mocking her with her tight stomach and creaseless face. She couldn't hold herself back any longer and she launched herself at the girl.

Sarah had failed to notice the small, drab woman staring daggers at her and sitting not six feet away. She had been far too wrapped up in her own predicament. It hadn't been finding the finger that had unsettled her so much as the fact that if what the police had suggested was right and Jon had become the serial killer's latest victim, where did that leave her as far as her child allowance and detached house were concerned?

All of a sudden, as if from nowhere, she had some crazy beast on her back, pulling at her hair and slapping at her face. She screamed out in terror as the woman on her back started screaming obscenities at her.

The WPC and PC who had interviewed the two women earlier came bursting back into the reception area and dragged Joanne off of Sarah.

"Now, can we all just calm down?" The PC sounded tired and both women regarded him warily, Joanne still panting from her energetic assault.

"It's been a very stressful time for you both, so let's just concentrate on getting you both back home," the PC ventured. Sarah swung about to face the PC.

"Hold on—I want to press charges; she just attacked me for no reason." The indignation in her voice was palpable. The WPC who was still holding Joanne by the arm turned to face Sarah.

"If you want to press charges Miss Lester, you are of course within your rights. However, these are exceptional circumstances and Mrs Hamilton here has just suffered a terrible shock, emotions are running very high for you and for her."

Sarah regarded the both the WPC and Joanne as the last statement hung in the air waiting to be addressed. The PC, sensing that a man had no place in the argument, held his tongue and did his best to blend into the back ground.

"Do you wish to press charges?"

"No. Take me home."

Sarah turned and headed out the door, the PC following behind her.

Then the WPC turned to Joanne.

"Christ, I wouldn't want to get on the wrong side of you."

Joanne gave a weary smile.

"Guess I must still have feelings for the cheating bastard after all."

The WPC held the door open for Joanne and they made their way to the squad car waiting for them outside.

Chapter 23

Dean arrived at The Tin Whistle at eight as previously arranged and saw that Mark was already waiting for him with a pint ready. He wandered over to the table, sat down, and took a long drink before acknowledging Mark.

"So come on then, what do you know?"

"Well the bloke's name is Adam, and he's usually down at Andre's every Friday and Saturday night."

"What time?"

Mark checked his phone briefly before responding.

"Well, according to my mate, he should be there in the next half hour—what do you want to do?"

"What do you think I want to do? I want to go down there and kick the living shit out of him. Let's go."

Mark downed the rest of his drink quickly and grabbed his jacket as they headed toward the door. Getting into Marks car the two set off at speed toward Andre's. Pulling up in the car park, they marched inside and ordered drinks—two lagers and a vodka chaser for Dean. They managed to find a small table in the corner of the room where they could watch the door.

"So how are we going to go about this? I mean, are you going to ask him anything or just twat him outright?"

"Not sure yet." Dean slurped his pint noisily.

The door swung open and three men strode in. Mark nodded at the first of the men.

"That's your man there. Adam Woodacre."

"So I see. Look, Mark, I don't want you to get involved in this. I'm going to wait until he goes to the bogs, follow him, and I'll meet you in the car after, ok?"

Mark looked across the room to where Adam was standing; he was busy laughing at the landlord with all his mates chiming as required. Mark hated that kind of bloke, all mouth and no substance. Mark could run his mouth with the best of them, especially if he'd had a few, but he had form. He wasn't necessarily proud of the reputation he had garnered, but at least he had a reputation. Adam Woodacre was a ponce, a lowlife piece of shit who liked to strut about like a big man.

"You sure you don't want me to come with you? To be honest, mate, I wouldn't mind kicking that shit eating grin back down his throat myself, and he ain't even done anything to me."

"Nah, you just get yourself back to the car. Ah, looks like we're on." Dean nodded toward the bar as Adam started to make his way to the gents' room.

The two men got up, one following Adam and the other heading for the car park.

Adam slammed the gents' toilet door open. His website's popularity had grown phenomenally within the last week. Other people had been posting items and this had given him a kick. To him, the fact that there were other people who shared his perverse mind-set had been a form of validation. As he stood in front of the urinal, he smiled a wide smile, lost in his reverie. He barely noticed the door swing open.

Dean stood in the doorway and watched Adam's back for a moment. Walking quietly up behind him, he stopped just inches from Adam's back before peering over his shoulder.

"Not as big as the one stood in front of me."

Adam jumped at the proximity of the voice. Doing up his jeans, he spun round to see who it was.

"What's your fucking problem?"

"Careful, Adam, you've gone and pissed all over your shoes." Dean hadn't backed off, and he now stood just inches from Adam's face. Adam looked down to check his shoes, and as he brought his head back up to Dean's level, it was met by Dean's forehead. The blow put Adam straight on the floor as Dean set about kicking him, blows landing on his stomach, legs, and back. Adam had no chance of fighting back through the ferocity of the kicks that were raining down on him, so he was busy trying to protect his head and face with his arms. Seeing this, Dean continued to kick at Adam's body, trying to focus on his kidneys. Dean had been on the losing side of a fight once and had taken a few blows to the kidneys, and he remembered how painful it had been. He had been pissing blood for a good few days after. Finally Dean tired and he squatted down next to Adam, who was dully aware that the onslaught had ceased. He looked Adam up and down.

"You'll be pissing blood for the next few days; however, if you ever go near Clare Heathers again, I'll be back, and next time I won't leave you with anything to piss with."

Dean hawked back in his throat and spat straight in Adam's already swelling eye.

Getting back up, he checked his reflection; apart from a small red mark on his forehead from where it had made contact with Adam's nose minutes before, there was nothing to indicate he'd done anything untoward. Glancing once more back at Adam, he left the toilets and met Mark in the car.

"Are we good?"

"We're good."

With that, Mark sparked the engine into life and pulled out of the car park.

Chapter 24

Robert Hollister wasn't a happy man. He was in charge of the estate to the south of Manning's Town. The estate was run from Shropshire approximately seventy miles away, and so it was up to him to ensure the smooth running of this particular part of it. The estate owned around forty thousand acres of land, ten thousand of which he was personally responsible for.

The estate would rent land and sometimes farm buildings to farmers in the area. In return the estate would be ultimately responsible for the buildings' upkeep. The estate had originally been set up as a trust fund by a wealthy landowner who didn't want the land to be sold off to the highest bidder after his death and fall into the wrong hands—the wrong hands being those of property developers or industry. He had wanted to make sure his farmers weren't forced off their land by large corporate companies; the flipside of the trust, however, was that the farmers could never actually own their land—the trust was not allowed to sell any of it off.

The reason for Robert Hollister's visit, however, was a specific building within this particular area of the estate: a derelict farmhouse. Its previous occupants had left over twenty years ago and the building had not been touched since. However, with the recent jump in house prices within Manning's Town, the estate had to been quick to pick up on the fact that the farmhouse was a prospective goldmine. Commuters would pay a substantially larger rent than most in order to have the peace and tranquillity this country retreat would offer.

In his opinion, moving non-country folk in would be a nightmare. Unfortunately, though, it wasn't his decision to make. All the land that had originally belonged to the farmhouse had since been divided up between the surrounding farms, which meant the only use the farmhouse would have would to be a family residence.

As he pulled into the top of the driveway, he had a prime view of the building; it may have been completely derelict, but as the morning sun streamed over it the view was breath taking.

There was a long sweeping driveway into the front yard area. Far in the background a hillside fringed by a wooded area masked the horizon. And Robert could see why people from the town would want to live in such a place. The seclusion and solitude it provided would serve as a balm in even the most hectic of lives.

As he manoeuvred his car onto the drive, he was once again reminded of how much work would be needed to bring this place up to scratch. The driveway was full of potholes, and as his wheels found another one and grazed the underside of his new Mercedes he cursed quietly under his breath.

The door to the property was wide open. Getting out of the car, he first walked round to inspect the damage done. There was a small scuff mark along the bottom of the skirts that troubled him even though he'd had to actively look to notice. He sighed noisily and made his way to the front door, checking to see if it was still attached; it was, but only just. Walking into what was once the kitchen; it was like travelling back through time. The kitchen cabinets were unfitted and painted, something he reflected, that you rarely saw anymore. What had once been carpet tiles on the floor were virtually all rotten and peeling up at the corners. Robert grinned to himself. It all reminded him of his youth. His parents had been farmers; in fact, before they had retired, they ran a farm less than ten miles from here. He could still remember the mornings; they always felt like the busiest time of the day. He would have to be up at seven to get ready for school, and as he was dressing in his freezing cold bedroom, he'd hear his mother in the kitchen below scraping the ashes from the hearth, ready to start the fire for the day. By the time he bowled into the kitchen she'd have all the breakfast plates laid out. His two sisters would already be there, bickering between themselves. And then his father would come in, bringing fresh milk for the day, and they would all sit down and have breakfast together, which, depending on the time of the year would consist of either toast or porridge. Once they'd all finished their breakfast, he would run back upstairs to have a wash in tepid water that the kitchen fire had only just managed to take the edge off of. By the time he got back down to the kitchen, his mother would be dashing around trying to find her keys to take him to school.

  Taking a final look around the kitchen, Robert made his way into the hallway; the stairs went off to the right, spiralling as they did so. He was under strict instruction from the estate not to go up there under any circumstances. He had been assured that the staircase would be rotted through by now, and clumsy footing could see him starting the renovation work earlier than intended.

Going back outside again, he decided to take a walk around to the back of the property to explore the possibility of turning the stables into a garage. A quick scan about told him everything he needed to know: they'd serve that purpose brilliantly, but a new roof would be required.

Pondering the idea of fitting patio doors into the main house, he strode over toward the old barns that had disrupted the view. The doors looked about fit to collapse, but a quick analysis of their situation couldn't hurt.

The first barn had no roof and the brick was already beginning to crumble. As Robert started toward the second barn the one directly in the line of view from the house, he stopped.

There was something just outside of it. Something was there, shining. It was in a pothole, which was probably why he hadn't seen it from the house. He walked over to investigate further and found a cigarette lighter. He bent and scooped it up; the cigarette lighter had once belonged in a car. It stuck out because everything around him that was manmade was in decay, but not this—this looked brand new, not tarnished, scuffed, or weatherworn in any way. Wondering if this place had become the chief hangout for the local kids, he put it in his pocket and continued into the barn. This barn, like the first, was in shambles with crumbling brickwork and gaping holes in the roof. Robert scanned the floor, wondering what it would take to have the lot removed and lay down some turf instead; a building this size would make a nice family a home, and the parents would want a garden for the kids.

As his eyes moved over the concrete flooring, his line of sight moved to the back of barn. There was something there, in the shadows. Maybe it was his eyes; the morning sun was bright outside, and although the roof needed replacing it was still dark enough inside to mask certain areas of the floor.

There is something there.

Robert felt a small chill going down his spine.

Maybe it's an animal—a fox?

No, it's too big for a fox.

His rational side kicked back in. He chastised himself for being afraid.

You're too far away from it to make that decision.

Maybe it's something the last tenants left behind, machinery or something.

As he drew closer, he could tell it wasn't machinery. His mind started to race.

A homeless person? He mentally scolded himself again. *Why would someone come out to the middle of nowhere to sleep in a barn? The house is a derelict but it would still be preferable to this.*

Just to be sure, he called out to the bundle, but there was no reply.

Well, that settles it—it's not human, so no need to continue any farther.

But he couldn't stop; his legs weren't listening, and something inside of him had to know what it was.

As he came up on the remains of Richard and Jon, he heard a scream.

One of them is alive.

Robert was unsure of how much time elapsed before he realised the scream was coming from him.

Before he knew what was happening, he had his mobile in his hand and was furiously pressing buttons.

Within thirty minutes, three police cars and an ambulance were there.

And Robert Hollister had been tranquilised.

"Sir, we've found two more." Henson's voice came through loud on Holt's mobile.

"God, please tell me *one* of them is Jon Hamilton."

"It looks like it, sir. The chap on top's missing the fourth digit on his left hand."

"The chap on top? Never mind, Henson, where are you anyway?"

"We're seven miles outside town. Come out of town as if heading towards Newton Leigh, and about four miles along the road there's a turn on your right, take it and follow the road for three miles, and the entrance to the farmhouse is on your left. I'll have a couple of uniforms standing at the top so you don't miss us."

"I'm on my way." Henson could hear Holt open his car door.

"Hurry, sir, the coroner's here already and he's getting impatient."

"Be with you in ten." And with that, Holt hung up.

Henson stared down at the phone in his hand for a few minutes. Why had it taken so long to get hold of him? They were in the middle of a major investigation and Holt was becoming the scarlet pimpernel—not good, considering Dennis Grant wasn't known for good-humoured patience. Dennis Grant was the acting coroner and had all the good temperament of a rabid dog. When he'd arrived on the scene and Holt hadn't been there, he'd spent ten minutes chewing Henson's ear and wouldn't tell him anything pertinent about the bodies at all. He'd referred to Henson as "boy," something that had gotten the young DC's back up straight away.

He said he wanted to speak to "the organ grinder, not the monkey," and had then gone on to berate DI Holt's slapdash attitude to the case in general. Anyone would think the man was in charge of the investigation himself.

Ten minutes later, Holt's car pulled into the driveway. Dennis Grant walked over to meet the upcoming vehicle, his head to one side, the most petulant look he could muster on his face. As the car pulled up and the door opened, Dennis opened his mouth to speak, seeing this Jimmy raised his hand.

"Dennis, I don't have time for this. I'm sorry I'm a little late." Dennis raised his eyebrows and went to speak again. Jimmy cut him off once more.

"However my DC was here and now so am I, so if you'd like to make a formal complaint please feel free, but for the time being can we just do what we're all here to do?"

Dennis turned on his heel and stormed back toward the barn.

Henson had seen the exchange between the two men and suppressed a grin. Holt was really good at cutting people off dead—he had a real presence about him when he chose to.

Holt was walking in Henson's direction and knew he wouldn't be happy with what little information he had garnered about the discovery.

"What do we know, Henson?"

"Well, sir, I believe the body on top to be Mr Jon Hamilton."

"And the other?"

"Not sure, we're rechecking missing persons. We think it might be a Richard Abbott—went on the list over a week ago."

The two men strode toward the barn, following the irritated Dennis Grant into the building.

"Who found the bodies?" Consulting his notepad, Henson answered,

"A Mr Robert Hollister, the estate manager for the area; you won't be able to speak to him yet, though."

"Oh yes, and why's that?"

"He's been tranquilised."

"Tranquilised?"

"Yeah, poor guy went into shock."

Holt was amazed but ultimately pleased to hear some compassion in the young DC's voice.

Walking into the dim barn, Holt was reminded of how secluded this area was; the killer had really done their research on this particular location. If the

PCs hadn't been standing at the top of the driveway, he'd probably have driven straight past. As he neared the bodies he started to smell the decay—they'd probably been here a while.

"Who owns these buildings?"

"Oh, they're part of an estate. We spoke to Robert Hollister's boss earlier, and apparently the place his been empty for over twenty years. They'd sent him down to assess the state of it and then they were going to renovate. What with the property market as it is, I guess they figured they could really cash in on it."

"Good job they did, otherwise we might never have found them."

Holt was surveying the remains of Jon Hamilton and Richard Abbott.

"Any idea of time of death yet?" Holt queried. Dennis Grant, having gotten over the previous set-to with Holt, answered.

"Around two weeks ago—this one was first, the other a week or so later. I won't know properly until we get them back into town, but it does look like the one on top was moved into this position post-mortem."

"What makes you say that?"

"Well, the discolouration of the feet, mainly; if the victim had died in this position the mottling would be all down the front of their body, including the face."

"What about rigor mortis? Surely it would have been practically impossible to move him after he'd died."

"Not necessarily. Rigor mortis only affects the

body after the first few hours, then after twenty-four hours the effect wears off and the body becomes pliant again."

"There's no doubt that the one on top is Jon Hamilton, then?"

"No, I don't think so. Build, height, and clothing fit, and of course there's this." Picking up Jon's left arm, he held out Jon's hand.

"He's missing his ring finger."

Henson pulled a small, sealed bag out of his jacket pocket, and held up the evidence bag to Holt.

"A cigarette lighter? To cauterize the wound, I assume."

"Looks like it. It was found over by the door. Before they knocked out Robert Hollister he mentioned he'd found it, obviously he had picked it up, so we'll need to get his fingerprints so we can rule him out."

"I very much doubt we'll find anything of any real use on it anyway. The killer's been very methodical up to now, and I wouldn't be surprised if it'd been left there to taunt us. Let's face it: he's miles ahead of us at the moment"

"Can I take that as a direct quote, Detective Inspector?" The voice was loud in the room and the arrogant mocking tone was one that could only belong to a certain type of person—press.

"What the *hell* are the press doing here?" Holt whispered angrily under his breath.

"Get them out now, and get these bodies covered up until they're gone. That's all we bloody well need." Henson went to make a move and felt a hand clutch his arm.

"Confiscate everything they've got—cameras, notepads, tape recorders, anything—and warn them that if any of this finds its way into any of their shit rag papers tomorrow, I'll be round with warrants for their arrests."

"What for, Inspector?"

"Jeopardising an on-going investigation, trespassing, and whatever else I damn well feel like. Now go."

It took little under twenty minutes to completely rid the farm of reporters. Once it was clear, Holt allowed the removal of the bodies.

"I want them back at the station and ready for identification as soon as possible, no need to draw that out any longer than necessary."

Henson nodded.

"Ring me when they're ready. I'll go and collect Mrs Hamilton myself."

Holt turned and headed back to his car. Dennis Grant marched up to Henson, who was watching Holt's retreating back.

"And where does he think he's going?"

Henson turned to look at Dennis Grant, whose mouth was still open.

"I didn't like to ask."

Holt had spoken to Loretta to let her know he was on his way, and, for the first time in a long time, Holt felt the urge to smile when she answered the door.

"I'm sorry to turn up like this."

"It isn't a problem, go through and make yourself comfortable. The kettle's just boiled. Is instant ok with you?"

"Yes, instant would be just fine."

Holt walked through into the living room and sat down.

Loretta brought the coffees in, and passing one to Holt she sat down and waited for him to start. Holt thanked her for the coffee and let out a long sigh.

"Honestly, Loretta, what's wrong with the world?"

Loretta sat patiently, waiting for him to continue.

"This town's being torn apart and all I seem to be able to do is watch. You know where I've just come from? A double murder scene. Two men—well, one man and one boy trussed up like a Christmas ham. I mean, here we are, trying to get into the mind-set of the killer, and the more I see the more I realise I just don't want to. Who wants to be able to understand the kind of insanity that's been happening recently?"

"Well, that's what criminal profiling is about—understanding the motives so as to anticipate the next move."

Holt nodded.

"I know, I understand the principle, but I'm going to have to accompany two women to identify their loved ones later on today. What am I going to tell them? We don't even know why they were chosen as victims, much less have any potential suspects."

"Do we know the cause of the deaths yet?"

"No, not yet, we're going to have to wait on the results of the post mortems."

"Well, once you know the results, you can always come back here and we can discuss them."

"Thanks, I do appreciate all your help, but to be

honest you've done enough, and besides, with more bodies turning up…" Holt left the sentence hanging, so Loretta finished it for him.

"You are going to be under the microscope."

"Not helped by the fact that the press seem to be getting extra information from somewhere."

"Extra information?"

"Well, I'm not entirely sure what they know or where they're getting it from, but let's just say I'm going to be under very close scrutiny and the last thing I need is certain factions questioning my competence."

"Understood. Well, I wish I could have helped more, but you're right, it's probably best if you keep your distance for now, if only for your reputation."

"Thank you for all your help, and not just with the case; to be honest I've been glad of the company."

"Me, too, I've quite enjoyed having someone to share a meal with."

"Maybe once the case is over we could meet up again in more social circumstances."

"That sounds great."

Loretta was following Holt towards the door.

"Take care of yourself and once again, thanks for your help. Until next time."

Loretta closed the door behind him.

Holt paused for a moment. He had never felt more alone in all his life.

Regaining his composure, he decided he'd head back to the station and see if Henson had any further ideas on who they were looking for. He smiled at the futility of the thought.

"Why were Richard Abbott's arms tied behind Jon Hamilton's back, sir? Do you think it was sexual?"

"Firstly, Henson, we need to establish if the body underneath is Richard Abbott's. The boy's mother is on her way. I hope for her sake it's not. Secondly, if it was sexual, why not remove the clothes?"

"I don't know, sir, maybe the killer was disturbed by someone or something and maybe that's why they dropped the lighter, rushing to get away."

"The whole place is a derelict, no one's so much as stepped in the front door in over twenty years, but while our killer's busy at work, an unsuspecting dog walker happens upon the farm? I don't think so. Besides, the cigarette lighter's given us nothing— the only DNA evidence on it belongs to the late Mr Hamilton and the only fingerprints to Mr Hollister. The killer was in no rush, believe me; if what Dennis suspects to be true is the case, time was not an issue."

At that moment, a WPC stuck her head around the doorframe.

"Mrs Abbott's here, shall I show her through?"

"If you wouldn't mind, and get hot, sweet tea on standby; even if it isn't her son, she's going to need it."

"Yes, sir." The WPC left the room.

"Dennis Grant says he thinks Jon was first to die, but why weren't they killed together? It would have been a lot less trouble."

Holt slammed his hands down on his desk.

"For Christ's sake, Henson, have you not listened to a word I've said?"

Stopping briefly to draw breath and calm himself, Holt continued,

"The killer doesn't care about trouble. He enjoys killing people in bizarre and unlikely ways, usually to illustrate some random point, all the time right under our noses, parading the mutilated corpses in front of us. I wouldn't be surprised if it was the killer who tipped off the press as to our whereabouts today, to humiliate us and show us up as incompetent fools."

Henson visibly paled at this.

"You really think so, sir?"

"Yes, Henson, I actually do. In fact, get onto the press office, find out who tipped them off about the bodies this morning."

"They won't tell us that, sir, you know how the press are with their sources."

"Well, you tell them that this is an on-going murder investigation, not playtime at school; they tell us who tipped them the wink or they're excluded from any more press conferences, ok"

As Henson opened the door to leave, the anguished wail of Mrs Abbott identifying her son could be heard.

Chapter 25

It had been a fortnight since Joanne had identified her philandering husband's body. Standing in the front row of the church, Joanne looked at the coffin in front of her, her children by her side, staying as stoic as possible. She felt bad for them; Jon had been a good father and the children had loved him dearly. The fact that he had been such a good father had been the only saving grace in the last five years of their marriage. She had never tried for a divorce, as she knew how much it would have hurt the children, and the last thing she wanted was to be the bad guy. Joanne had changed almost beyond recognition since Jon's death; her life was now her own again. Jon had never tried to repress her in any way; she had done that herself, always believing in her marriage vows even after he had so callously dismissed them. She had started taking pride in her appearance once more. She had always been well turned out, but she was very conservative in her dress. Her hair, which had been streaked with grey, was now a lustrous gold colour thanks to her regular trips to the hairdresser's. She suddenly seemed to personify confidence, always meeting peoples eyes, speaking up and making sure she was heard. It was almost like she had been leading someone else's life up to now, always waiting for the time when she could emerge. She had felt eyes on her as she had walked into the church with her children. She knew she looked stunning all in black; despite the four kids she still had a very tidy figure, something she was determined to flaunt from now on. She had already had some interest shown in her by some of her late husband's friends. But as much fun as flirting was, she had no interest in taking it any further; she had her own money now and she had no intention of wasting another seventeen years of her life on a man again. For the first time she could plan and the first port of call would be the solicitor to check the will. Once she could be assured that Sarah Lester wasn't getting a penny, she would book a long holiday for her and the kids. They would need a break after burying their father. Then when they got back, she would set about finding someone to run the chain of sandwich shops she now owned. She intended to be a lady of leisure from now on, and if she could find someone suitable, she could relax and just let the business take care of itself.

As the priest started to waft the incense around the coffin, Joanne stole a moment to look toward the back of the church. Dressed in a short black dress, Sarah Lester sat sobbing. Joanne noticed how, despite her tears, her makeup wasn't even smudged, and every now and then she would cast her eyes around the mourners. Joanne rolled her eyes; even at her lover's funeral Sarah was looking round for her next Jon. Joanne had called and invited Sarah on the proviso that she stay at the back and well away from her and her children. Sarah had sounded apprehensive at first, but once Joanne had pointed out that she wasn't about to create a scene in front of her children at their father's funeral, she had accepted. The main reason for her attendance, however, was rather more cynical than wanting to say a final goodbye.

As Sarah sat at the back of the church her mind was focused solely on what came after the church service; she wanted to know if she had been included in his will—she had reasoned that that might be why Joanne had invited her. She now well over three months pregnant, and decisions had to be made; if he hadn't left her anything, she had decided to have an abortion.

As the funeral was closing, Jon's coffin was taken from the church and placed into the hearse, followed by Joanne and her children. Joanne took her children to the first car and got them all inside. Closing the car door, she turned and walked over to where Sarah was standing. Sarah hardly recognised this petite woman standing serenely in front of her; she had dropped ten years since their last meeting. Joanne reached into her purse and retrieved a five-pound note, which she handed to Sarah.

'This is your pay off. Spend it wisely, because you will not get another penny from my late husband's estate. Stay away from me, stay away from my kids, and enjoy your life.' Her voice was calm but firm, a tone that brooked no arguments. Sarah nodded.

Sarah Lester, for once in her life, knew she was beaten. She'd ring the hospital first thing tomorrow.

Satisfied her point had been made; Joanne went to join her children.

Chapter 26

Adam Woodacre was confused. He had gone to log onto his website tonight and found it had been shut down. The first thing he'd done was ring Tom, the co-host of his website, Tom was as confused as he was. In a way, Adam was slightly relieved; running a website for the last month had been the closest thing Adam had ever had to a real job in years, and he didn't enjoy the constant upkeep. When he and Tom had first set the site up, Adam had believed Tom would do the day to day running of it, but after the first week Tom had handed the administration side over to Adam, claiming his nine to five job was demanding more and more of his time. Work was an alien concept to Adam; his parents had supported him his entire life, and he had been given everything he needed. He had gone to university and tried several different courses before finally settling on a history of arts degree. It kept his parents off his back and had no real merit in the real working world. It also meant his parents would keep him on the payroll of their business, which, in time, would become his business. Adam wandered through into his bathroom, switching on the shaving light and checking his nose. It had been a week since the altercation at Andre's and the bruising had almost completely gone.

Today was quite a special day for Adam; he'd had his eye on this particular lady for some time now—well, some time for Adam, anyway. She wasn't his usual type. She was quiet and unassuming, and he'd had to take the sensitive approach with her. They'd had a nice chat and ended up swapping numbers. Adam had changed his routine after the altercation at Andre's and had decided to give it a few weeks before he graced the bar again. It had turned out to be a blessing in disguise; he had started frequenting a wine bar round the corner from him. And that's where he had met Sophie. He had had the dawning realisation that he had slept with most of the women in his particular circle, and picking up women was fast becoming boring. He didn't have to work at it and Adam felt he needed a challenge. It had seemed a shame that all their webcams and all the work it had taken to get Sophie round would go to waste. Sophie was after all, to be the latest leading lady on his website. All of his cameras were set up in his bedroom, now all he needed was Sophie to arrive and the show could commence. Sophie had certainly been a challenge, and secretly he got quite a kick out of seducing the more conservative women. Most of the women he'd posted on the web had been easy; they'd slept with most of the town already, so being on the Internet was a natural progression for them. He knew he'd have to be careful until she'd drunk his special party cocktail, as he'd made up so much crap about himself that he couldn't risk her getting wind of how full of shit he was.

    He'd taken a line of coke when he'd gotten in and he was starting to buzz. Like this, he was invincible. Adam walked through into his pristine kitchen and started to make himself a coffee. Walking over to the kitchen table, he pulled his laptop over and opened it. It took Adam just a few moments to find the page he was after: the website that had originally alerted him to the fact there was a market for voyeurism in all its extremes. The website was dedicated to cruel and depraved individuals who took the human instinct of morbid curiosity a little too far. He had decided he could post tonight's exploits on it, and it wouldn't hurt to see what he was up against. A new video had been posted that featured someone having their throat slit—that was getting big hits. Adam wondered briefly if his videos would be gritty enough.

Adam was just scrolling through some images on the screen, trying to decide which video to download first when the doorbell rang.

She's early—obviously can't control herself any longer.

A lewd smile on his lips, he walked into the hallway and toward the front door on his way he stopped briefly to check himself out in the full-length mirror.

What woman could resist?

Smile plastered on his face, he flung the front door open, but faltered.

"Who the hell are you?"

Using the confusion on Adam's face as an opportunity, the masked intruder lurched at him and planted a damp handkerchief over his mouth. After a couple of seconds of struggling, the fight left him and his body became limp.

Manoeuvring Adam's body into the wheelchair, the killer removed the mask. Covering Adams legs with a blanket, the assailant pushed the wheelchair back into the lift.

Adam came to in a small room he didn't recognise. He wasn't in his apartment anymore, though, that much he was sure of. The coke had worn off now and he was red-eyed and tired. Looking around him, he noticed a figure in the corner of the room, and it started drifting towards him.

"Is this a set up? Whose idea was this?" Adam was smiling in the direction of the figure. He was amused; as far as he was concerned this was all an elaborate practical joke.

"Hello, Adam, I'm your conscience. You seem to spend most of your time ignoring me, so I'm afraid I've had to step into real life to have myself heard."

"Ok, where's the camera?" Regarding the figure before him briefly, he added,

"Or the padded cell?" The figure stood stock-still in front of him, the angelic white mask almost luminous in the flickering candlelight.

"Adam, you've spent a lot of time as of late watching—for what I can only assume is your perverted entertainment—differing degrees of degradation and humiliation. To compound this you have not just participated in rape, but even had the audacity to post your crimes on your website."

The mask paused to allow Adam the time needed to process the information.

"I must say I find it most unfortunate, in a world

that is already full of horrors, that people such as you would not only actively seek misery out, but also take such great joy in participating in such a graphic way." The mask paused once more, waiting for realisation of the situation to dawn on Adam. Confusion crossed his face and then left, taking with it all the colour.

"Have you…have you told the police?"

"Oh, I don't think we need to bother the police; they have enough to do trying to catch me. So, seeing as I seem to be taking up so much of their valuable time, I thought it might be nice if I lightened their workload by dealing with you myself."

Adam looked unsure for a moment and then the knowledge of what he was being confronted with hit him; this was the killer, the man who'd been terrorising Manning Town.

"And I don't think we need to burden our already overstretched prisons with you. You must be aware of what I do, my work is gaining notoriety, however, you may not be aware as to why I do it. Something that the police have yet to work out also, although I think by now they must have some idea. I am choosing people who have broken laws in some way, not necessarily the laws of the land, but the standard laws of morals and ethics that are needed for a society to live harmoniously. I am judge, jury, and executioner, and you, Adam Woodacre, are guilty."

"Guilty? Guilty of what? Rape? I didn't rape anyone, those women came back to my place of their own free will."

"I'm not interested whether or not you raped, that's a law of the state—the police deal with that."

"So what, then? What have I done to deserve this?" Adam's voice had turned into a pathetic, nasal whine.

His persecutor watched Adam from behind the mask with disgust. Adams whining was only giving further justification of why this kind of social pruning was necessary. If Adam had thought that his vulnerability was gaining him sympathy, then he was sorely mistaken. The fact he expected a level of sympathy or empathy when he had clearly never felt either was salt in the wound.

"Voyeurism, and you've done well in asking me, as the punishment is intrinsically linked with the crime." Adam watched the masked man turn and walk to the edge of the room. Picking something up from the corner he came back and started setting it up. Adam shifted uneasily in his seat, watching as a tripod was set up in front of him. On top of the tripod was a small phone, which Adam recognised at once—it was his.

Seeing Adams recognition a smile replaced the sneer beneath the mask.

"Yes, it's your phone. Fitting, don't you think?"

"What are you going to do?"

"Well, Adam, I want to send a very clear message to all of those similar to yourself, and you're going to help me." Mentally wiping his brow, Adam let out a sigh.

"Sure, yeah, no problem. What do you want me to say?"

"No, Adam, I don't think you understand—you

are the message."

Adam paled, and suddenly his body came alive underneath him, his arms writhing about in their bonds, his legs struggling to find purchase. All of his efforts, however, came to nothing; he wasn't going anywhere. His mind refused to believe that all was lost, trying desperately to concoct an idea of escape, each one more ludicrous than the last. His captor watched as all the sanity left Adam's eyes, as he struggled against his binds and when satisfied he was spent, reached down to the floor and picked up a gag.

"Now, I think we've had quite enough histrionics for one evening.'

Adam became quiet once more and he stopped fighting.

So this is it, this is my last day

Almost obligingly, he let his captor place the gag round his mouth.

Reaching back down to the floor, the masked man retrieved a dessertspoon.

Tom Webber was knackered; he'd been out all last night, coked up to the eyeballs, and had gone into work red-eyed and remorseful.

Why did he always listen to Adam? The guy was obviously a maniac. He didn't have to go to work the next day, though. The day had been made slightly better by the fact that he could tell everyone at work about his 'mad' evening, embellishing wherever necessary. Going into his kitchen, he switched the kettle on and grabbed the jar of instant coffee from the shelf, spooning out two generous measures into a mug. He thought back to the first time he'd made Adam a coffee; the pompous git had spat it out. Apparently Adam was far too good for instant coffee.

If Tom was honest with himself, he didn't actually like Adam; in fact, none of his mates liked Adam. They probably didn't like him, either; he was constantly with Adam, agreeing with everything he said and did.

Adam was a Grade A wanker; however, the guy had money, and he wasn't afraid of splashing it around, meaning that nights out with Adam cost little more than a round. Adam's latest fetish was a website dedicated to degradation and humiliation—either animals or humans, it didn't matter. All his mates, Tom included, would go to the website regularly to watch the latest spectacle. The idea that the acts portrayed on them were real had not entered their heads or they just didn't care. Whenever they came across people opposed to such things—usually women—their attitudes would rapidly change, along with their beliefs and anything else necessary to avoid getting slapped and facilitate getting laid. Since they had set up their website, Adam had become even more unbearable. He was starting to believe he was invincible, and although Tom got a kick out of it, he didn't discuss the site in front of people in a public place. The last time they were in Andre's, he'd all but advertised the site—he seemed to have lost the volume control for his voice. A couple of women had gotten up and left, something Adam hadn't noticed, but Tom certainly had. He'd had to take Adam aside, calm him down and explain that not only was talking about the site a huge risk as far as the police were concerned, but also how were they going to get any more girls on their site with him broadcasting the site's existence?

As Tom logged onto his computer, he heard the message alert go off on his phone. Putting his coffee down on the kitchen work surface, he went through into the living room to retrieve his mobile. He pressed ok and waited a few minutes for the video to stream. He was sure it was another twisted video from Adam. He wandered back through to the kitchen to his coffee, glancing down every now and again to see if the phone had finished downloading. When the image came up on the screen, it caused Tom to do a double take.

Sometimes Adam would do or say something that shocked Tom; Adam had the most warped sense of humour he'd ever encountered. But this was something else. Even for Adam. This must have taken some setting up. It was, as usual, a grainy image, but it was definitely Adam staring back at him through the screen. Then a cloaked figure wearing a theatrical mask came up on the right of the screen. The video had no sound, but Tom doubted it would have made much difference, as Adam was gagged. Tom grinned as he watched the masked figure move toward Adam with what looked to be a spoon.

This must have taken him weeks to organise!

The look on Adam's face was priceless. Adam's head had been taped to the back of the chair, making it impossible for him to move his head. As the masked figure moved in view of the camera,

Tom's view of Adam was blocked. As the figure moved back out of the line of sight revealing Adam, Tom took a sharp intake of breath; Adam's eyeball was hanging by its nerves outside of its socket. After a moment Tom laughed out loud; the make-up was fantastic—it looked so *real*. Tom continued to watch in fascination as once more his view was blocked. Tom was stunned by the sheer inventiveness of his mate's twisted mind. This time when the cloaked figure moved away, the other eye was gone. Adam's face a grotesque mask of horror in the half-light. The masked tormentor started moving toward the camera, picking it up from its stand and bringing the focus in on the holes in Adam's face that had once housed his eyes. Slowly, the camera panned down the agonised face, coming to a stop on Adam's neck. A small blade suddenly appeared and viciously stabbed at his throat, sending a long stream of blood at the camera lens. Once the blood had ceased to flow, the video went black. After a few seconds, it seemed the reason for this temporary loss of vision had been to clean the screen. The camera had been put back in its original position, once more showing Adam, this time as a corpse. The focus started to shift; it was zooming in on a placard hanging around Adam's mutilated neck.

'This is what voyeurs get for watching things they shouldn't.'

Tom snorted into his coffee, quickly tapped out a brief message, and hit the send button.

Standing in front of the late Adam Woodacre, the

killer started to dismantle the tripod. After a few minutes Adams phone gave a beep to alert the owner to a text message. The noise was so loud in the sparse room that the phone was nearly dropped in shock. Opening the text the screen read: *"Nice 1 M8, see ya at Andre's at 8."*

A reply certainly hadn't been expected.

The cloaked figure's fingers moved deftly across the keypad, entering two letters and hitting send.

"OK."

As Tom pulled into Andre's car park, he was still going through Adam's prank in his mind.

He was a little thrown by the message he'd gotten back.

"OK."

He'd just pulled off the stunt of the century, and all he had to say was "OK?"

He was either modest or he was in a rush, and for a man with no need of a job, it was hardly likely to be the latter. And knowing Adam as he did, it wasn't likely to be the former, either. Adam was notoriously arrogant, and was silently despised by all who surrounded him, even his mates—especially his mates, Tom admitted to himself.

Parking up his 206 he got out, slamming the door behind him. He pointed the remote behind him, and as he crossed the car park he heard the reassuring sound of the doors locking. He always did it with the nonchalant look of a man that believed any female eyes in the area were trained on him.

As soon as he got through the doors of Andre's, he was hit by the familiar smell of beer and cheap perfume. He saw Paul and Stuart propping up the bar, halfway through their beers, and he shouted a greeting as he walked over to them.

Stuart was busy trying to chat up the new barmaid, and by the looks of things, he wasn't getting very far.

"I told you, Stu, she's in my bed tonight, you can have her tomorrow," Tom announced to whoever was listening.

"Nah. Thanks, mate, I don't fancy your seconds."

The girl blushed furiously, shot a withering look at all three men, and flounced off to the other end of the bar.

"Second thoughts, Stu? Maybe not 'til after a few beers; she looks like a girl that could benefit from the old beer goggles." Tom said this loudly in the direction of the barmaid.

All three blokes fell about laughing.

"Well, that's buggered up the chance of getting served this evening."

Tom decided to spare the barmaid further blushes and changed the subject.

"Enough of that shit—did you get that video from Adam?"

"Sure did, that's one twisted bastard. How long do you think it took to plan?" Stu was grinning at Tom.

"Oh, I don't know, you know what he's like—he's probably been planning it for months. He doesn't have much else to do, does he?"

"Tell you what, though, he doesn't half know how to pick his timing. I was halfway through me breakfast. Where is he, anyway? He was supposed to be here at eight."

"Ah, it's only ten past."

"Yeah, fucking hell, it's a good job he doesn't have to work; he wouldn't last a week. Be late for his own funeral, he will."

As Tom finished speaking, the door at the end of the bar swung open and Alan, the bar manager, appeared.

"Alright, Webber, thought I heard your dulcet tones."

Smiling broadly, Tom turned to him.

"Alright, Al, think you might need some more bar staff."

"What you on about? I've only just taken Helen on. You've not been on at her already?"

As he said this he looked up the bar to where a very pissed off Helen was standing.

"For fuck's sake, lads. Could I just be allowed to take on one new member of staff without you lot fucking her or fucking her off?"

Tom laughed riotously.

"But we're your best customers, Al, mate. You've got to keep us happy, not the other way around."

Stu, who'd already necked his second beer, piped up.

"Yeah—you hear that, love?" Directing this down the bar at the now quite worried Helen.

"Anyway, Webber, I've got a bone to pick with you."

Tom, putting on a mock serious expression, leaned over the bar toward Alan and lightly covered his hand with his own.

"Now, now, I like you, Al, mate, but we can only ever be friends."

His stooges once more laughed on cue.

"Shut up, you tosspot. No, I'm on about using this place as a fucking post office."

Shaking off Tom's hand, Alan crouched down and rustled about, trying to find something underneath the bar.

There was a brief exclamation when he found what he'd been looking for. Emerging once more from behind the bar, he chucked a parcel not much larger than a ring box at Tom.

"What's all this about, eh? Having your mail delivered here—been kicked out again, have you?"

It was a well known fact Tom couldn't hold a flat for much longer than a month, or at least until the bills started to come in. He spent most of his wages the first week he got them. He liked to act like the big man at least once a month. Out every night buying rounds, doing coke, fixing up his car, anything to prove he could live like Adam, too. But when the person you aspire to be most like is a work shy, arrogant, unreliable megalomaniac, life can prove to be tough.

Now, though, looking down at the package, he knew he hadn't arranged for anything to be sent here. His two mates were looking on expectantly, waiting for him to open it. Moving swiftly, he tore open the package.

It was a small box, obviously made for presenting jewellery. Opening the hinged lid, he heard a harsh intake of breath as his mates closed in around him to get a better look. Staring back at all three of them was an eyeball that looked worryingly real, the nerve endings fashioned into a loop, and through the loop a heavy gold chain was threaded.

"Isn't that Adam's chain?" Stu asked.

"Yep." Tom's mouth had dried out in a matter of seconds, and his voice was barely more than a whisper.

"What about the thing on it?" Paul queried.

Nobody answered.

If this was a prank, it had gone way too far.

If it wasn't, it didn't bear contemplating.

As Tom, Stu, and Paul walked into the police station, they had the look of guilty men. They'd performed small criminal acts since childhood, taking drugs and committing petty acts of vandalism. Only Tom and Adam had moved into the real crime area—date rape. Stu and Paul knew about their website, but what they didn't know was that all the women had been drugged before hand. And Tom wasn't about to tell them, or, for that matter, the police. Tom and Adam had always liked to think they were above the law. They'd often start fights just to get a lift home when they were too battered to find their cars. They wore their distrust of the police like a badge, as a status symbol, like they believed they were slightly dangerous men, living just outside the law. Strutting about like wild boys, sometimes donning a 'mockney' accent to add credibility, even though they'd never set a foot south of Cambridge.

In reality they were typical middle class boys, and the closest they'd been to being gangsters was watching the Kray's. Now, as they approached the police station, they were all apprehensive. They were known in town for being pranksters, and Tom thought they might not be taken seriously.

All three of them had left Andre's and gone around to Adam's flat, and when they'd had no answer, they'd decided they ought to tell the police about their little gift.

Well, Tom's little gift, and if Tom were being honest with himself, it wasn't fear for Adam's safety that had found him at the police station tonight but fear for his own. The package had, after all, been addressed to him. Tom had already decided that it wasn't a prank and that Adam had fallen foul of the local serial killer who'd been running the town recently. And, taking into account the message hanging round Adam's neck, it had crossed Tom's mind that he might be next on the killer's hit list. Paul and Stu, who in any other circumstances would have laughed off such a supposition, seemed unusually concerned. With the recent spate of murders that had Manning's Town gripped at the moment, even Paul and Stu were concerned. Even so, knowing something and speaking it out loud were two very different things. As Tom was still lost in thought, Paul's voice echoed in the background.

"What do we say when we go in?"

"I don't know, Paul," a tired sounding Stu answered.

"Well, shouldn't we decide what we're gonna say before we go in?"

"What you mean, like, 'Excuse me, Officer, me

and me mates were down at the drinking pit tonight and we were given an eyeball on a chain.' Something like that, you mean?"

Hearing this, Tom piped up,

"Look, we're gonna have to tell them everything—about the video, the package, and the fact that we can't find Adam."

"You tried him again on his mobile yet?"

"Yeah, must be over ten times now. I'm telling ya, it ain't switched off; the line just goes dead. If it were switched off, it'd either ring through to another number or to his voicemail."

As Stu finished speaking, the door to the reception area swung open and a young PC came to the desk. Spying the lads, who had a good five years on him, he put on his most official tone.

"Evening, lads, and what can I do for you lot tonight?"

Tom, already addled with fear and annoyed at being spoken to like a child, walked up to the counter. He opened the box in his hand and threw it across the desk. The young PC almost gagged at the contents, and then his expression changed from pompous to one of grave concern. Picking up the phone next to him, he rapidly punched in a number. Silence resounded in the room as the PC waited for the Holt to pick up the phone at their end. Finally the silence retreated.

"Inspector Holt, sorry to ring you at home, but it seems there's been a development."

Holt was sat in his living room at home staring out of the window lost in thought, when the phone had rang. The sudden noise had startled him.

"No problem, Peter, what kind of development?"

"Well, there's three men at the station now…" Tom was gratified to hear they'd been promoted to men; at least this meant he was being taken seriously.

The PC continued,

"They've got an eyeball, sir."

On hearing that, Holt was suddenly fully alert.

"Get it to Dennis Grant now. I'm coming in."

Holt hung up and the PC stared at the phone for a second then replaced it in its cradle. He looked back up at the three men.

"DI Holt's on his way. Do you want a coffee while you wait?"

As Holt came through the doors, he saw the three men; they were dressed like rejects from a Hugo Boss advert. They were all looking reasonably sheepish, and Holt wondered for a brief second if he could trust a single word that came out of their mouths. He looked over at the PC behind the desk for confirmation that these were the men and the PC nodded his confirmation. Holt walked up to the desk.

"Who are they? Where did they find it?"

"There's a Tom Webber, Stuart Harvey, and Paul McNamara. They said it'd been delivered to the bar they're locals at—Andre's on the high street."

"Right, and it was definitely a human eyeball?"

"Definitely."

Holt turned to face the three men.

"Right, chaps, I think we need a little chat. Who was it who received the item?"

Tom looked up wearily and acknowledged himself with a nod.

"Right, could you follow me through, please?"

Tom got up and followed Holt. Holt held the door for Tom before addressing the other two.

"I take it PC Bryant has taken all of your details. I'll send some officers through in a minute who'll take your statements."

As Holt and Tom entered the interview room, Tom felt the first wave of fear flood over him.

Holt sat him down.

"Would you like a coffee, tea…?"

"No, I'm fine, thanks. Look, am I going to need a solicitor or anything?"

"Why would you need a solicitor? You haven't done anything wrong, have you?"

Holt wasn't sure why he was being so antagonistic, but he didn't feel sorry. Tom Webber had the look of someone who could stand to be taken down a peg or two.

Tom was watching Holt uneasily.

"No, but I thought if I was a suspect or something I might need a lawyer."

Holt stretched back in his chair, comfortable in his environment, which made Tom all the more uneasy. Noting this, Holt decided to allay his fears.

"You're not an anything at the moment, Mr Webber, this is just a chat, a chance for you to tell us the exact course of events that led up to you having a human eyeball in your possession."

As Holt finished speaking, the door to the interview room opened and a somewhat harassed looking DC Henson stuck his head round.

"Sorry I'm late, sir."

"No problem Henson, just hurry up and sit down." Despite Holt's reply he was clearly annoyed that he had been kept waiting by his junior.

Henson quickly manoeuvred himself around the interview table and sat just behind Holt. There was a moment of tension when Henson caught Tom's eye.

Holt couldn't quite put his finger on it, but it seemed there was something like glee coming off of Henson.

"Ok, Mr Webber, this is my colleague DC Henson, he'll be sitting in on this, if you don't mind."

Tom nodded, but it was clear to all in the room that he was not pleased by this fact.

"Could you start at the beginning, please?"

"All right," Tom started, taking a sideways glance at Henson before continuing.

"About five o'clock this evening I got a video message from Adam's phone— " Holt interrupted him.

"I take it Adam is the guy reportedly missing?"

"Yeah, that's right, Adam Woodacre. Well, I thought it was him sending me another video that he'd downloaded off the Internet." Seeing the confusion on the older copper's face, Tom stopped to attempt to explain.

"Basically there's a website people can post videos or pictures on—"

"Are these images legal?" Holt queried.

"Yeah, I'd have thought so, it's a really popular website, if it was illegal surely it would have been closed down by now."

"Sadly it's not always the case. Please continue," Holt added.

"Well, they show things like…" Tom was obviously struggling to find the words to describe, and Henson took the opportunity to jump in.

"It's a website for sickos and perverts. Sex, beatings, RTAs, even executions."

Holt swung round at this.

"What?" For a second he forgot he was on duty.

Henson started again.

"Sick people send in clips of depravity, sexual and not. Isn't that right, Tom?" he added, clearly enjoying the discomfiture of the man in front of him.

Still painfully aware of the tension between the two young men, Holt spoke up.

"Can I have a quick word with you outside, Henson?"

"Yes, sir." The two men left the room.

Once out in the corridor and making sure that the door to the interview room was closed Holt rounded on Henson.

"What the hell is going on in there?"

"Sir?"

"Don't play cute with me, kid, you two have got history."

"All right, we used to go to school together. Tom Webber, Adam Woodacre, and the rest used to make my life hell."

"Is that going to influence your work today, Henson? Because if it is, I'm afraid I'm going to have to ask you to step down from this case." The threat had the desired effect: Henson looked crestfallen.

"No, of course it won't, sir."

"Good, then let's have you acting less of the school boy and more like the policeman you're supposed to be. Right, now that's out of the way, what's this site all about? Please, God, tell me it's not as bad as it sounds."

"I'm afraid it is, sir. I went on it once—a mate told me about it and I didn't believe him. I didn't sleep right that night."

"Can't anyone do anything about it?"

"People have tried to shut it down, but it just pops up again under a new name. That's the problem with the net—you can't police it."

Holt grunted and opened the door to the interview room.

"Sir, one more thing."

"Yes?"

"These guys are renowned for playing practical jokes, so—"

Holt cut him off.

"If I get one whiff of any such nonsense, I'll charge them all with wasting police time."

Hot had been opening the door to the interview room as he'd said this, and Tom, who had been waiting for them to come back in had heard it.

As Holt got inside, he sat back down opposite Tom, face set like stone.

"So you thought Adam was sending you one of these videos, and…"

Tom went on to relive the chain of events that had led to him being sat there.

Holt sat for a moment, staring at the young man in front of him with a combination of utter amazement and wonderment at what he'd just been told.

"You mean to tell me you *watched* Adam being tortured and didn't think there was anything wrong with that?"

"I know what you're thinking, but I thought it was a prank."

"You watched as your supposed friend had his eyes gouged out and his throat slit and you though it was a prank?" Holt's voice was getting dangerously low again.

"Yes. Listen, what could I have done anyway? This psycho's got Adam's phone, he knows my number—what are you gonna do about it?"

"We're doing all we can at the minute, but I have to be honest with you, we always seem two steps behind this guy, and from what you've just told me, that's not about to change anytime soon. The killer's becoming more ambitious if the video you told me about is anything to go by."

Tom sat for a minute and stared at Holt as if he'd just dropped out of his nose.

"You mean to tell me this guy's going keep butchering people until he slips up—if he slips up? Can't you trace Adam's phone? Doesn't it send out a signal?"

"Yes, we could do if it was switched on, but it doesn't seem to be. I can only assume the killer's either disposed of it or it's been left with the corpse, and as you no longer have the video on your phone, we're powerless to know where the body might be."

"So you're not going to do anything? I might have well not bothered coming in."

"I've got people out looking for the body—derelict farms, industrial units. The killer seems to be favouring them so far, however… If there turns out to be no body and your little friend Adam turns up unscathed, it won't be the killer you'll have to look out for."

Holding Holt's gaze steadily, Tom answered back just as forcefully,

"If Adam turns up now, you can just wait your turn—trust me."

"Ok, then lets' go back to the person wearing the mask. What did it look like?"

"It looked like a mask; it was white, they were wearing a black coat—I don't know, the picture was blurry. Funnily enough, I wasn't concentrating on the mask; I was kind of fixated on something else."

Holt, who'd had his elbow resting on the table, moved a weathered hand up to his face and rubbed at it in exasperation.

"Listen, Mr Webber, I'm sure you're in shock, very tired, and probably confused with the situation, but you've got to start realising that you're the closest we've got to an eyewitness. We would really appreciate if you could just *try* to remember anything about this person; the only other people who could have given us any kind of description of the killer are lying on slabs at the morgue. Do you understand what I'm saying?"

"Ok, ok, point taken. Thinking about it, he seemed quite small in stature—slim, you know. The mask looked like one of those ones you see at the theatre, you know? The smiling face and the crying face. That's all I know."

"Ok, Mr Webber, thank you for your time. If anything comes back to you, please feel free to get in touch."

Chapter 27

Holt received the call at half past two in the morning. The body of Adam Woodacre had been found.

Not wanting to waste any time, he'd managed to pull additional resources and had had extra men working solidly for the last twenty-four hours scouring the surrounding countryside for derelict barns, warehouses, anything that would fit the killer's profile. It had been a hunch of Holt's that the body was out of town, and it turned out his instinct had been correct.

As Holt pulled on his clothes hurriedly, he realised he'd have to wear the same shirt he'd had on yesterday—not usually a problem, but he hadn't gotten home until eleven, a little over three hours ago, and he'd left his clothes in a crumpled heap at the bottom of his bed. He hadn't had much time recently to tackle the ever-growing pile of dirty clothes sitting in his laundry basket that was threatening to overspill—that was if his clothes didn't walk out themselves first.

Wandering through into the bathroom, he started to lather up his face to shave. When he saw himself in the mirror, the reflection took his breath away. He looked easily ten years older than he was. Purple rings hollowed out his eyes, deep creases ran across his forehead, and his crumpled shirt finished the look off, giving him the appearance of a homeless man who hadn't seen a bed or a sober day in years. Mentally promising himself a long trip abroad when this case was complete, he felt a sudden rush of depression, often connected with being overtired and the early hours. It suddenly dawned on him that he might never find the killer. As soon as the thought entered his head he dismissed it; it was too horrific to contemplate and he didn't think his mind could such a thought at the moment, especially considering it was teetering on the brink most of the time these days.

Walking through to the kitchen, Holt switched on the kettle. He was in a rush, but he couldn't leave the house without a cup of tea; it wouldn't be fair to his colleagues. Ordinarily he would have had two, but there wasn't time for that this morning. He wouldn't have another cup until he got home again, whenever that would be. He never drank tea at work—mainly because it was never strong enough, but also because he associated tea with home.

When he'd made his tea, he walked through into his living room, and sitting down on the sofa he forced his mind back to the reason he was once more being deprived of sleep. Adam Woodacres body had been found, and from what he was able to garner from the somewhat overexcited PC at the other end of the line, he was exactly as Tom Webber had described him. His phone—the one that had been used to send the video clip had been found in his hand—was smashed beyond recognition. Although Holt had yet to see the scene, he could imagine it: the buttons of the phone hanging out, the screen cracked—he imagined the phone would illustrate a telecom version of its owner's demise. The killer did seem to love making sick little points.

Holt's eyes fell upon the crack in the curtains of his living room, remaining unfocused as his mind raced behind them. He'd always had a habit of doing that, almost like meditation. His mother had told him off for it as a boy.

"Don't stare, its rude," she'd say.

He tried once to explain he wasn't looking at the person, but through them; his mind was elsewhere and he was never conscious of it, which meant, of course, that it was almost impossible to control, as a child anyway. As he became older, he would actively search out inanimate items to focus on.

Now, staring through the curtains, he pondered what the killer wanted.

Was it fame? Did they want to get caught? Most psychologists believed that serial killers possessed a desire to be caught so they could take full credit for their work, make it into one of the books on serial killers of which there were so many. A multimillion-pound industry, where books, films, and television series were always big hits.

Holt, on the other hand, preferred to believe that serial killers just became complacent, that they didn't want to be caught, but ended up being victim to another human condition: being human. Nobody was infallible.

Holt preferred his reasoning because, by his own admission, it allowed him to rest easier at night.

And what about Jack the Ripper? His true identity was never realised, and he went down as one of the most infamous killers in history. People liked the mystery.

It had always sickened Holt that Jack the Ripper's name was still the topic of Hollywood films and numerous documentaries. Many people had become rich off of him, or, rather, his victims. The man himself was never brought to justice and most likely went on to live out his life in full while his victims lay in paupers' graves outside of the city that were unmarked and uncared for, the forgotten characters in a twisted fairy tale that spanned a century.

Holt couldn't get them justice, but he could claim justice for the families of this killer's victims. Holt thought back to Mrs Abbott, Matt Reynolds's girlfriend who'd gone into premature labour when she'd discovered her partner's demise.

Holt screwed his eyes closed. Mrs Abbotts scream as she had identified her son had reached right through his consciousness and into his dreams. The feral scream of someone who knew they'd never see their loved ones again, never see them laugh or cry, never hold them ever again. Those screams never left a person; they served as a reminder that humans were just animals, when the part of the brain that repressed baser instincts and set the human race apart from their mammalian cousins shut down, unable to process the gravity of the situation they were dealing with. At that moment a human, if confronted with the perpetrator, would attack; the most rational of minds would struggle to control the consequences in that scenario. Sometimes Holt wished he could let the families loose on such a person for them to exact their own punishment.

Holt finished his tea and got up, switching off the lamp beside him and taking his cup through to the kitchen. He grabbed his jacket and left his apartment.

Holt arrived at the derelict barn at half past two. He had the windows of his car wound right down in a bid to stop his eyes slamming shut, the chill in the air befitting the circumstances. He brought his car to an abrupt halt. Getting out, he saw Henson scurrying toward him. Holt wondered briefly if the lad ever went home; he always seemed to be there to welcome him at the crime scenes.

Holt looked around him; this place was pretty much exactly the same as where the last two bodies had been found. How many more places were there like this? It was perfect for the killer—deserted, forgotten about—he must have known he wouldn't be disturbed.

He would have to speak to the director of the estate again, which he didn't relish the idea of, as the last time he'd had to they'd almost come to blows. The man was upper class, and clearly had been riled by the fact that the murders had taken place on his land—not for the reasons that most might've have expected, however. He was annoyed because it meant having to put the renovation work back several weeks and the rent would have to be dropped, as no one would want to live in a house where a murder had occurred.

Now Holt was going to have to go through it all again, although maybe he could get Henson to do it instead. Slightly assuaged by that thought, he walked up to Henson.

"Barn again?"

"Yes, sir."

Holt walked straight past Henson toward the skeletal building at the far end of the yard.

He saw Dennis Grant's van at the mouth of the building. He walked through the police cordon and made his way into the barn.

The forensic cameras were flashing further illuminating the scene. As Holt stared at the body of Adam Woodacre he was taken aback; it was almost identical to how he'd imagined it while sat in his living room less than thirty minutes ago.

At the Police station, several hours later Holt had assembled the whole team. He had called the meeting at eight o'clock, which had meant officers who had been helping in the search for Adam Woodacre had been pulled back in. They were all stood staring at him with bloodshot eyes.

"So we've got five bodies, no leads, and a town on the brink of insanity. Not that the papers are helping."

Holt paused his address, looking for Henson. As his eyes rested on him, he continued,

"Any news on who tipped off the press yet, Henson?"

"Afraid not, sir, you know what they're like."

"Well, that's not bloody good enough. I want a name by midday, else I'm going down to their offices myself."

"Yes, sir." The tension in Henson's voice was back.

Holt's audience was watching him warily,

wondering where his next attack would be aimed.

They were all exhausted and as frustrated as Holt at the unfurling nightmare happening within their small community. But they were also tired, hungry, and could have done without the verbal battery.

Looking out across the drawn faces of these men and women, Holt suddenly felt a stab of shame; they were all doing their best, but he felt so utterly helpless.

"Listen, I know you're all shattered and I appreciate that a lot of you haven't slept properly in the last twenty-four hours, but the fact remains that there's a lunatic out there who isn't about to stop. Each murder becomes more daring. This last murder was even sent to the victim's friends' mobiles. The killer is making a statement, daring us to catch him, while all the time laughing at us. I want everyone's full cooperation on this case. I don't want any more 'leaks' to the press. Is that understood?"

Holt took a minute to look round at the stony expressions on the faces in front of him and felt his cheeks redden with guilt. He couldn't bring himself to believe any of these officers would jeopardise the case voluntarily—most had as much invested in it as he did. Either someone had let something slip by accident, or—what Holt thought to be more likely—it was the killer himself who had done it, to add still more pressure to the underfunded police force. Holt knew if the killer wasn't caught soon his people would start to break, and that was a scenario he really didn't want to contemplate.

Chapter 28

Clare had started the evening with Hannah in a small quiet bar. They had decided between them that they had needed to get out, even if it was just for a few hours. They both realised they were in danger of becoming recluses and to regain control of their lives they'd have to start reclaiming it a bit at a time. However, after a few Bacardis, they felt almost back to normal and were becoming louder.

"It's great to be out again."

"You're not kidding, we were becoming hermits."

"Listen, Clare, I'm going to have to go soon, my mum's coming round early tomorrow. She's decided there's something wrong with me and is using it as an excuse to come round and take control of my life again." Hannah rolled her eyes.

"So I take it you want to go home early to do a clean up?"

"Got it in one. This is the woman who checks dust on skirting boards; she'll have the skin off my back if she sees the state of my kitchen at the moment."

Clare burst out laughing and nodded her acknowledgement. Her flat had become an absolute mess of late; with her laboured attempts at study and her need for a drink every day, housework had finally filtered through to the bottom of her priorities pile.

"Fair enough. Well, give me a ring tomorrow once you've got rid of your mum."

"Will do. Are you staying?"

Hannah was putting her jacket on.

"Yeah, I might have one more drink. My mum and dad said they'd probably be coming in here tonight and it'd be nice to see them."

"Lucky you, I wish I could say that about my parents."

Clare smiled at her. Hannah stopped for a moment before heading to the door.

"Are you sure you're going to be ok here on your own?"

"I'll be fine, I'm only five minutes from home."

"Ok then, hon, speak to you tomorrow."

"Take care."

Hannah had left twenty minutes ago and Clare had finished her drink. She did another cursory scan of the bar. It didn't look like her parents were coming out after all. Although the bar was busy, she didn't feel threatened at all. The average age of the customers looked to be around fifty-five. All had come out to enjoy a sociable evening with their friends, family, or colleagues. This would have been exactly the type of place she and Hannah would have avoided at all costs a few months ago, but now it was what they had both needed—a gentle step back into the social real world. She got up to get her coat.

Dean had been watching Clare from the other side of the bar for the last half an hour. He had finally admitted to himself earlier that day that he still loved her and had tidied himself up, originally planning to go and see her at her place. But when he'd seen her and her friend Hannah leaving the flat, he'd decided to follow them instead. Now it looked as if his patience might be about to pay off.

"Clare?"

Clare's head spun round. She'd know that voice anywhere: the man who'd been so kind as to re-spray her car free of charge. He sounded genuinely pleased to see her.

"Dean?"

He was moving toward her from the other end of the bar. How was she supposed to react? She had often imagined how she would react when she bumped into him again. She hoped she looked nice, despite the fact that she knew she shouldn't care. A quick glance in the mirror behind the bar put that argument on ice: her eyes looked red, her face puffy, and she'd managed to spill some of her drink down her top not five minutes before. A large part of her wanted to tell him to fuck off, but the small part of her that was still withstanding the alcohol realised it might be nice to talk to someone.

As Dean got closer, she cringed inwardly; he looked great. She was ashamed to admit it to herself, but she still wanted him.

"Look, Clare, I'm sorry about your car, it's just—"Dean was looking sheepish.

"Look, just forget it. We've both been going through a rough time. Let's just leave that for now. You look well."

It was a statement of fact, but she hoped it didn't sound so.

"Yeah, you, too."

A kindly lie; that was all she needed.

"Do you want a drink?"

Before she had chance to answer, he spoke again.

"I miss you, Clare. Just have a drink with me would you?"

Before logic could make a move, she'd accepted.

Finding a table they sat down and three hours and numerous drinks later she had to admit she was enjoying his company. It had been just like before the split, before her life had imploded.

"Would it be ok to walk you home? I don't like the idea of you walking home alone; there are loads of drunken tossers about, and they've still not caught that killer yet."

Clare looked him straight in the eyes; she knew it was a bad idea. All that crap about worrying about her safety was a ruse to get her into bed, but at that moment in time she didn't care.

"Yeah, sure, that'd be great. Cheers."

Getting up, he moved closer to her, wrapping an arm around her waist, and they moved together toward the door.

"You did what?" Even through the phone Hannah's voice was so loud it almost shook the plaster from the walls.

"I slept with Dean. You know this is your fault; if you hadn't left me in the bar last night—"

"Oh no, I am not taking the blame for this one. And what about what he did to your car?"

"He apologised."

"Oh, well, that's all right, then." The statement

was loaded, but Clare chose to ignore it.

Both women were feeling relieved to have something other than the assault to focus on.

"So is it all back on, then?"

"No, it was a one off, no more no less."

"You sure?"

"Yes, I'm sure. I've got enough going on without starting all that crap again."

"Fair enough. Now, on a completely separate note, have you seen the latest? They've found another two bodies."

"What?"

"Yeah, really nasty, actually. They were found together."

"Together?"

"Taped together; one guy starved to death, the other had been taped to him and left to die."

"Oh, nice one, Hannah, I was just about to get my dinner."

"Sorry, but it's gross, isn't it? I mean, who thinks up these things?"

"A sick individual, I guess. Anyway, you got anything planned three weeks from Saturday?"

"No, why?"

"Well, I thought we could try going to that new spa—oh, what's it called? The Retreat. They've got a special offer on that weekend and I thought we could take advantage of it. They do facials, massage, and I hear they've got a great gym."

"Well, you can sign me up for the massage and facial, but you're on your own in the gym. All I want to do is relax."

"Well, it was just an option. So shall I book us in

for the Friday and Saturday night, then?"

"Yeah, that sounds great."

"Ok, well I'll get onto that now. I don't know about you, but I could do with getting out of town for a while."

"Me, too. See you later, hon."

"Yeah, see you later."

Clare hung up the phone and returned to the living room. She was relieved Hannah hadn't judged her too harshly. Smiling to herself, she picked up the brochure for The Retreat and started flicking through its pages, deciding what treatments she was going to have. For the first time in weeks, Clare was starting to feel in control of her life again, and that pleased her.

Chapter 29

Holt sat in his flat and stared around at the bare walls surrounding him; he'd never bothered to redecorate when he'd moved in. Now, looking around him, he wondered at himself, a fifty-five-year-old man who still didn't want to settle down. It was a characteristic that had eventually driven his wife away. She'd never known him, not really. Truth was, he didn't want her to; for her to know him she'd have to know his secrets about his upbringing. Things he didn't like to think about, let alone discuss openly. He couldn't let her know for two reasons: firstly, by divulging secrets that still haunted him, he was readily handing her a stick with which to beat him with whenever they had an argument; secondly, if that happened, he was petrified his reaction would turn him into the person he despised most in the world—his father.

All children are scared of the bogeyman, a fictitious character that lurks under their bed and only appears when the bedroom lights are out. Only the bogeyman isn't fictitious, and it didn't live under the bed; it hid in every drinking cabinet in the country, and, for the most part, stayed there. Sometimes, though, it made an appearance. It did so in his house most evenings. His father was a prison officer, a role he'd take home with him. The routine was always the same: he'd come home and his first port of call was the drinks cabinet. By the time Holt was going to bed, his father would be steaming drunk and spoiling for a fight, and he'd always find one. Unfortunately, Holt was usually the one on receiving end. He'd be black and blue from the neck down, and his father, who was always so repentant the next day, would lavish affection on him for a couple of days before the cycle started again. After the beating Holt would lie on his bed, tears staining his reddened cheeks, and wonder what the inmates at the prison would think if they knew the way Officer Holt spent his evenings. For the first few years his mother had tried to intervene, but all that did was earn her a black eye and infuriate his father more. Eventually she had given up, and even though Holt had previously wished she wouldn't get involved, the realisation that no one was going to try and save him had hurt more than the beatings. The last bit of resilience left with his mother's back as she walked out of the room.

Yes, the bogeyman was alive and well; to this day Holt had lost count of the reports of domestic violence where alcohol was involved. The reason for his distrust of psychologists and psychiatrists probably stemmed from the fact that he'd been made to keep secrets since he was born. Lying about his mother's bruises, keeping his arms and legs covered all year round to avoid awkward questions about his own abrasions. One night, when his father had been in an even more fearsome mood than usual, he'd broken Holts arm in three different places. Watching his father from his hospital bed as he played the concerned dad had looked so alien to Holt that it was all he could do to stop himself laughing out loud. Psychologists and psychiatrists tried to break those boundaries down and get into your head, forcing you to confront upsetting issues from your past. Holt sometimes wondered why they should want to do that; at the end of the day there was a *reason* these things got hidden so deeply.

Alcohol lived in every home in the country, acted as your best friend at first, made you more confident, helped you unwind, helped you forget. Then once you'd pledged your allegiance to it, it took everything—your livelihood, your family, and finally your life. Holt thought the reason he hadn't wanted children was because he was afraid what they might turn into: chav, goth, or gobshite. But now, on closer reflection, he realised that it wasn't what he feared they might turn into that had stopped him; it was what *he* might turn into. When his wife had finally turned forty and was being deafened by the ticking of her biological clock, she'd given him an ultimatum, one he couldn't accept, and he'd reluctantly had to let her go. He couldn't blame her; it was his hang-up, not hers.

The recent killings were making headline news and putting his police station under very close scrutiny. It was starting to feel as if every day was lasting a year; each week he became more and more tired. He forced his mind back onto the case again.

He would go back to Andre's and speak to the landlord again. He must have wondered about a package being delivered to one of his regulars there. He knew the package had been hand delivered and left outside the back door. But it was still the best lead they had. Besides, it gave him the opportunity to ask about a fight Tom Webber had said Adam had been involved in two weeks prior. Holt retrieved his mobile from his pocket and rang ahead to let the landlord know he was on his way. Then getting up, he slung his jacket on for the second time that day and headed for the door. Getting into his car Holt drove to Andre's lost in his thoughts. Ten minutes later, he arrived in the Andre's Bar car park.

Within Andre's, the landlord; Al Marsh, stood nervously by the door waiting for Inspector Holts arrival When Alan had taken the call and found that the chief inspector had wanted to speak with him again, his stomach had dropped. He knew he hadn't done anything to warrant the fear he had felt, but funnily enough that hadn't helped. These murders were national news, and he didn't like the idea that his bar would come under scrutiny. Once upon a time someone had said, 'All publicity is good publicity.' Al wondered if that particular person had ever had an active serial killer use their business as a postal depot. He couldn't help thinking that if they had they wouldn't have had that literary gem tripping off their tongue quite so readily. Since the news of his bar being associated with a murder victim—along with the fact that the killer was well aware of the bar's location—trade had dropped off quite substantially. He had only had the bar for six months and it'd been the busiest place in town for five of those. Now he wasn't sure if it would make it to Christmas. He only hoped that this Inspector Holt was going to have something good to tell him and that he wasn't going to be looking for more information that he didn't have. One look at the man, though, had told him that good news couldn't have been further away.

As Holt walked into the bar and saw Al waiting for him it saddened him. He knew the man had been waiting for his bar's reprieve, to be told the killer had been caught and the eyeball thing had been an elaborate prank so he could return to a normal existence again. 'Normal.' Holt couldn't remember the last time he'd felt that. He got out of his car and walked through into the bar area with Al.

"Would you like a coffee or anything?"

Holt sat down.

"No, I'm fine, thank you."

"Ok. So what was it you wanted to ask me about? I've told you everything I could about that night."

"I know, but I was just wondering if you knew anything about the fight Adam had?"

"Adam in a fight? Are you insane? He liked to play the big man, but that's as far as it went: play. Bloody hell, he could have a row, gobby bastard that he was, but for all his bravado, he couldn't make it physical; it'd smack too much of hard work. Besides, he loved his looks too much to risk a broken nose."

"Well, a broken nose he got. In your toilets two weeks ago."

"Two weeks ago?"

"Yes."

"That's strange…"

"What's strange? What do you know?"

"Well, two weeks ago I was working the late shift. One of my barmaids had fallen through, incidentally because of that lot."

Holt's eyebrows rose. Al noticed but continued,

"I was taking some empty barrels out the back for the brewery to collect and I heard raised voices coming from the gents' The gents' room backs up to the car park and the window was open. I remember it because I couldn't believe Adam had finally been caught out. Some old boy was chewing him out about some bird. Oh, what was her name? Clare—yeah, that was it, Clare. It only stuck 'cause that was the name of my first missus and she messed me about similar like. I didn't know he got hit, though."

"Did you see the other man?"

"Yes, I did, actually. He came flying out the back way a few minutes later, got into a beaten up Peugeot, and drove off."

"Can you remember what he looked like?"

"I can go you one better than that: I know him. Only in passing, that's why I didn't recognise his voice at first, but he works at Hamilton's Auto Care. Dean, I think his name is."

"Well, thank you for your time, Mr Marsh, you've been a great help."

"No problem." Al watched as the somewhat dazed Inspector Holt left his building for what Al hoped would be the last time.

Holt arrived at Dean Matthews's house just before four o'clock. He had picked up Henson en route and had explained the situation. The two men approached the front door. Holt knocked on the door and then turned to Henson.

"When he answers, I want you to leave the talking to me. We are not bringing in a suspect; we just need him in for questioning, ok?"

Henson nodded. The door swung open in front of them.

"Hello."

Lauren Matthews looked the two men up and down and knew at once they were police. That was all she needed; the last two weeks had been absolute hell, with Dean acting more and more irrationally and Jon's demise. Which she had only found out about courtesy of the local paper. She hadn't known how she was supposed to feel about it; she had spent most of the last nineteen years wishing he was dead, but now all she was left with was guilt. The last time she had spoken with him they had left on bad terms, even though he had only come round to try and protect her son—their son. He was trying to give her a chance to get him in line without involving the police. She had known at the time that Dean had overheard their conversation and was now aware of his paternity, but they had never discussed it openly. Dean's behaviour had become more aggressive ever since hearing about his estranged father's demise. Lauren wasn't sure if this was due to the fact that when he had last seen him they hadn't exactly been the best of friends, or whether he begrudged the fact that someone else had gotten to him before he did. Now, though, Lauren was concerned. She knew the two men in front of her were policemen not because she was a criminal matriarch, but because she recognised them from the TV. They were the detectives working on the serial killer case.

"Hello, Mrs Matthews, is Dean in?"

"Yes. What do you want with him?"

"Mrs Matthews, if it's all the same to you, we'd rather discuss that with Dean."

Lauren, who was holding the door open with one arm, creating a defensive barrier between the detectives and her home, turned and shouted over her shoulder,

"Dean, there's someone here to see you."

A door down the hallway swung open and Dean, who had been expecting Mark, swaggered out, grabbing his coat off the banister and making his way to the door. As he saw who was standing there, he stopped dead. He recognised them instantly.

"What do you want?"

"A word, if that's ok with you. Down at the station."

"Well, it's not ok with me. I'm waiting for someone."

"That's a shame, but I'm sure your mum wouldn't mind making your excuses."

Holt smiled warmly at Lauren Matthews as he said this. Lauren, sensing Dean was about to retort once more, stepped in.

"I think you'd better go with the detectives, Dean. I'll let Mark know when he gets here."

Knowing he was beaten, Dean continued putting his coat on and trailed after Holt and Henson as they went to the car. During the journey Holt took the opportunity to glance at him when he could in the rear view mirror. He didn't look like an archetypal psychotic killer; he looked like a stroppy teenager.

Holt knew deep down that he couldn't be their guy, but he still needed questioning. Once at the station Holt got out of the car and opened the door for Dean before shepherding him inside and into an interview room. Gesturing for Dean to sit down, Holt took the seat opposite him.

"Do you know why you're here?"

"Well, given you're the coppers investigating the serial killer case, I guess it's 'cause you assume I know something."

Holt didn't like Dean's surly attitude. When he was his age, he'd have been a lot more humble if he had been found in this situation.

"We understand you knew the late Adam Woodacre?"

"Know him? No, I didn't know him. I knew *of* him."

"How?"

"Well, let's just say it was a personal matter."

"About what?"

"Like I said, it's personal."

"Well, that's a shame, but guess what? This is a murder investigation, so consider all rights pertaining to personal matters revoked."

"It was about my ex. He'd been having…relations with her." Dean's face had darkened. And Holt was reminded how close to a boy he still was.

"So what did you do?"

"I found out where his regular haunt was, waited until he went to the gents', and followed him. I gave him a bit of a slap, but he was still very much alive when I left."

"I know that, but is that how you left it, or did you feel the need to pay him another little visit later on?"

"Look, anything I felt toward him I unloaded on him that night. He seemed to have gotten the point. So what reason would I have to go and see him again? He didn't come wailing to you lot; I had no reason for additional reprisal. Anyway, I'm not capable of doing that to another person."

"Doing what? The details haven't been released to the press."

"Detective Inspector Holt, this is a small town. Everybody knows everybody here. That video was sent to three people's phones. Those three people know other people; a story like that doesn't take long to circulate."

Holt sat back in his chair. He knew what Dean was saying was true, and he knew he wasn't the killer.

"Could you tell me where you were at six o'clock on Friday night a week ago?"

"I was at work, all day through to half past seven."

"Oh yes, you work at Hamilton's Auto Care, don't you? Funny time of the night to be open until, isn't it?"

"We've been very busy recently."

"And why might that be?"

"Well, I imagine its partly to do with our great service and reasonable prices, but I suspect it might also have something to do with the fact that the owner was found dead the other week. What do you think?"

Dean's voice was dripping with sarcasm, and although he didn't appreciate it, Holt knew what it felt like to have the world and his wife wanting to be part of the macabre chapter in the town's history.

"Of course. Unfortunately for you, Dean, you can be linked to two of the victims."

"Look, I'm not the person you're after."

"Didn't think you were, but you must admit it is coincidental. If you know any of the other victims, this would be the time to volunteer the information." Holt knew he was clutching at straws, but it was an obligatory question under the circumstances.

"Well, now you mention it, yes, I did. The first guy, he was my chiropodist, and the other guy—you know, the one found with Jon—was my long lost brother. Now that would be a coincidence."

"What? How do you mean a coincidence?'

"Well, Jon Hamilton was my father, not so you'd notice, though. I only found out a couple of weeks ago."

"That must have made you quite angry."

"Yes, of course it did. But before you say anything, no, I was not angry enough to kill. My idea of making him pay was more cash orientated."

"Why did you decide to tell me?"

"You'd have found out eventually, and then you'd probably go and accuse me of withholding information, and besides, I've got nothing to hide." Dean was staring at the floor, avoiding Holt's direct gaze.

Holt regarded the young man in front of him for a moment. His honesty had thrown him. Getting up, he walked over to the door and opened it for Dean.

"You're free to go for now. Henson, could you get a car to take Mr Matthews home?"

Chapter 30

Joanne was feeling exhausted but happy. She had just got back from Greece with her family, and she felt exhilarated. She had turned heads while abroad, even with her children in tow. A few men had even asked her out for dinner.

She picked up her suitcase and slung it onto the bed. Opening it, she looked at the contents and smiled to herself. It was a very different suitcase to the one she had packed last time she and Jon had been away. She had always been very aware of dressing her age, something she had always believed meant dressing in drab colours, so she became little more than a shadow. Now her suitcase was bursting with vibrant colours. She had even bought a bikini, something she hadn't had since before she had met Jon.

Harry, her eldest, burst into her bedroom.

"Can I go over to James's this weekend?"

"What, all weekend?"

"No, just Friday night, there's a gig in Leicester we're going to go to."

"How you getting there and back?"

"James's mum's taking us and picking us up."

"Well, I've got to go take your sister clothes shopping this Saturday. I'll leave Chloe with your Auntie Sue. You two can get a lift in with us, and that way James's mum only has to do the one trip."

"Ok, great, I'll go and tell James now."

Harry charged back out of the room. Joanne turned back to the suitcase and started unpacking. At that moment, the doorbell rang. She called out,

"Harry? Can you get that, please?"

She heard the front door open, muffled words, and then Harry shouted back up the stairs to her,

"Mum, it's for you."

Joanne was slightly confused; she wasn't expecting anyone until three, when Sue said she'd be coming over. Once again leaving her suitcase, she made her way downstairs. Joanne was shocked to see Detective inspector Holt standing there.

"Hello, Mrs Hamilton. I don't suppose I could have a few minutes of your time, could I?"

"Of course, come through to the kitchen and I'll put the kettle on."

Holt smiled his thanks and followed her through to the kitchen. Holt sat down while Joanne filled the kettle.

"I must say, Mrs Hamilton, you're looking very well."

"And that surprises you, I suppose. Why aren't I in my widow's weeds sobbing in the corner? Well, I didn't have a very happy marriage, Inspector. I had been attending counselling for it for over a year. Loretta suggested divorce, but I didn't want the kids to end up resenting me."

"Loretta Armstrong?"

"Yes—do you know her?"

"Yes, I've heard of her."

Holt was reluctant to say any more.

"I take it Jon went with you to the sessions?"

"Well, he was supposed to, but he always seemed

to have someone better to do."

Holt picked up on the bitterness in her voice and didn't push the subject any further. Instead he took the cup of tea from her gratefully and waited for her to make herself comfortable. Once Joanne was settled, she looked up at Holt.

"So how can I help you?"

"Well, it was something about your husband."

Holt wasn't sure how much she knew about her late husband's affairs and so wasn't too sure how to tackle the question he had to ask.

"What about him? Detective Holt, please just ask me what it is that's on your mind."

"Did you know your husband fathered another child before he met you?"

"I could have guessed as much. Who?"

"Do you know a lad called Dean Matthews?"

"Yes, he used to work at the garage. Jon mentioned him before."

"Dean only found out himself a few weeks before your husband went missing."

"Poor kid. Ah—that might explain the car, then."

"The car? What car?"

"About a month ago, Jon's car was vandalised; at the time I just thought it was one of his exes, but thinking about it now, Dean's involvement would make more sense."

"You don't seem very surprised."

"That's because I'm not; my late husband was an incredibly selfish individual. How's Dean coping now?"

"He seems ok. He's back working at the garage; the guy you've got managing the place took him back on as he already knows the place and the way things are run—" Holt suddenly stopped dead. He realised that Joanne might not be overly happy about her late husband's illegitimate child being back on the payroll. He hoped he hadn't spoken out of turn.

"I hope you don't mind me telling you this."

"Mind? Why should I mind? The garage has been doing great business recently. It's not quite the cash cow that the shops are, but it still turns over a good amount. I have complete faith in the manager there, and if this Dean Matthews is good enough for him, then he's good enough for me."

Holt was relieved and also a little shocked by this tidy business-like little woman sat in front of him. She didn't even seem to be shocked by the fact that her children had another sibling.

"My indifference bothers you, doesn't it?"

Holt was taken aback by the frankness of the question and paused before answering.

"No, it doesn't bother me. You get on with your life for your children's sake. We have all had to protect people at certain stages in our lives, even when all we wanted to do was curl up on our own."

"I don't want to be on my own, Inspector Holt, I've spent the last seventeen years of my life on my own. My husband checked out of our marriage years ago. I continued to play the dutiful wife, of course, always labouring under the illusion that one day he'd come back to me, realise what he had. Looking back, I now know that I was as much to blame for the breakdown of our marriage as he was. If I'd made a stand all those years ago, I could have saved not just myself but my children from the misery of being in a loveless home. I didn't have the courage to do that; it took a lunatic to remind me who I was."

Holt sat and absorbed the words she spoke. If he was honest, as much misery as the killer had created, for the most part people had seemed to gain from the destructive path left in his wake. The woman sitting in front of him now was living proof of that. He'd never had believed this was the same woman he'd met all those weeks ago. It was almost as though the ending of Jon's life had triggered the reanimation of hers. And although he wasn't happy about how this had come about, he couldn't wish it wasn't so. Joanne and her family seemed to be flourishing under its effects.

Chapter 31

Clare was slightly concerned. She hadn't been feeling right for the last few days, and she wasn't sure why. Her temperature didn't seem to be up. She had packed her bag for the weekend and had had to pop to Boots to pick up some toothpaste. She had paid at the dispensing counter, as the queues for the main tills were busy. As she had stood there she had noticed the pregnancy tests, and although she was sure it was just her own paranoia at work, she decided to get two. Whatever way it went, she knew she'd want a second opinion. Now she was stood in the bathroom in the beautiful twin suite she'd booked for herself and Hannah weeks before, and she couldn't feel less relaxed. She'd agreed to meet Hannah for lunch; Hannah had wanted her to go with her for a massage, but Clare had wanted to check first, just to put her mind at rest. So she had told Hannah that she wanted a lie-in. Now, as she stood there waiting for the inevitable time to pass, she felt removed from her surroundings. The first test had come out positive. Believing it must be a mistake she had employed the other test. As the time ran out, she went to check it. Positive. Clare's stomach dropped. She checked her watch; she had an hour before she was supposed to meet Hannah. If she went now, Hannah wouldn't need to know. Grabbing her mobile, she punched in the number. After only seconds, the recipient answered.

"I need to see you. I'll be at yours in ten."

Ending the call, she chucked her phone in her bag, grabbed her car keys, and charged out the door.

In Mannings Town at her office, Loretta sat back in her chair. She'd been taken aback by Clare's abruptness on the phone and she was worried. Clare should have been enjoying her weekend; she deserved it after everything she'd gone through lately. But she had sounded stressed. Loretta wondered briefly if the website had reappeared again, but as quickly as that thought came to her it left. She had ensured that couldn't happen. Her IT friend had been very helpful with the situation. So what was it that made Clare feel the need to drive six miles back into town to see her? She went through the office into the tearoom. Switching the kettle on, she leant back against the counter and started going through all the possibilities, but she was still no wiser by the time the kettle had boiled. She spooned large measures of coffee into two mugs. After adding milk, she took both mugs back through into her office. Placing the mugs down on her desk, she sat down and swivelled her chair round to look out the window. Contemplating the building site that now made up her view, she wondered how much longer the council was going to take with their offices. Lost in thought about the rising council tax, she jumped when Clare tapped quietly on her door.

"Hi, sorry about this."

Loretta smiled at her gently and beckoned her to take a seat.

"What can I do for you?"
"I need your advice."
"About?"
"Pregnancy."
"What? You're pregnant? By whom?"
"Dean."
"Your ex Dean?"
"The very same."
"When did this happen?"
"A few weeks ago. You know, I told you Hannah and I were going out for a quiet drink."
"Yes."
"Well, we did, and it became a slightly louder drink. She had to go, so I stayed to finish my drink and there he was."
"You seem very calm about the situation."
"No, I appear calm because I know I can trust your advice, and to be honest it's a relief to tell someone."
"So nobody else knows? Not even Hannah?"
"Hannah knows I slept with him, but not about the pregnancy, no."
"What made you decide not to tell her?"
"Because I think I know what I want to do and I'm pretty sure you will agree. Hannah, on the other hand, wouldn't."

Loretta understood what Clare was saying and decided to voice it.

"Is she pro-life, then?"
"No, far from it. She's been pro-choice since I met her—about everything, incidentally, not just that." It was a weak attempt at humour, but Loretta knew why she'd done it.

"So if she's pro-choice, why are you worried about telling her?"

"Because she is pro-choice as far as rape and underage pregnancy are concerned, or if carrying to full term is going to be mentally or physically damaging. Otherwise she'd say it was being used as a form of contraception."

"So she wouldn't be supportive, then?"

"No, I think she would support me and that'd make it worse."

"Right, well, would you like me to make the appointment?"

"Oh, could you, please? How long will I have to wait?"

"I'm not sure; I'll let you know when I do. Now, I don't want you to worry about this anymore. I'll sort it out and I'll come with you if you like."

Clare smiled her gratitude.

"I want you to get up, plaster a smile on your face, go back to the spa, and enjoy your weekend. I'll ring you Monday night."

"Thanks."

Clare got up and did as she was told, and now, with her load lightened, the smile on her face was genuine.

As Clare arrived back at The Retreat, she felt ten times lighter. Even though Clare had originally been introduced to Loretta professionally, she now felt there was a real bond between them. She knew that Loretta must have felt the same way. Even though her profession was pre-determined to be caring, all the ways she'd put herself out for Clare recently had been more out of friendship than professionalism.

Beaming, she let herself back into the suite. Relieved not to find Hannah there waiting for her, she went into the bathroom and tidied herself back up again. Just as she'd finished straightening her hair, she heard Hannah let herself back into the room.

"You better be up by now, hon, I have just had the most orgasmic ninety minutes and I've worked up quite an appetite, so you better be ready for lunch."

Clare swung the door of the bathroom open.

"I'm ready, all right?" Hannah looked her up and down approvingly, a broad smile on her face.

"Yeah, I'd say you are. Come on, then."

Hannah opened the door once more.

"After you."

Clare was still grinning to herself as she let herself back into her apartment. She had really needed the break, but she only fully appreciated how much now. Walking straight through into the bedroom, she threw her bag on the bed and decided she would unpack later. It had been a tonic to be in such a feminine orientated environment, and, more importantly, not having to justify it to anyone.

Wandering through into the living room, she grabbed a bottle of wine from the fridge and settled herself on the sofa. Flicking the TV on, she started scrolling through the options for the evening's entertainment. She was busy debating whether she should opt for comedy or drama when the phone rang into life. Believing it to be Hannah ringing to recant the weekend's highlights, she answered without thinking.

"Hiya, hon."

"Clare?"

Clare suddenly sat up.

"Dean?"

"Were you expecting someone else, by any chance? It's been a while since you've called me 'hon.'"

"Yeah, I was expecting Hannah to call. I've only just got back, actually; we went to The Retreat for a couple of days."

"We?"

"Hannah and me. We had a bit of a girly weekend. So how are you?"

"Me? I'm fine thanks, all things considered."

Clare, sensing a manipulative movement, tried to head it off.

"So are you seeing anyone yet?"

"No, I've been kind of busy."

"Oh yeah? What with?"

"Well, nothing much, finding out who my father was just in time for the local serial killer to mow him down and then being taken in for questioning about it—you know, the usual."

Clare felt herself buckle.

"Really?"

"Yes. I did leave you a message about it."

"Sorry, my phone's been playing up, I can't retrieve my voicemail."

Dean wasn't sure if this was true or not, but decided to let it slide anyway; it was a relief just to hear her voice again.

"Anyway, how have you been?"

"Dean, I don't know what to say."

"What can you say? I know this might sound selfish, but I've got nobody else to talk to. I don't suppose I could see you sometime? Just to talk, of course."

"Of course you can, anytime."

"Anytime?"

"Yes."

"How about now? It's just that I was out walking earlier, and I found myself outside your building."

Clare's ability to empathise overrode her usual caution.

"Of course, I'll come down to meet you now."

Clare hung the phone up and slipped her shoes back on.

She hadn't stopped to contemplate the fact that a man who had been questioned about the recent murders had been sat outside her apartment waiting for her living room light to go on.

Grabbing her jacket, she slung it around her shoulders, and picking up her door keys, she left the security of her home without a second glance.

Dean was waiting by the front door of her building when she got to the bottom of the stairs. She went over and let him in.

As they got back into her apartment, Clare walked into the kitchen.

"Would you like a drink?"

"What've you got?"

"Well, I was going to have a glass of wine."

"I'll join you, then, if that's ok?"

"Of course."

Clare returned to the living room with another

glass. Passing it to him, she sat back down on the sofa.

Clare poured the wine, waiting patiently for Dean to start talking. She was rewarded after only a few minutes. Dean took a long drink of the wine and sat back in the chair.

As he explained the last months events, Clare sat open-mouthed. She waited for him to finish and regaining her composure she refilled both their glasses..

"How do you feel about it all now? I mean, did you go to his funeral?"

"No, it didn't seem right somehow, and besides, his wife doesn't know about me, so she'd probably have wondered what I was doing there."

"Have you been to the grave?"

"Yeah, a couple of times, I'm usually half cut when I do, though. I don't know, Clare, this all seems so surreal. A couple of months ago I was so happy, I had a great job, a gorgeous girlfriend, and no idea that I was working for my father. Now it's all fucked."

"Of course it's not. It's shit, I'll give you that, but at least you've got your job back now."

"Oh yeah, great, my job, which I only got back because Jon—sorry, Dad—wound up dead."

"I know we aren't going out anymore, but I'm always here for you—you know that, don't you?"

Clare was unsure as to what else she should say to him. After everything he'd gone through over the last few weeks, anything she was going to say would sound hollow.

"Yeah, I know you're here for me. I still love

you, you know. I'd do anything to have you back."

"Let's not go there, shall we? It's not good for either of us."

"Oh, right, sorry. Am I making you feel uncomfortable? 'Cause I wouldn't want to do that."

The sarcasm was apparent.

"Dean, I don't want to get into that again."

"So you say it's ok if we talk as friends, but only if we talk about things that you're ok with."

Clare looked at Dean and realised he'd been drinking before he'd turned up at her apartment. She hadn't noticed it before, or maybe she had and had put it down to him being upset, but either way she was starting to feel threatened.

"If you're going to be like that, then I think you should just go home and get some rest."

Dean watched Clare and he seemed to soften.

"Ok, sorry, I didn't mean to go off on one. I'll go."

Dean got up and made his way to the door. Clare got up and followed him.

"You can ring me tomorrow if you like."

Dean didn't answer.

Clare, aware she might have upset him, followed him to the top of the stairs.

"I do mean it, Dean, I do care for you and I want us to be friends."

Dean turned to look at her.

"I know. Take care, yeah?"

Clare smiled at him.

"I will, and you, too."

"Can I get a hug—just as a friend?"

Clare smiled and stretched out to hug him. He

hugged her back, and for a moment she realised that she did miss him. She wanted him back, but now wasn't the best time for either of them. So when he went to kiss her, she kept her resolve and pulled away. He went to kiss her again, so she pushed him away lightly.

"I know you want me back, Clare. Why are you doing this to us?"

"I can't at the minute, Dean, please understand."

"Oh, I understand, all right. You've moved on. You don't need me anymore. Well, you can't fucking push me around anymore, Clare."

"Dean, don't be like that." Clare stretched out a hand to Dean's shoulder

"Oh, just get fucked." And grabbing Clare's hand off of his arm, he shoved her backwards.

Clare, who had been standing on the top step, faltered as she tried to regain her balance, but it was too late and she went crashing to the bottom of the stairs.

"Clare!"

Dean watched as Clare's body remained prone at the bottom of the stairs. Rushing down to her, he reached into his pocket and grabbed his phone.

"Ambulance please, Coventry House, Manning's Town."

After listening carefully for a moment, he answered,

"My name's Dean Matthews. Can you hurry, please?"

Dean hung up the phone and Clare started to stir. "Clare? You ok?"

Clare's eyes opened slowly and tired to focus,

then they started to close again.

"No, don't fall asleep again. Talk to me, talk to me, please…"

Dean, stayed by Clare's side until the ambulance arrived twenty minutes later. Dean watched as the paramedics bundled Clare up.

"Could I come, too?"

The ambulance driver looked him up and down.

"Of course you can."

Dean jumped in the back of the ambulance and held Clare's hand. Nervously, he looked up at the paramedics.

"Is she going to be ok?"

"Yes, she'll be fine, it's a nasty knock, though, so we're just taking her in to check her out. Did she lose consciousness at all?"

"Yes, she's been going in and out since it happened." The paramedic nodded and went back to tending to Clare.

Dean climbed into the back of the ambulance and they departed for the hospital. During the journey Clare regained consciousness. Dean stayed by her side while Clare was checked over and finally left to rest in a hospital bed

She turned to Dean.

"I'm going to be fine; they're only keeping me in overnight as a precaution. Why don't you go back home and get some rest?"

"I don't feel right leaving you. I mean, it's my fault you're here now."

"Don't be silly, it was an accident; I know that. Just go home, I'll be fine."

"Ok, if you're sure. I'll give you a ring tomorrow

and come and pick you up."

"You don't need to, I'm going to ring a friend—she'll come and get me."

Dean looked dejected for a moment and Clare hoped he wasn't about to lose his temper again. She could do without a scene at the minute. She still felt groggy and all she wanted to do was rest, not pander to his insecurities. Dean got up and grabbed his jacket. Leaning forward, he kissed Clare gently on her forehead.

"Well, at least give me a ring tomorrow so I know you got home safely."

"I will." Clare smiled weakly at Dean and he left.

Clare breathed a sigh of relief, and relaxing back into the bed she let herself drift off to sleep.

Dean walked out of the hospital and took a deep breath, reaching into his pocket and pulling out his phone. After trying Mark's mobile and only getting his answering machine, he left a brief message.

"All right, mate, could you come and pick me up from the hospital?"

On the other side of town Mark had heard his phone ringing and hadn't answered; he had been in the middle of doing a deal with a new supplier. Once his business had been concluded, he checked his phone, jumped straight into his car and headed for the hospital. Dean was waiting for him outside the front doors. Hurriedly going over to the car, he got in.

"Fucking hell, you took your time."

"Well, I wasn't sat by the phone waiting for you

to ring, you know. What you here for, anyway?"

"Clare fell down the stairs."

"*Fell* down the stairs?" Dean picked up on the tone of Mark's voice and turned to look him in the eye.

"Yes, *fell* down the stairs."

"What, and you just happened to be there, did you?"

"Yes."

"That's a lucky coincidence...that you were there to bring her in, I mean."

"If you've got something to say, Mark, say it, or shut the fuck up."

Mark decided to leave it and turned the car out of the car park. He gave it a few minutes before he spoke again.

"Where do you want to go, then?"

"Pub."

Once Dean and Mark had found a table inside the Tin Whistle, Dean explained what had happened. Mark had listened in silence only stopping to get more drinks in. As the evening had progressed Dean had become more intoxicated and three hours and a trip to the off-licence later, Mark had watched as Dean staggered off in the direction of home.

Dean had made the decision to walk back past Clare's apartment block on his way home. As he passed, he decided to stop and roll himself a joint. He still felt tense and wouldn't be able to sleep properly until he knew Clare was safely back at home.

Crumbling the dope into the paper, he started trying to work out how it had come to this. These thoughts didn't last long however as his drunken state was making multitasking an impossibility so giving up, he focused his attention solely on the joint After several attempts at rolling, he finally managed to cobble something together and lit it, and drawing deeply on it, he sat down on the wall opposite the apartments. As he felt the stress, alcohol, and dope taking its toll on his body, he decided to pull his legs up and lie back on the wall. One hand held the joint, and the other held a beer can on his chest. Lifting it up, he took another swig. He was starting to get warmer as the alcohol started to have its desired effect, lulling him into an alcohol induced state of unconsciousness. Suddenly, a car turned onto the road.

As the last binds of consciousness loosened their grip, he was vaguely aware of the car slowing to a halt beside him.

Loretta had arrived in time for Clare to wake up. She had been contacted by a doctor at the hospital at Clare's request and had been asked to pick her up in the morning. Now she waited while the doctor checked Clare over once more. As the doctor came back through, he approached Loretta.

"Dr. Armstrong, I'm pleased you could come. You were the only person Clare wanted us to contact."

"Is she ok?"

"Oh yes, she's fine, although…"

"What?"

"Well, I'm not sure if you were aware or not, but Miss Heathers was pregnant."

"Was?"

"Yes, I'm sorry to say the fall terminated the pregnancy."

"How does she feel about it?"

"Well, ok from what I can ascertain, although she didn't have much to say on it. I just thought I'd let you know to avoid upsetting her any further."

"Thank you, is it ok for me to go and see her now?"

"Of course, go straight through."

Loretta walked onto the ward and up to Clare's bed. Clare, seeing her smiled broadly.

"So how are you feeling?"

"Ok, thanks."

"Well, I'm glad you're ok. So now what do you want to do about Dean? It was Dean, wasn't it? The doctor told me a young man accompanied you to the hospital."

"Yes, it was Dean. We had a bit of an argument last night and I lost my balance on the stairs—it was an accident."

"Are you sure you shouldn't contact the police?"

"He's been going through a bad time recently; he came round 'cause he needed someone to talk to."

"If you're sure—"

"I'm sure."

Clare looked around quickly and then leaned in toward Loretta.

"The fall did have its advantages: all the benefits of an abortion without the guilt. Now I can tell Hannah about the pregnancy; I've been feeling bad about keeping it from her."

Loretta was unsure what stance to take on such a

statement and so smiled at her.
"Shall we go, then?"

Chapter 32

Lauren Matthews sat in the kitchen, holding her head in her hands. Alcohol had a lot to answer for. She had been drinking every day since Jon's death. And now her body was giving away tell-tale signs. Her face was bloated, her eyes bloodshot. After spending her lifetime up until now addiction free, she still wasn't aware she had a problem. To those around her, it was becoming more obvious by the day. Alice had seen what was happening to her mother and had tried to warn her, but Lauren couldn't seem to function without the aid of her trusty bottle of vodka. She'd never witnessed an addiction before and so she continued, blissfully unaware of any connotations. Every day seemed to start the same with the hair of the dog, by lunchtime she was drunk and by midevening ready to sleep.

Getting up gingerly, she moved to the fridge, grabbed a bottle of water, and sat back down again just as carefully. Lauren heard the bathroom door slam and the familiar pounding down the stairs.

"Hi, Mum, how's your head?"

It was a taunting question, but Lauren didn't have the strength to deal with the antagonism this morning so let it slide.

"Is your brother getting up today or not?"

Lauren had tried talking to Dean a few times since Jon's demise, but she just couldn't get through to him. It seemed that every day he drifted further away. She knew he had no respect for her now, but lately she couldn't help feeling he didn't even love her anymore.

"Well, I wouldn't know—he's not here."

"Where is he, then? Mark's again?"

"I don't know, Mum, I'm not his bloody keeper."

"Are you deliberately trying to piss me off today, Alice, or is this just another of your teenage charms?"

"Well, what do you want, Mum? If you want our respect you have to behave like you deserve it."

"Are you really trying to lecture me, Miss Thing? How about you show me the respect that I, as your mother, deserve? I earned that giving birth, looking after you, bathing you, feeding you, and every other thing you pair of ungrateful bastards demanded. I did all of that on my own, and what do I get in return? Back chatting, strop-throwing, law-breaking wankers."

Alice stood stock-still. She had never heard her mother use that kind of language, and in such a brutal way, before, and certainly never directed at her. Unable to match her mother's verbal ferocity, Alice decided the best statement she could make would be to make none. Alice turned on her heel and slammed out of the house.

Knowing she had gone too far, Lauren went to the cupboard, pulled out the half empty vodka bottle, and poured herself a large measure. Sitting back down, she took a long drink before replacing the glass on the table. Cupping her head in her hands once more, she started to sob.

Picking up the bottle and glass, Lauren went

through into the living room and switched on the TV, sitting down she held her glass in one hand and the phone in the other waiting for Dean to ring.

By the time Lauren fell asleep the bottle was half empty and the phone was still quiet.

As the front door slammed, Lauren woke. Looking around her she realised night had stolen up as the only light in the room now was the light from the TV. She jumped up from the sofa, fully expecting Dean to walk in.

"Mum?" Alice peered round the corner of the door into the living room. Lauren allowed herself a moment of disappointment before answering.

"Hi, sweetheart. Look, I'm sorry about earlier."

"I'm sorry, too. Is Dean back yet?"

"I don't think so, pop up and check his room, would you? I'll go and see what we've got in for tea."

Lauren heard Alice bolt upstairs and got off the sofa, wandering through into the kitchen. Switching the oven on, she checked the freezer for a pizza and grabbed the salad from the fridge. Throwing the salad in a bowl, she drizzled dressing over it before returning it to the fridge.

Alice came dashing back through into the kitchen.

"Doesn't look like he's been back."

"I'll try him on his mobile again"

Picking up the phone, Lauren punched in Dean's mobile number. The phone went straight to voicemail.

"Dean, could you give me a ring when you get this, please? Are you planning on coming back home at any point?"

She hung up the phone and looked at Alice.

"Well, I guess there's no point in waiting for him. I'll get the pizza in the oven."

Chapter 33

The foundations for the new county council buildings had already been dug, and the cement mixer was all lined up ready for use the next morning.

One of the bonuses behind the position of the new buildings was that it was in no way overlooked; the premises had been too large to construct in any central location. The nearest building to the site housed some offices, but as office people tended to clock off at five, this certainly wasn't a cause for concern. Most people in the town had objected being set out on the edge of the town, but for hiding a body it was perfect. The idea had been fantastic, a flash of inspiration, and now the groundwork had been established. The unconscious Dean was dragged from the back of the car. The car had been parked as close as possible to the porta-loos. Once inside, Dean was bound and gagged, making it impossible for him to move or make any noise. Once Dean was secure, the door was locked from the outside with a coin and a sign was hung on the door.

"Out of Order."

As morning broke across the building site, Charlie, the building's foreman, got out of his truck.

Already in a spectacularly bad mood from the berating he'd received from his wife just five hours earlier, he leant against his vehicle and perused the site. He wasn't gong to be up to much today, and had decided that the day was going to be a short one. It was Friday morning, and they always had a short day before the weekend; it kept the lads happier about having to work Sunday.

Bloody council. Anyone else and he'd have told them to stick it.

As he saw Stu pull his car into the site, he walked in its direction. As Stu parked the car up and opened his door, Charlie called out.

"We'll just lay the first layer today—is that all right with you?"

Stu, seeing the black rings beneath his boss's eyes, grinned.

"Fine by me, mate. Louise been giving you shit again?"

"Yeah, she only wants to go on fucking holiday to the Maldives, of all places."

"I see, nice and pricey."

"Tell me about it, I told her that we couldn't afford it just on my wages, and if she was set on going she could try getting off of her fat arse and getting a job."

"Oh, aye, and how did that go down?"

"Well, let's just say I've got a lump on me head the size of a tennis ball."

Stu laughed.

"Come on, then, the others should be here soon, let's make a start; the sooner we get done, the faster we'll be down at the pub."

Loretta watched with mild amusement as the

builders clocked off for the day. Briefly she wondered how they got away with it she knew councillors were already getting peeved by how long the build was taking. Oh well, at least her afternoon sessions wouldn't be marred once again by the sound of heavy drilling along with the occasional shout out of inextricably linked swear words.

Loretta started to think back to Clare. She had been so unfazed by recent events. She had just lost a baby, but you would never know it to look at her. Loretta had spoken to her once since she'd gotten back from the hospital and Clare had told her that Hannah knew all about it now. Loretta was relieved she had another person to confide in. She knew how close Clare was to Hannah, and that pleased her almost as much as it worried her. Clare had a lot of work and study ahead of her, and if she, Loretta, were being honest with herself, she knew that a close friendship was always going to be a hindrance. The time and energy such relationships consumed left precious little left for anything else. She knew from bitter personal experience that closeness to people could cloud judgement; it had been a lesson she'd learnt the hard way many years before. She occasionally wondered what her patients would think if they knew all that had gone on in her life before she'd chosen a life of therapy. She'd done the whole staying with a man for the sake of a misguided sense of love thing. She had been kept at the beck and call of another, never having the freedom to even go to the local shop on her own for fear of offending. Deliberately being beaten about the legs to insure she hadn't the confidence to wear skirts. Alcohol being the driving force behind all of the attempts at control. She knew that her patients must be aware on some level that she had a history that they could relate to in one way or another. It was what made her so good at what she did, unlike her peers, who, despite their best efforts to hide it, were quoting textbooks for the best part of their sessions. Loretta never condescended or patronised the people who came to her for help. She approached them as friends, and they responded well to her open handed approach to therapy.

She allowed her mind to wander back to Holt. She missed his company. It had been so long since she had allowed herself to feel anything for any man that she almost hadn't recognised the feelings. Once again her belief in closeness clouding judgement was proven to be correct, as when she was denied his company and she took a step back she could see it clearly; she felt a real attraction to him. Now all she wanted was for him to find a reason to seek her out again; she certainly wouldn't be the one doing the running, it went against her pride. She had wasted her time in the past, chasing around after a man who had little more than a passing interest in her wellbeing and she wasn't about to do it again. Even though she knew that Holt wasn't that kind of man, deep wounds left scars.

Her secretary finally broke her train of thought.

"Loretta, your next appointment's here—Mrs Francis."

"Ok, send her through."

Loretta cleared her desk and waited for Mrs Francis to knock.

Chapter 34

Lauren was becoming frantic. She'd tried Dean's mobile again this morning and this time the line had gone dead. His mobile was switched off now and Lauren was unsure what to do. She wished she had a number for Mark, but she had never wanted to ask for it—a clear act of disdain on her part. Grabbing her coat, she left her house and jumped in the car. She knew that her best chance of tracking Dean down was Mark. Even though it was a weekday, she knew where she would try first: The Tin Whistle.

As she pulled into the car park, she started imagining what she'd do if she found him in there, drinking and joking with Mark. She'd skin him. Marching through the door—almost knocking a man from his feet—she stopped a minute and scanned the bar. Over in the far corner by the pool table, Mark was standing with another of his friends, laughing raucously.

Mark stopped laughing as he saw Dean's mother heading straight for him. He knew she had never approved of him and in a way he didn't blame her for that—to him it proved her to be a good mother. Mark was the first to admit that he wasn't a great influence; maybe if his mother had been a bit more like Mrs Matthews he wouldn't be in the position he was now. Moving home month after month, unable to keep a job, and just scraping enough of a living by petty crimes to subsidise his meagre benefits money. He didn't show much respect to anybody, but Mrs Matthews was different; he wanted her to like him. Even though she could barely keep the contempt out of her voice when speaking to him, he still enjoyed her attention.

"Hello, Mrs Matthews." Mark's voice, as ever when addressing Lauren, was courteous.

"Don't you 'hello' me, you shower of shit. Where's Dean? I've been ringing his phone for the last two days and the little bastard isn't answering." Mark was taken aback by her aggression.

"I haven't seen him in a couple of days now. Why? Hasn't he been home?"

"No, he bloody well hasn't. No call to let me know he's ok—nothing. So where is he?"

"I'm sorry, Mrs Matthews, I've no idea." Mark's voice was so earnest it caused Lauren to pause, and the colour drained from her face. Mark watched as she shrank in front of him, and all of a sudden he became concerned. Now that he thought about it, he hadn't had so much as a text from Dean since the night he picked him up from the hospital, not even to tell him that Clare was all right.

"You said you saw him a few days ago—where?"

"Here, he went and bought some drinks from the off-licence and was heading toward home when I left him."

"Oh God, what am I going to do?"

Mark, sensing she actually needed him for once, stepped up.

"What we're going to do is get into your car and go straight to the police."

Lauren looked slowly up at Mark, and for a

moment he could have sworn he saw a flicker of gratitude pass behind her eyes.

"We?"

"Yes, I'm coming with you; I know you don't think much of me, but he is my mate. Come on."

Mark grabbed his coat from the back of the chair, nodded at his mates, and left with Lauren.

All three of his mates watched him leave, mouths open.

As Dean started to come to, his eyes felt heavy, as if they had been glued shut. Staring around him, he tried to work out where he was. It looked like a porta-loo. His hands and legs were bound and he had been gagged, which made his attempts to shout out useless, and as he struggled for breath, he started to black out again.

The next time he woke it was due to a noise: car tyres on gravel.

There was a car pulling up outside. Thinking that the prankster must have become bored with his stunt, Dean struggled to get himself upright.

The door opened slowly. Dean's eyes struggled to adjust as they came into focus on the masked face now peering down at him. Suddenly he was struck blind as the mask clicked a torch into life and inspected the dishevelled Dean.

Dean tried to shout out, but the gag foiled the attempt.

Watching Dean, the masked stranger spoke softly.

"If you can promise to remain calm, I will remove the gag, and we can converse like the civilised people we are."

Never taking his eyes off the mask, Dean nodded abruptly.

"Ok, then." Pulling a knife out of what seemed like nowhere, the masked stranger leant forward slowly.

Natural instinct kicked in and Dean squirmed, trying to get away.

"Now, now, stay calm. You don't want me to slip; you might get a nasty nick."

Dean remained still and allowed the gag to be cut from him.

Dean took a few moments to stretch his jaw and get the saliva back into his mouth again.

"You're the one the police are looking for, aren't you? From the papers."

His captor nodded slowly.

"You're going to kill me, aren't you?" Dean didn't know why he felt so calm; he'd always known his life was leading up to a moment, but he'd never imagined this would be it. Now here he was, and he felt almost serene.

"First of all, have you any idea why you're here?"

Dean shook his head.

"It has come to my attention that you are heading down a slippery slope, Dean. Luckily for you—hard as that may be to believe at this moment—I don't think you've gone beyond the point of no return. So I'm going to give you a chance of survival. Whether you accept this chance or not is entirely up to you."

Deans mind was racing, but he kept his counsel. Something told him that a sudden verbal outburst would not be well received.

"Now, in order for you to survive, you're going to need to remain calm, so I will administer an anaesthetic—only a little, but enough to knock you out."

"What? You think I'm going to let you stick me with a needle?"

"Dean, I don't think you have much of an option, and besides, if you go into this conscious, there's a very real possibility that you'll start to panic. And if that happens, there's a good chance the air within this plastic box will run out sooner than either of us want and you'll simply suffocate. If you are unconscious to start with, your breathing will remain, hopefully, slow and steady, giving your rescuers more of a chance of freeing you alive. Your feet and arms are bound, so your best hope is to remain calm and let me give you the anaesthetic, otherwise this discussion is over. Now, what's your decision?"

Unable to speak his response, he slowly nodded.

"Clever boy."

The masked stranger reached down into the bag and retrieved a syringe.

Lauren's car screeched into the police car park and she and Mark jumped out of the car.

"Thanks for coming in with me; Alice's still at work. I'm sure there's nothing to worry about and he'll probably be there when I get home…"

Lauren was aware she was grasping at straws, but it was all she could do. Mark was keeping his counsel; he didn't see any point in saying out loud what they both feared.

As they walked into the police station, Mark could feel the hairs on the back of his neck stand up. He had been in this place more times than he cared to remember, and he was concerned as to how his presence might be received.

The door to the reception area swung open and a young WPC appeared.

"Can I help you?"

"Yes, my son—he's been missing for two days now."

"I see, what's his name?" The WPC had pulled a pad out.

"His name's Dean Matthews, he's nineteen, and he hasn't been seen since about eleven o'clock Wednesday night."

"Ok, Mrs Matthews, do you have any recent photos of him?"

'Photos? Oh, of course. No, sorry, I didn't think to bring any, but I'll go and get them now.' She turned to face Mark.

"Do you want to stay here and fill them in on what you know? I won't be long."

Mark watched her leave and went to sit down to wait for her. As he was waiting, the door to the station swung open.

Holt looked round the waiting area before walking up to the desk. He gestured toward Mark

"What's he doing here?"

The WPC looked unsure for a moment.

"He's here with a Mrs Matthews—she's here to report her son as missing."

"So where is she now?"

"She went home to pick up some photos for us.

Do you know him, then?"

"Oh yes, I know Mark."

The WPC sensed his tone and decided not to question any further. Instead, she picked up her paperwork and returned to the back of the station, leaving Mark with Holt. Holt, sensing Mark was nervous, walked over and sat down next to him.

"It's been a while since you've come here voluntarily, Mark."

"Yeah, well, exceptional circumstances an' all that."

"Really? So what's happened, then?"

"My mate Dean's gone missing, and what with all the murders going on, I thought I'd come down here with his mum to report it."

"Why couldn't she come on her own? I don't see why she'd need you tagging along."

"Well, I thought she could use a bit of support."

"Oh, don't tell me you've suddenly acquired a conscience. My bullshit meter couldn't take the load."

"I know you don't trust a single word I say, but it's true—she's a good person. Anyway, that ain't the only reason I'm here; I was the last person to see him alive."

"When?"

"Wednesday night. Look, Inspector Holt, is there any chance I could tell you something before Mrs Matthews gets back?"

Holt, who looked shocked by his conspiratorial tone, nodded.

"Follow me."

Mark followed Holt through into an interview

room and sat down.

"So what did you want to tell me?"

"First of all, I don't want this going any further. I mean, I don't want you to say anything to Mrs Matthews—she's worried enough."

"Well, let's just see what you've got to say first, shall we?"

Mark looked unsure but continued.

"I got a phone call about seven Wednesday night; it was Dean, he wanted me to go and pick him up from the hospital."

"Yes."

"Well, I thought something was up with him, so I went to pick him up, and it turns out he was there with his ex. He said she fell down the stairs, but I don't know, he seemed edgy."

"Edgy how? Do you think he pushed her?"

"Well, I wouldn't want to say either way; I just thought you should know. You know about Dean and Adam having a fight, but do you know why?"

"No, tell me"

"Well, I can't be sure—Dean was quite touchy about it—but it might be worth looking up Clare Heathers, Dean's ex—the one who ended up at the bottom of the stairs Wednesday night."

"What connection do you think this Clare Heathers might have with Dean's disappearance?"

"I don't know, I don't think she has anything to do with it, but there was something going on between Adam and Dean and I think it probably had something to do with her."

"Really? Here's what I think happened: Dean Matthews, the only person we've had that's even close to a lead, has gone missing. He had connections to at least two of the victims and was becoming paranoid about it. You and he concoct this story in the pub one night to throw us off the scent—any of this sounding familiar?"

"You don't really believe he had anything to do with this, do you? Come on, be realistic, he's not an angel, but he's no murderer."

"No, I don't believe he's responsible for the murders, but I do think he may know something of use to the investigation, and, worryingly, I think the killer might have worked that out, as well."

"So what are you going to do about it?"

"Everything we can to get him back in one piece." Holt was rubbing at his brow, and Mark was made painfully aware of how desperate the situation was becoming. He had known Detective Inspector Holt for the best part of ten years on and off in a professional way, and not once had he ever seen him so rattled. At that moment, the WPC stuck her head around the doorframe.

"Sir, Mrs Matthews is back."

Chapter 35

Clare was sat in the middle of her living room, papers and folders and various books littering the floor around her. She was busy studying Freud and psychoanalysis. It was not really an accepted psychology anymore; it was taught more as an example of how not to practice.

Just as she'd decided that Freud was no more than a psychological sadist, the phone rang into life. Swiftly grabbing the phone, she hit the button to answer.

"Yep."

"Oh, nice telephone manner."

"What? Oh, Hannah, hi, sorry about that, I'm a bit busy at the minute."

"I'm sure you are, but I need to tell you something."

"What?"

"Never mind that, just let me in, would you?"

Getting up from the floor, Clare walked to the front door and opened it with the phone still to her ear. Not waiting for an invitation, Hannah brushed straight past her, grabbing the phone away from her as she went. After hanging up, she put it down on the coffee table and waited for Clare.

Clare wandered back through into the living room.

"And hello to you, too. What do you want? I'm in the middle of some work."

Hannah passed her eyes over the floor before looking up disapprovingly.

"So I see. It looks like a bomb's gone off in Paper Chase. Jesus, Clare, have you ever heard of a table?"

Ignoring her, Clare went to put the kettle on.

"Well, seeing as how you're here now, I could probably use a break. Do you want tea or coffee?"

"Tea, please."

Bringing the two cups of tea back into the living room, she handed one to Hannah before sitting down.

"What's all this about?"

"I'm glad you asked. You know Helen who works at The Tin Whistle?" Clare stared blankly back at Hannah.

"Well, I've known her since school, but anyway she was working yesterday and Mark was in."

"Dean's mate Mark?"

"Yes, and apparently some woman came in bawling about her son."

"And?"

"It was Lauren Matthews."

"Dean's mum?"

"Apparently no one's seen him in a couple of days."

"Are you sure? No offence to your mate, but it's a well-known fact that pissed people talk bollocks."

"That's what I thought, until I saw the news."

Hannah picked up the remote and clicked the television into life. It was just past six and the local news was still busy reading the headlines.

"Possible fifth victim in the on-going murder

case in Manning's Town. Police have just released this photo of Dean Matthews, who hasn't been seen since late Wednesday night. Police are anxious to speak to anyone who may have knowledge of his whereabouts."

Clare grabbed the remote from Hannah and switched the television off. Sitting back down quietly, she stared into the distance.

"Clare, are you ok?"

"Every time things seem to be evening out, something happens. Things are never going to be normal again, are they?"

Standing up, Hannah walked toward Clare and sat down next to her, taking her hand. She looked Clare in the eye.

"No, hon, I don't think they ever will be for you; you've been through too much. But you don't honestly have any sympathy for him, do you? Clare, he pushed you down those stairs, he aborted your baby—don't waste your time on him."

"Hannah, he didn't push me down the stairs, I told you he didn't. It was an accident."

"Yes, an accident that would never have happened if he hadn't been here in the first place. Look, don't worry about it, just go back to your work and I'll call you in a bit, ok?"

Clare nodded and Hannah let herself out.

Glancing back down at her books, feeling more confused than she ever had, she slid back down onto the floor and proceeded to try to understand Freud.

Chapter 36

Holt pulled out the chair for his desk, still reeling. He'd gone to meet his journalist buddy for lunch in the hope that he'd be able to shed some light on the mystery caller who had been leaking sensitive information about the case He never thought for a minute he'd get a name, and he had already decided it must be the killer. Never in his wildest nightmares had he seen it coming.

Henson was the not-so-mysterious mystery caller.

Now he was uncertain of how to deal with the information. He was the senior officer; it was up to him. He wished he had someone to talk to about it. But it was no good—he would have to decide what to do. He absentmindedly checked his watch and rubbed at his brow. Henson would be in any minute now. In any other situation Holt would have been furious, but Henson was the only other person who had any real idea of the pressure of the case, aside from Loretta. He had become used to having him around, as irritating as he was at times. Technically he had every right and every reason to throw him off the case. He'd not only jeopardised the case; he'd jeopardised his own career. And what about the feelings he'd had about the calls? He'd been so sure the killer had been making them. Should he just automatically dismiss those feelings now just because he knew who the caller was?

He still hadn't decided how to deal with the

situation that was rapidly unfurling in front of him when Henson strolled in. Holt watched as Henson went and got himself a coffee from the vending machine, anger bubbling up inside of him.

"Henson, my office now."

Henson looked up from his coffee, and for a moment there was a look of confusion, then realisation.

Still holding his coffee, Henson walked toward Holt's office, all the officers had noticed Holts ton and were now watching Henson with interest.

Holt waited for Henson to enter his office and slammed the door. Rounding on him, Holt stared him straight in the eye.

"Anything you'd like to share with me?'

Trying for time, Henson faltered.

"How about the fact that you've been tipping off the press as to the whereabouts of the bodies."

Henson stood agog; he wasn't sure what to say.

Seeing the confusion on his young colleague's face, Holt continued,

"It was you tipping off the press. Did you get your nice, tidy little back hander? Exactly how much were they paying you?"

Henson started to answer and Holt cut him off.

"Was it worth it? Your thirty pieces of silver? Honest to God, Henson. You've put everything at risk—the case, your career..." Holt paused, to give Henson time to speak.

"I don't know what to say, sir, I never told them anything confidential."

"You told them where the bodies were; they virtually followed me down the driveway at Jon

Hamilton and Richard Abbott's crime scene."

"Sir, you don't believe I am responsible for these atrocities, do you?"

Holt regarded him for a minute.

"Now why would you say that?"

"Well, you seemed so sure that the person tipping off the press had something to do with the case."

"Yes, and I was right, wasn't I? But no, I don't believe you're the killer; for a start, you don't have the bottle. I've got to tell you, Henson, I'm at a loss as to what to do about you now."

"Are you going to inform the rest of the station?"

Holt stared at him.

"No. They're under enough stress at the minute. Ordinarily I'd take you straight off the case, but that would just arouse suspicion, so I'm going to keep you on. But this isn't over, Henson, and I need your word that there'll be no more leaks to the press."

"Are you sure you want to keep me on the case?"

"Well, no. But given the circumstances, I'm going to take a chance on you. Don't let me down." Holt made his way across his office and opened the door.

Henson took his cue and left the office.

Henson left Holt's office absolutely annihilated; he had felt pushed out ever since Holt had seen fit to bring Loretta in on the case. He had never trusted her. Realistically he knew it was down to his latent insecurities, but he felt now more than ever that she and Holt needed to be brought down a peg or two. And he knew that the best way to do this was to discredit Loretta. How he could do that he wasn't sure, but in the meantime he was going to try and win Holt's trust back.

He had met up with Thomas Webber an hour ago, and after a few drinks he had let Henson know about the sordid side line he and the late Adam had had. Henson had been shocked by Tom's apparent willingness to talk about the website, but he knew that Tom had still been concerned for his own safety. Fear of death always seemed to have a funny way of loosening tongues. Henson had assured Tom that he wouldn't be charged if he could tell him anything that might be of importance to the case. Tom had told him everything, including the fact that the website had been closed down by a third party. This had sent a shiver of excitement through Henson; it made sense that whoever had closed down the website might also have been responsible for Adam's demise. The fact that he had gone missing the same day the website was shut down spoke volumes to Henson, and he had excused himself to the toilets to call a contact of his. The person he'd spoken to was a journalist and partly the reason why Henson was in bad odour himself, and if he could use him to vindicate himself then all the better. Half an hour later, Henson had received a text with a name and contact address.

He decided to follow it up straight away, and within twenty minutes he was sitting outside of a house. Getting out of the car he double checked the address and once satisfied he knocked sharply on the door. After a few moments the door was opened by a slight man in his late fifties.

"Can I help you?"

"Hello, Mr Jenkins?"

"Yes."

"DC Henson, I was just wondering if I could have a minute of your time?"

"Yes, of course." Mr Jenkins opened the door to let Henson inside.

As Henson walked in he looked around; papers and books littered the hallway, and as he made his way through to the living room, he wondered when was the last time the carpet had met with a vacuum cleaner.

Mr Jenkins, noticing the look on the young DC's face, spoke up.

"I live alone—can you tell?"

Henson smiled at him and, moving some books on the sofa managed to make enough room to sit down.

"Would you like a drink at all?"

"No, I'm fine, thank you, sir."

Sitting down in an armchair, Mr Jenkins made himself comfortable.

"So how can I help?"

"Well, Mr Jenkins, I got your name and address from Jo at the Manning's Mercury."

"Ah, Jo, I know Jo. How is he?"

"He's fine, thank you. He told me you're an expert with websites and I was wondering if I could pick your brain?"

"I wouldn't say I'm an expert, but I'll do my best."

"A website was closed down a few weeks ago and I was wondering how much expertise would be required to do that."

"Well, it isn't something everyone can do."

Mr Jenkins got up and moved toward the computer. Switching it on, he waited patiently for it to start up.

Henson had moved to the computer, as well, and had his hand on the back of Mr Jenkins's chair, peering down at the screen.

"What was the name of the website?"

"Peep Show."

Mr Jenkins stopped what he was doing and turned to look at him.

"Well, I can tell you now who closed that site down: I did."

"You did?"

"Yes, I had a call from a friend asking me if I could, so I did."

"And the name of your friend is?"

"Loretta Armstrong."

Henson felt his stomach drop.

"Well, thank you for your time, Mr Jenkins."

Before Mr Jenkins had a chance to respond, Henson had gone.

Holt had just gotten back to the station after a brief conversation with Clare Heathers about Dean and the late Adam Woodacre. Although she clearly wasn't at all distraught about Adam's death, Holt didn't see any reason why she would be. When she'd mentioned the assault, Holt had been shocked, although he could see why she hadn't reported it in a country where the laws seemed to only protect the perpetrators. He had to be careful in his questioning and had been incredibly relieved when he had rang

Henson's mobile and it had gone to voicemail. Clare had assured Holt that the only people she was aware of who knew about the assault were the people involved. Although she couldn't be sure be sure of whom Hannah Simpson may have told. Holt had left a voicemail on Miss Simpson's mobile making a somewhat oblique reference as to what he wished to her speak about.

Going into his office, Holt sat back down at his desk. He sat staring at the incident wall, where all the photos of the victims were posted along with various information about their lives. His eyes kept going back to the first victim; they still didn't know who he was. Ever since the body had turned up, they had been scouring the missing persons, but the case had been so unrelenting that precious few leads regarding the victim's identity had come in. Holt was starting to believe that he might be the key to the investigation. The attack had been so meticulously planned and so much more ferocious than the subsequent murders. But somehow Holt felt there was more to these cases than he was seeing. The more Holt thought about it, the surer he became; find the first victim's identity and that would lead them to the murderer. Holt reasoned that the murderer must have been aware of this, too. Using fire as a method to kill had served two purposes: firstly, it was an agonising way of killing someone; and secondly, it ensured a difficult identification process. All the dentists in the area had been checked and none of them could shed any light on the first victim's identity. They had managed to get a break with his shoes, though; they had been an expensive limited edition pair, and after a few calls they had located a handful of shops up and down the country that had stocked them. The stores checked how many pairs of size tens they'd sold in the last six months, and then lists of dentists within a ten-mile radius of the shops had been sent copies of the deceased's dental information. It had been a long shot, but given that they had little other information to go on, it was worth a try.

As Holt sat back in his chair and continued to stare at the mystery victim, his office door slammed open. WPC Wright stood there looking flushed.

"Inspector, we've got a positive ID on the first victim. His name was Simon Reeves, fifty-two, lived in South London, went missing three months ago. He had a record Sir, he'd been to prison for-" Holt cut her off

"Murder."

"Sir—did you know him?"

"I was his arresting officer, first murder case I worked…"

At that moment, his mobile phone, which had temporarily lost reception, beeped into life again, signalling the arrival of a voicemail message. Holt, still reeling from what he had just heard, dialled 1 to retrieve it. A crackled message started to play to him.

"Inspector Holt, my name's Hannah Simpson—you left a message. I'm just calling to let you know that the only people who new about the assault were Clare and myself—oh, and Clare's counsellor, Loretta Armstrong. I know you are investigating murders, but I can speak for Clare and myself when

I say that we'd really appreciate it if the information regarding the assault and our names didn't make it into the papers. We've only just started to get our lives back and could do without a dozen journalists turning up vying for the lurid details. Anyway, if when you get this message you need to know anything else, you know where I am. Thank you."

Holt felt his stomach drop. His eyes went back to the incident board, his mind whirling.

Matthew Reynolds, the second victim, had been referred to anger management via Loretta Jon Hamilton, the third victim, had a wife who was seeing Loretta for marriage difficulties. Richard Abbott, the fourth victim, he couldn't be sure about, but he wouldn't be surprised to find that either he or a close family member had been getting 'professional' help. Adam Woodacre had been a date rapist whose victims had included patients of Loretta's. And now Dean Matthews, someone who had 'pushed' his ex down a flight of stairs, had gone missing. An ex who was directly related to Loretta.

The WPC looked concerned; she had known that the revelation of the victim's name was going to create a reaction, but she wasn't prepared for the look on the inspector's face now. She had expected relief or determination, but there was none of that. There wasn't any expression at all; there didn't seem to be anything behind his eyes.

"Sir?"

Holt's mind snapped back and he looked up at the WPC.

"I can't believe I've been so stupid; all the time

I've been looking for a link between the victims, and I honestly believed there wasn't one. And all the time the link was sitting there feeding me information." With that, Holt grabbed his jacket from the back of the chair and charged out of the office. Practically running from the building to his car he jumped in and slammed the door behind him. Sparking the engine into life, the car tyres shrieked as he sped out of the car park.

Holt was furious as he drove. How could he have been so blind? She'd tricked him; she'd led him to believe she was helping with the case when all the time she'd been using him to make sure she'd always be one step ahead. Tears started rolling down his face at the betrayal. He'd started having feelings for her and believed she felt something for him. And what about all the victims, tortured and murdered so callously while he'd enjoyed dinner made by the same hands that had caused all the carnage? He'd almost had one of his own thrown off the force because of this woman

His mind was filled with snippets of past conversations and distracted, he had had to swerve hard to avoid a car pulling out in front of him. He cursed the driver quietly under his breath and then resumed his thoughts. By the time he got to Loretta's office car park, he was practically foaming at the mouth. He was shocked to see Henson's car sitting outside the front door. The surprise of seeing it forced him to recompose himself. Leaving the car and straightening his tie and jacket, he strode purposefully through the door. The receptionist was nowhere to be seen and he continued through to

Loretta's office. The door was open as he approached.

Inside at her desk, serene as ever, sat Loretta. In front of her Henson had his hands on the desk, almost shouting a series of questions at her. Loretta, who had been quietly regarding the young DC, looked up slowly, catching Holt's eye.

"Hello, Inspector." Her voice sounded different somehow, cold.

As soon as Loretta had spoken, Henson swung around to face Holt.

"Inspector?"

"How did you get here before me?"

"Wright radioed me and told me about the phone call; I figured you'd be coming straight here. Also it turns out that the good doctor here was responsible for the shutdown of Adam Woodacres website."

As Holt went to query the statement, he faltered. Loretta, who now had Henson's back to her, had picked up the fountain pen she had been using, and in one fell movement plunged it deep into the side of Henson's neck.. Holt ran forward and held Henson as he slid to the floor, trying to keep the pen steady so as not to make the wound worse. Cradling Henson's head in his lap, he called for an ambulance and additional support. He looked at Loretta with contempt as she settled back into her chair. As Holt looked up at her, his voice was barely a whisper as he spoke.

"Why?"

"Don't worry, he won't die. You have to admit he was irritating, and I don't appreciate being barked at. This should quiet him down some. Maybe now he'll have a little more empathy for victims of violent crimes. You know, you should be thanking me; that pen cost a lot less than sensitivity training courses, and the benefits will stay with him for his whole life. Maybe you could put the idea forward at your next annual review."

Holt knelt, staring at Loretta with incomprehension. Was this really the same woman he had relied upon? She had seemed so understanding and made him feel at home in her apartment. He watched her as she sat calmly regarding him.

"Why aren't I trying make my escape? Is that what you were about to ask?"

"Yes."

"Very simple: I don't want Dean to die."

"He's still alive?" Holt was amazed; never would he have believed that that boy wasn't dead already.

"You're surprised. You know, I'm not a complete monster, and besides, I want to spend some more time with you before my inevitable carting off to some secure wing."

"What do you mean spend some more time with me? As soon as this comes to light, I'll be taken off the case for personal involvement."

"So you'd agree we've become close, Holt? You know, I'm actually quite fond of you."

"Exactly—they certainly won't allow you to be interviewed by me." Holt paused then, looking down once more at the wounded Henson.

"And besides, I don't ever want to see you again." Holt's voice was flat.

"You surely don't expect me to volunteer the

information to anyone else? This is our investigation. I want to see if you've learnt anything from me these last few months."

Holt sat staring at her.

"I'm not patronising you for the sake of it; I believe we can all take something from this experience. Whether they allow it or not is inconsequential to me in the long term. I fear Mrs Matthews and the delightful press might think otherwise, however."

As she finished speaking, police and ambulance crew burst into the office. Quickly the paramedics rushed to Henson and removed him. The PCs waited for Holt to acknowledge them. Holt, still stunned, turned to face Loretta.

"Loretta Armstrong, I am arresting you for the murders of Simon Reeves, Matt Reynolds, Jon Hamilton, and Richard Abbott, for the abduction of Dean Matthews, and for assaulting a police officer"

Holt turned to face PC Bannerman.

"Read her her rights and get her to the station."

Holt turned and left, leaving a confused PC Bannerman to deal with Loretta.

Holt found himself back at his car, and opening the door he got inside. Sitting there, he contemplated what had just happened. In his rear view mirror, he watched as his one-time ally was shepherded into the back of a squad car. He felt almost lightheaded as he put the key in the ignition. Following the squad car out of the car park, he proceeded back to the station.

At the station, Holt went to the interview room where Loretta was waiting.

"Hello again, Jimmy." Loretta's voice had become warm once more, and this irritated Holt.

"My name is Inspector Holt." Holt kept his voice flat.

Holt was aware she was mocking him, but he ignored it. Holt felt exhausted, even though he'd heard that Henson was going to be ok. He now knew, sitting in the same room as the local serial killer and his once close friend that he didn't think he could deal with the upcoming interview and interrogation.

"Where is Dean?"

"He's safe. So tell me, Inspector Holt, have you missed me?"

Holt was caught off guard by the question. He decided to be honest, hoping that this would please her enough that she would let him know where Dean was.

"Yes, I did." Holt had his elbow on the table with his hand supporting his head.

"You are still shocked, aren't you? That a woman could have done this."

Holt forced his face up to meet her gaze.

"To be honest, yes."

"Well, I have no sympathy for you, then."

Holt was confused by the statement, but decided to leave it and try another line of questioning.

"Why the mask?"

"We all wear masks every day of our lives, we pretend to be different people to different people. Why do we do that?"

Holt was becoming frustrated; he wasn't sure he was capable of getting a straight answer out of her, and exhaling loudly, he sat back in his chair

"Do you think you could give the pop psychology a rest for a bit? You know you can help yourself—you can tell me where Dean is." Holt quietly hoped that the directness of the question might elicit a useful response.

"Tell you? Why would I tell you? It's up to you to work it out; believe it or not, you are capable. Think about it."

Holt sat thinking for a minute, the hardest thing he'd ever had to do. He had to force his mind to calm down enough for logical thought to return.

What did he know about Dean? He was young and reckless, not averse to mixing with the less acceptable side of society, but still living at home with a mother and younger sister. He was only nineteen and had a hot temper, not helped by binge drinking and occasional drug use. For all intents and purposes, he was a CHAV.

"He's a CHAV."

Completely ignoring the statement, Loretta looked up at Holt.

"Do you know what I do? I help people—I protect them from themselves. True, recently I have become a little more hands-on in my approach to therapy, but the results are undeniable."

"What? Butchered bodies littering the landscape—that's your idea of good therapy, is it?"

"You aren't listening to me, Inspector. Maybe you should go and find Dean." Loretta's voice was friendly, almost advisory.

Holt got up and left the room. It was the first time in his career he had been dismissed by a serial killer.

PC Bannerman was waiting as Holt left the interview room.

"So where should we start searching?"

Holt thought back to his previous meetings with Loretta.

"Bannerman, do you know what CHAV means?"

"CHAV? Trouble, as far as I'm concerned"

"But does it mean anything? A shortening of something?"

"Well, the word CHAV is an acronym."

"What for?"

"Council Houses And Violence."

"Council houses? But Dean doesn't live in a council house, but maybe that's not the point." The last part was spoken quietly, as if underlining the point to himself. Suddenly Holt's gaze snapped up to meet PC Bannerman's eyes.

"Bannerman, what's the biggest council house or building you can think of?"

"Well, the council offices, obviously, but they haven't even laid the foundations for them yet."

"Maybe somebody's already started with our Mr Matthews. Notify the ambulance crew and let's get over there."

"Yes, sir."

Just over an hour later, Dean had been discovered in a porta-loo on the council offices building site. The relief of finding him had had a noticeable effect on the mood of the entire police force. The ambulance crew had checked him over and he seemed fine, although still a little groggy from the effects of the anaesthetic that had been administered, the packaging for which had been found, quite helpfully, with him. Holt decided to go with Dean to the hospital, and as Holt got into the back of the ambulance, he turned briefly to PC Bannerman.

"Could you go and pick Mrs Matthews up and bring her to the hospital, please?"

"Of course, sir." Bannerman's face split into a wide smile; the relief of going to tell a relative good news for a change was evident.

In the ambulance, Dean was drifting in and out of consciousness; clearly the strain of the last four days had taken effect. From what Holt could make out, after the initial anaesthetic had been given, Dean had found himself awake a little later with no idea of what time it was, as it was dark. Dean had started to panic. In that moment of panic, Dean had felt something knock against his leg, and he realised water had been left for him. He hadn't wanted to drink it, but given his circumstances, he hadn't had much choice. After that, Dean had drifted in and out of consciousness until the police had found him. The water bottle was coming to the hospital with them for analysis; Holt wasn't sure exactly what they'd find, but if it turned out the water had been laced with sleeping tablets, he wouldn't be surprised.

Just over a mile away on the other side of town, a squad car pulled up outside Lauren Matthews house. PC Bannerman got out of the car and replaced his hat. Looking across at WPC Wright, he smiled.

"I never thought I would going to be giving good news to Mrs Matthews."

"I know, it is a bit unreal, isn't it? I can't believe we caught her. Finally I can get a proper night's sleep."

Walking up to the front door, Bannerman took a deep breath and knocked. After a few moments the door swung open. Mrs Matthews's face was drained of colour and the look in her eyes told them they were the last people she wanted to see.

"Have you found him? Is he dead?"

She was so consumed by her own terror that she had failed to notice that both the officers were smiling.

"No, Mrs Matthews, far from it. We've come to take you to him, he's at the hospital.'

"Hospital? Oh my God, what happened to him?"

"As far as we can tell, nothing; he's in one piece."

"Oh thank God, thank God." She broke down into sobs and WPC Wright took her by the arm and led her to the car. As Wright opened the door for Lauren, Alice came running up the street, a look of confusion and fear on her face as she saw her distraught mother being helped into the back of a squad car. Seeing this, Bannerman moved quickly.

"It's ok, love, your brother's been found alive and well, and we're just taking your mum to see him now—do you want to come, too?"

Nodding at Bannerman, she followed her mum into the back of the car. Bannerman pulled the Matthews' front door closed, making sure the latch had dropped, and he went to join the crowd now waiting patiently in the car.

At the hospital Holt waited at Dean's beside until Bannerman and Wright arrived with the Matthews family. Lauren Matthews practically ran the length of the ward to her son; she barely noticed Holt sitting on the other side of the bed. Eventually she looked up.

"So you've caught him, then?"

"Yes. The killer has indeed been apprehended."

Lauren sat for a moment, digesting all that had happened in the last few days. Holt got up to leave, and as he did, Lauren caught his eye.

"Thank you."

The words had barely been a whisper, and Holt felt his demeanour starting to crumble. He nodded at Lauren and left the ward.

Chapter 37

Three months—almost to the day—after the apprehension of Loretta Armstrong, the serial murderer, was found guilty on all counts. A cheer had resounded in the courtroom as the verdict was read out, and as Holt had walked into the police station following it, everyone had taken a turn congratulating him. But despite everyone else's obvious happiness at the verdict, Holt still didn't feel right. Something still didn't fit, and he couldn't work out what it could possibly be. He had spent the last three months continually returning to the case, trying to piece together where his doubts were coming from.

Holt walked into his office and sat back down at his desk. No sooner had he done this than there was a knock at the door.

"Yes?"

Henson, who had recently come back to work following his incident with Loretta, stuck his head round the door, grinning wildly.

"We did it, sir, we got her."

"Yes, we did." Holt's voice was low and flat.

Henson walked in and took a seat.

"Aren't you happy?"

"Yes, I suppose I am, but it's just…I don't know, there still seem to be a few things that don't quite fit."

"Like what?"

"Well, like when Jon Hamilton went missing, I was at Loretta's apartment."

"Obviously she went out after you'd left."

"Maybe, but why would a woman in her fifties with an exceptional career record suddenly decide to throw it all away? Why wait until now? We now know that what Simon Reeves did thirty years ago must've been the trigger as he was the first victim. But why wait until now to get even when she had so much to lose?"

Henson shifted uneasily in his seat.

Holt's mind went back to the day they had found out Simon Reeves's identity. A message had been left on Holt's voicemail from Hannah Simpson, who had received his message about questions relating to the assault on herself and Clare Heathers. She had been the one to inform them of the involvement between Clare and Loretta.

"Henson, how would you describe the death of Simon Reeves?"

"Well, calculated, ferocious… I don't know sir, what do you want me to say?"

"Ferocious—doesn't that suggest something to you? That whomever was responsible had a lot of anger? And how likely is it that you'd carry that anger with you for thirty years? You couldn't; it would destroy you. You wouldn't be able to concentrate on anything, much less build a career on trying to help people similar to the person who wronged you. But then how did she know? Sue had no sisters, cousins maybe…maybe a friend…?"

Henshaw was confused, he was fairly sure he was no longer required for the conversation

"What do you mean?"

"Often people charged with domestic abuse are asked to seek anger management. Loretta will have seen hundreds of cases throughout her professional career. Is that the behaviour of someone who hates abusers and thinks they're all damned? No, she was trying to protect women from ending up in the same position."

"The same position sir?"

"Yes, the same position as Sue…"

Henson looked concerned.

"Maybe you should take a few weeks' holiday, sir, get out of the country and just relax. I think you're thinking on this too much. I mean, we've got her, sir, she's confessed, case closed."

Holt looked up at Henson.

"Perhaps you're right. Well, I'm going to call it a night anyway."

Holt got up, smiling at Henson, and removed his jacket from the back of his chair. As he opened the door for Henson, he wondered briefly if what he was about to do was a good idea.

Chapter 38

Lauren Matthews was making the tea; since Dean had come home, he had been a different person. It was almost as if he'd gone from childhood to adulthood in the space of the four days he'd been missing. He had gone straight back to work as soon as he could, and he was actively enjoying it. Even Mark had noticed a difference in him. Mark was now a regular caller at the house; the shock of Dean's disappearance and subsequent reappearance had seemed to have had a profound effect on him, as well. He had his own flat now and was doing an apprenticeship at another garage. Lauren was pleased to see him these days, which was proof in itself as to how much he had changed. She was busy making a lasagne for dinner and had just finished sprinkling cheese on top of it when the doorbell rang. Wiping her hands quickly on a tea towel, she went to answer the door. A small, well-dressed woman was waiting for her.

"Mrs Matthews?"

Lauren nodded.

"I'm Joanne Hamilton, may I have a minute of your time?"

Lauren nodded and beckoned her inside. Joanne followed Lauren through into the kitchen, and noticing the freshly made lasagne she nodded toward it.

"That looks nice."

Lauren, unsure as to what this woman might want, smiled.

"Thanks, though I'm not sure if it'll taste any good. Would you like a cup of tea? I was just going to have one myself."

"That'd be lovely. Thank you."

Joanne felt comfortable around this woman; she hadn't been too sure how she'd be received. But in all the years of Dean's life, Lauren had never intruded on Joanne's family life or demanded anything from Jon. Knowing what she knew now, she was not sure she would have been so understanding in Lauren's position. Joanne sat down at the table as Lauren strained the tea and placed a cup in front of Joanne. Lauren joined her at the table.

"I'm sure there are things you want to ask me, and I'll try to answer them as well as I can."

Joanne looked shocked at this.

"No, I have no questions. I know what my late husband was like, and I know that you ended up being discarded like I was. I would never have any quarrel with you. In your case, I was the other woman." Joanne was smiling at the end of the sentence. Lauren appreciated the fact that she was trying to make light of Jon's many indiscretions and returned the smile.

"When will Dean be back? I'd like to speak to you both together if possible."

As if in answer to the question, the front door slammed open and two men could be heard making their way to the kitchen. Dean burst into the kitchen, followed by Mark. Joanne was taken aback by how like his father he was; she hadn't noticed it before, or maybe she had and just hadn't acknowledged it.

"All right, Mum?" Dean was grinning, and then he noticed she wasn't alone. He recognised Joanne and his manner changed.

"Hello, Mrs Hamilton."

"Would you two like a cup of tea?" Lauren got up and put the kettle back on. Mark followed Lauren over to the kettle.

"Yes, please, Mrs Matthews."

"I've told you, you can call me Lauren." Lauren's voice had a chastising quality and Mark seemed to redden around the ears a little. He recomposed himself quickly.

"What's that I smell?"

"Lasagne—that ok with you?"

"Fantastic."

Mark grabbed the mugs from the cupboard and stayed next to Lauren while she made the tea.

Dean, who was still shocked to see Joanne in his house, sat down at the table. Joanne, noting his confusion, was first to speak.

"I suppose you're wondering why I'm here?"

"Well, yes, if I'm being honest."

"I've come to tell you that I've decided to get rid of the garage, and I wanted to tell you in person."

Dean looked crestfallen.

"Can I ask why? I mean, I'm no expert, but I thought it had been doing great business."

Joanne opened her handbag and pulled out some papers.

"It has. Which is a good reason to pass it on now;

nobody wants a failing business."

"Do you have a prospective buyer yet? Are they keeping any of us on?"

"Well, that's entirely up to him—and her, for that matter."

"Do I know them?"

"Well, I'm looking at them right now."

Dean's heart skipped a beat.

"Me?"

"And your mother, yes."

Lauren, who had only been half listening to what was being said, spun round.

Dean wasn't sure if he understood properly.

"Is this a wind-up?"

"Well, here are the deeds—what do you think?"

Dean scanned the pages; she was serious. Still in shock, he passed them to his mother.

Lauren looked over the papers and then stood staring in shock at Joanne.

"I'm stunned. I don't know what to say. Thank you."

"Don't thank me; you deserve it. Jon could never provide stability, but maybe this will. Anyway, I suppose I better be going. Thanks for the tea."

Joanne closed her bag and got up. Dean shot a quick look at his mum, who seemed to have already anticipated this and spoke up quickly.

"I don't suppose you'd like to stay and have some lasagne? I've made enough to feed an army."

Joanne smiled.

"Well, Harry, my eldest, said he was going to pick up KFC for everyone tonight, and I've never been a great fan of fast food."

"That's a yes, then? Fantastic." She turned to Dean and Mark.

"Why are you two still here? Nip to down to Tesco's and pick up a bottle of champagne, and when you get back you can lay the table."

Smiling widely at the two women, Dean and Mark headed back out again.

Chapter 39

Holt's car swung into the prison car park. Parking up quickly, he slammed the brakes on and got out. He walked into the main reception and straight up to the officer at the reception desk.

"Hello, you've been expecting me."

The prison officer recognised the man in front of her and ushered him through. Holt was led through to a room where Loretta was waiting.

Loretta was sitting as serenely as always, a small smile playing on her lips.

"Hello, Inspector Holt."

Holt sat down.

"How did you know her? Was she your cousin? Friend?"

"Who?"

"Sue Lawrence."

Loretta looked shocked for a moment.

"Sue Lawrence?"

"Yes, Sue Lawrence and don't pretend you don't know who she is, she's the reason Reeves was chosen in the first place isn't she? Only thing is I don't know how you knew her. There is one thing I do know for certain though…"

"Really? And what's that?" Loretta was becoming agitated.

"You didn't do it." It was a statement.

"Do what?"

"You didn't kill those people."

"Really? The evidence would point to the contrary." Loretta's voice was low, but her back was straight and she was looking Holt dead in the eye.

"What evidence? The only concrete evidence we have is that you are responsible for Dean's abduction and the attack on DS Henson."

"Yes, I miscalculated with Dean."

"Bullshit. The one thing I know for a fact is that the killer never miscalculated things. You never meant for Dean to die—you just wanted us to think he would. You wanted all the evidence to point to you."

"I'm sure I don't know what you're talking about. Maybe the papers were right; you are past it."

Holt sat back in his chair for a moment.

"No, I'm sorry, that's not going to work this time. You can question my ability to do my job all you like, but I know I'm right. Who did it, Loretta? Who are you protecting?"

"Protecting?"

"Yes, you said it yourself—you protect people from others, from themselves. I thought I understood the motive when Simon Reeves's identity came to light, but I was wrong, I was seeing it from the wrong prospective. It's taken me three months to realise that the murder of Simon Reeves was an immediate reaction—the ferocity of it, the need to obliterate him completely. It doesn't square that someone who had known what he did and lived with it for the best part of thirty years would suddenly decide exact their revenge. So who did you tell?"

Loretta regarded Holt for a moment and smiled at him once again.

"I'm impressed—you clearly have a knack for psychology, Inspector Holt, or maybe that's your copper's nose busy twitching. But I'll think you'll find that whatever it is bears no consequence in the real world. I've confessed to the murders and you have no real evidence, forensic or otherwise, to the contrary."

"So you will quite happily spend the rest of your life incarcerated for coldblooded murderer?"

"Coldblooded? I think not. If you disagree, then may I politely request you go back and visit the victims' bereaved?" Loretta sat back in her chair and Holt leaned in.

"I don't think a single one would say they're happier now."

Loretta leaned in to meet Holt's gaze.

"What people *think* and what people *say* rarely square with each other; why do you think my ex-career is such a booming industry?"

Knowing there was nothing more to say, Holt got up and left.

After Holt had gone, the prison officer came in to collect Loretta.

"Come on, then, let's get you back to your cell. You know, you've got another visitor booked in for this afternoon—Clare Heathers."

Loretta looked at the PO and smiled.

"Oh, lovely, she's a nice girl. She's interested in becoming a psychologist herself.'

The PO returned the smile and led Loretta back to her room.

Clare was driving to the prison. When Loretta had first spoken to Clare about her own disastrous ex-relationship, it had been a revelation that had at first made Clare feel better about her own pitiful relationship history. But Clare hadn't been able to stop thinking about it, and it had built into a rage. This woman who had helped so many through mental anguish had once been the victim of a sadistic bully. It didn't seem right to Clare, and after a few weeks she had managed to track him down. Simon Reeves had done everything but laugh in her face, and that had been the final straw for Clare. Loretta was now her mentor, and as far as Clare was concerned, mentors didn't have tragic backstories. Once she'd disposed of Simon, she had felt relief. It hadn't been until speaking with Hannah that she'd realised that Loretta was far from an isolated case. After Simon's disposal, it had become easier for Clare to justify the eradication of some other people that had caused her and her friends pain. Hannah's ex, Matt Reynolds, had been next; Hannah had still known a lot of Matt's routines and had unwittingly helped Clare. Hannah had mentioned that she had thought of using the spare key he kept on top of the light fitting next to his front door to let herself in and call the speaking clock. Clare had talked her out of it; she had had other plans for Mr Reynolds. Once more Clare had felt the relief wash over her once she had finished her task. Jon Hamilton had been selected thanks to Dean; when Dean had first found out about his paternity he had left a drunken message on Clare's phone, even alluding to the fact that he had a new mistress, Sarah Lester. It hadn't taken Clare long to track down her apartment. During Jon's abduction, she had taken Jon's keys, assuming, quite correctly, that he would have a key to Sarah's apartment. Leaving the finger in the ice-lolly had been a particularly gratifying addition to the tableau.

Richard Abbott had gone out with Clare's cousin briefly—just long enough to introduce her to the wrong type of people—and she was now, thanks to his introductions, a heroin addict. He had been a remarkably easy target, as had Adam Woodacre, with his reputation and the fact that she already knew exactly where he lived. Clare just wished she had had a camera when she had surprised him.

Now, though, she felt remorse—not for any of her victims, but for the woman she revered taking her place in a prison cell. Loretta had worked it out that Clare must have been responsible for the murders. While visiting Clare in hospital the night she had lost the baby, she had told Clare that she knew. Loretta had been to her apartment and brought her an overnight bag, and she had found the mask. When Loretta told her she planned to help her, Clare had thought she had meant going to the police. And when Loretta told her not to contact her again, Clare had assumed it was because Loretta hadn't wanted to be associated with a murderer. She noticed that the mask had been removed and she had thought Loretta had taken it to the police. So Clare had kept her distance and waited patiently at home for the police. When they hadn't come, she had been confused, but when she saw Loretta's 'confession' across the front page of all the newspapers she had been shocked. If she were being honest with herself, she was still in shock. But she couldn't leave it any longer, and had rung to arrange a visit.

Three hours after Jimmy Holt left the prison, Clare sat in front of Loretta.

"Why did you do it?"

"You know why I did it. You must continue with your studies, and you can't come back here again, either. I recommend that you leave the area."

"Loretta, I'm the one who should be sat there now, not you." Clare's voice was a whisper.

"You have your whole life ahead of you, Clare; you have the ability to become a fantastic counsellor. But never lose sight of the ones you're protecting.

About a year ago, a girl came to me for help. Her partner was violent towards her and she didn't know what to do. I told her she should leave him and report him to the police. So she went back home and told him it was over. It created an argument and a neighbour called the police. The police turned up, arrested him and took him back to the police station. However after interviewing him and her, they decided to drop the charges and he was sent on his way.

I don't know what happened in the hours following his release but I do know the consequences. She was found with her head staved in by a neighbour the following morning. He claimed temporary insanity. That it had been an argument that had gotten out of hand. They had a record of repeated visits by the police to their address. Their relationship had a history of being, shall be say—troubled. And with the right amount of tears and remorse in the courts, he received eight years. I imagine he'll be out in four."

Clare knew what this was: it was reasoning. In an ideal world she; Clare, would be in prison. But this wasn't an ideal world, and every day it seemed to slip a little further away from achieving it.

Clare got up and smiled at Loretta.

Loretta returned the smile.

"Just remember to keep up the good work."

As Clare went back to her car, she felt almost lightheaded. Getting her mobile from her bag, she decided to ring Hannah.

"Hi, hon, what are you up to?"

"Nothing much—why? Do you want to meet up?"

"Yeah, I've got to talk to you about something. I'm thinking of moving, and I wondered if you wanted to come with me?"

Clare hung up the phone confident that Hannah would be on her doorstep by the time she got back. Throwing her phone down onto the passenger seat, she put the car into gear and left the car park without so much as a backward glance.

Three days later Holt arrived back at the prison. Loretta took the visitor request without question.
"Hello again DI Holt."
"Hello again… Sue."

Dear Reader,

I see you've read to the end and I'd just like to take another moment of your time to thank you for downloading Perfect Intentions. I genuinely hope you enjoyed it. For me entertaining you, the reader, is all I want to do.

If I may make a small request of you, if on completing this book you have enjoyed the journey we've been on together, please leave a positive review. It's good reviews that ensure I can continue to entertain. And as such that makes you, the reader, my priority.

With that in mind, please feel free to contact me via my website, twitter or Facebook as I'd love to hear from you.

As, I'm sure you're aware, Perfect Intentions is not the end of the journey and I hope you'll be joining me for the sequel.

Wishing you all the best and I'll see you again soon,

Leona Turner.

Printed in Great Britain
by Amazon